Petals for Deadly Power
Martha Monteval

Paperback ISBN 978-1-915193-92-6
Hardcover ISBN 978-1-915193-93-3
eBook ISBN 978-1-915193-94-0

Cover Design by Moonpress | *www.moonpress.co*
Editing by Jennifer Murgia
Interior Design by Martha Monteval

Visit my website at www.marthamonteval.com

About the book

This book contains subject matter that might be triggering for some, including violence, torture, murder and death, reference to domestic violence, emotional abuse and neglect.
This book also contains considerable profanity and sexually explicit scenes.

To the beings who fight for what they want
and don't give a shit about the consequences.

Prologue

Her onyx crown lay in the middle of a pool of black ink, black blood, and black feathers.

The splashing noise of his steps towards the limp body of his beloved echoed in the chamber where everything and nothing happened.

"Where have you been?" Her voice was but a whisper, yet that was more than enough to make him tense.

"I was busy." He continued approaching the stone slab where her naked body was confined to.

He would never get used to the astonishing beauty of this female before him. Her long dark hair billowed down the pale, almost translucent skin of her chest. Her black feathered wings protruded from her perfectly sculpted back. The same back he had kissed more times than he could count.

"In what world did you think *being busy* was a tolerable reason to ignore me?"

"I would never ignore you, my queen," he swore.

"You wouldn't." Her pitch-black eyes opened then, pinning him in place just as the four Cardinal-red shackles kept her limbs restrained for over two centuries.

Indeed, he knew how much the female hated the manacles and chains made of red crystal. He was aware of how much she had suffered trying to recover some of her freedom. Even the ability to freely move one arm or a leg would give her temporary satisfaction. But even that was too much.

He knew of her agony and despair, because countless times he had wiped her black tears from her pale cheeks, wishing he could take her pain away.

She, who never cried, had allowed herself to break in his company.

She, who never broke, had allowed him to put her pieces back together.

She, who never loved, had allowed him to desperately and irreversibly fall in love with her.

And wasn't love the most dangerous, fiercest weapon one could yield against the rest of the world? Wasn't love the starter of countless fires that could burn the world down to ashes and ruin?

His fingers stroked the only red thing in the chamber other than the chains and handcuffs.

Her lips trembled at his touch as she exhaled. "Please," she rasped. The darkness in her eyes glittered, begging for more.

More love, more passion, more desire.

More ways to make the remaining time of her curse less lonely and desperate. More ways to keep her mind off the bloodshed she would inflict when it was over, and she was free again.

Because when that time came, the world would never be the same.

Nothing would ever stop the queen again.

The male who loved her with every fiber of his being glided his finger from her red lips to her bare breasts, tracing them while the female slightly arched her back and held onto the stone underneath her, inhaling sharply.

The red crystal of her handcuffs and the rattling of the crystal chains echoed in the chamber.

Whenever the curse broke, he wouldn't miss meeting the love of his life in his dreams. He wouldn't miss the constant fear of waking up when he was with her, being torn away from ravishing her in this chamber.

Yet he would miss having the queen exposed and chained for him to devour. He would miss her compliance and the symphony of her moans.

He doubted an unleashed queen would ever be obedient again. And while he couldn't wait for her to come back to real life and freedom in full force, he would not waste the few opportunities he had left.

His fingers roamed from her breasts to her wrists, and in case the shackles weren't enough, he pinned her wrists down over her head.

His silver eyes glittered in anticipation, in admiration and awe.

He would never get enough of loving the Cardinal Queen.

1

Hope

Once there was a girl raised in the woods who killed through life to survive.

Now there was a woman looking through the crystal walls of the rooftop safe house in the capital of Thyria, the four-petal guarded island controlled by the Organ Mandor.

Hope Nevada's jaw clenched as his face crossed her mind.

The Organ Mandor and his immense magic, unmatched to any other panom in Thyria. Who happened to also be her father. The same man who killed her mother, Aurora. And the very bastard Hope couldn't wait to kill to avenge the death of the strongest woman she had ever encountered. The woman she had learned everything from during her twenty-four years living in Verdania.

Cardinals, how she missed her mother. Even if Aurora Nevada had kept the most important truths of Hope's life locked away for many years, with the excuse of keeping her daughter safe.

The three biggest secrets had been that panoms existed, and the Cardinals had blessed these males and females with the power to control magic; that Hope possessed panom magic in her blood; and that she had said blood because her father was the Organ Mandor of Thyria, making her the rightful heir of Organ House and successor to the throne.

Not a day went by without the sharpness of her grief and anger stinging her chest. She would walk down a corridor and visualize the black blade that felled her mother coming out of nowhere, only for it to fade in her imagination before it could graze Hope's own chest.

That her father had also tried to kill Hope with the same Black Lawful Stab mere minutes after slaying Aurora probably didn't help keep such visions at bay.

Hope wondered if the visions would go away when she finally killed her father. Not *if* she killed her father, but *when*.

The human beings carrying on with their lives in the streets of Corentre under the sunset didn't know about any of this, of course. Not that they could do much with that information, anyway.

A quick knock on her door was followed by the entrance of a smiling, white-haired young woman with ocean-blue eyes.

"Are you coming? I think they're ready," she said. Nina Avert didn't need to say more. Hope knew perfectly well who was ready for her. She had been waiting for them to stop arguing for the Fifth knew how long.

"Thanks." Hope smiled back. "Do you want to join?"

"It would be a great idea to know how to slice someone up the way you do, you know? But I much prefer learning from Indianna about other ways to slice beings up."

Hope chuckled. "All about healers' vocation, calling, and all of that."

"There is healing involved, sometimes. Most times." Nina raised her eyebrows as if trying to prove her point.

They walked through the wide apartment towards one of the largest and brightest rooms. It had recently been named "Badassery Suite", after a few complaints from certain beings about why calling it "Learning Room" was *boring as fuck*, and "Research Nook" was *too formal for their own good*.

Nina muttered a quick "See you later" before disappearing behind a black door where she and Indianna spent the most part of their days looking after Nina's brother, Raoul.

After months of worrying whether Raoul was safe, Hope knew what a relief it was for Nina to know her brother was conscious, and within reach, both mentally and physically. After they had rescued him from the Beftac Center for Injured Beings, his mind hadn't been his. And even now, sometimes he had episodes when one could doubt whether he was truly a human being. Or if he thought like one.

But at least he was alive and awake. That was something.

The first thing Hope saw when she entered the Badassery Suite were two red-haired twins arguing at the back. The second thing, next to the archway she just crossed, was an amused, black-haired man looking at said twins.

"Are you having fun?" Hope asked her half-brother.

Without sparing her a glance, the corner of Jake's lips tugged upwards.

"You have no idea." He bit his bottom lip while looking at the fieriest twin in a way that Hope was surprised didn't take her clothes off. But luckily or unluckily for Lenna, panom magic was not controlled with eyes but hands.

Jake opened his hand and Gave himself a bowl full of light pink petals with an edible appearance. At the crunchy noise of Jake eating one, Lenna turned her neck from her twin sister Ayla to him.

"Are you taking the absolute piss, Jake Coralt?"

For a moment, Hope thought Jake was going to offer Lenna some petals, but maybe something changed his mind. The something was likely to be the stunning flame-haired woman with golden eyes that was now storming towards them.

"Fucking corolla snacks?" Lenna's hands were on her hips, marking the generous curves of her body even more than her black, tight shirt and its very low neckline already did.

"You can have some. But please, carry on arguing." His voice was full of mischief.

Lenna's red, full lips frowned as she inhaled sharply. "You know where you can shove the Cardinals-damned corollas?"

Jake tilted his chin slightly upwards. "Are we talking about shoving things up deeply?" He looked around, a smile slowly spreading on his features. "I don't mind a bit of an audience, Brachyan. I'm all in."

"You *wish* you were all in. Sadly, the only thing going in right now is your snack affair." Lenna opened her hand, and a single corolla appeared between her index and middle finger. A corolla that she licked absolutely, shamelessly, and slowly while Jake's eyes darkened.

The woman with green eyes and smoother hair than her sister's wild-fire-looking waves sighed. "Can you two stop teasing each other so we can do something useful?"

"But teasing *is* useful, dear Ayla," Jake said, closing his hand and Taking the bowl away as he walked towards Lenna. "And you always look so fucking sexy."

The heir of the North House curled her upper lip in disgust, looking at her twin and the dark-haired man devouring her with his silver eyes. "Cardinals guide me somewhere out of here. Hope, shall we make a start?"

"Are we doing magic or blades?"

"Magic. Our disagreement was about who should lead and what we should practice," Ayla explained.

Because Hope had received no formal panom training, and the Brachyan sisters had. Lenna's Panom Guidor had been the man teasing her, and Ayla had learned from the Ruler of the South House.

Yet a certain person with night and pine scent had been teaching her as much as Hope could imagine any Panom Guidor doing.

"I told my beloved sister that you already know the basic stuff and can control each petal of your panom mark, but she insists on practicing more. I wanted to take it a step further and think about how we could use the powers and combine them in different real-life scenarios."

"Because knowing *the basic stuff* is not going to take her very far," Ayla told Lenna. "She has to fully control and own each power, so the more she practices, the better. And it would be useful for us too. It has only been a few months since we had the Fifth Ceremony and I don't know about you, but I feel I barely know my magic at its core."

Hope wasn't used to being talked about in third person when she was in the same conversation. But regardless of that, both sisters were right.

"We could practice each power individually and use them in scenarios that could happen in reality. We can combine powers, but working together towards the same goal," Hope said.

The twins nodded, and Hope didn't miss the slight narrowing of Jake's eyes.

Being outlaws chased by the Roix—the military organization of Thyria commanded by the Organ Mandor—there was a vast number of scenarios they could encounter. It was ironic that the fugitives the roixers were so desperate to find were hiding in an invisible safehouse atop the highest building of the busiest square of Corentre. Right under their nose. Or *above* their nose.

"If we Give a pretend scenario, we might be biased by already planning how to fix it. Jake, would you honor us?" Hope asked.

Lenna lifted an eyebrow, as if she wasn't used to hearing *Jake* and *honor* in the same sentence.

There hadn't been a noise by the archway, but Hope felt a presence that made her look. Her almost black irises locked with the blue eyes of the devastatingly beautiful man staring at her. His smooth dark hair fell casually over his inked shoulders, his metallic arm and his biological arm were crossed over his broad chest.

Ciaran Castel didn't say anything. A slight dip of his chin was the only visible greeting. He just observed Hope, his eyes not moving from hers, as if the rest of the room or the world were empty and meaningless.

"It would be my absolute pleasure," Jake said.

2

Lenna

What the Cardinals' fuck was this woman thinking?

That Hope had asked Jake to give free reign to his imagination, creating a scenario for them, meant three things.

1. Hope had no clue her half-brother's mind was as dark as they came.

2. She was utterly dauntless.

3. They were about to be in for a treat, and Jake would make sure it wasn't an easy one.

The growing side smile on the face of the gorgeous man Lenna spent day and night worshiping was a dangerous reminder that Jake did not like limits or boundaries. Well, he *liked* them in the sense that he enjoyed stepping on them, breaking and twisting them until they were dust.

As if Jake had read the honest worry in her frown, he whispered in her ear, "Don't be so worried, my golden girl. You wouldn't be my woman if you didn't like a challenge."

Lenna wanted to threaten him and tell him to be careful with what he came up with, unless he wanted his balls to suffer challenges in multiple ways, but she bit her tongue. Maybe it would truly be a useful chance to practice the four powers they had mastered. Especially if they were planning to obtain the Fifth Power in the near future.

"Don't break my house," Ciaran warned from the archway.

"I wouldn't dare," Jake said. "I can behave like a civilized guest."

Lenna lifted her eyebrows. "That doesn't mean you do."

Jake winked at her, and her blood wanted to warm up thinking about all the ways he was everything but civilized and controlled. Her blood didn't have time, though.

Jake's arms expanded in front of his chest, and he opened his hands—those *very* skilled hands— and Gave a floating red crystal orb in the middle of the Badassery Suite.

Lenna hadn't missed the damned orbs.

As soon as it appeared, Ayla, Hope, and Lenna readjusted their positions. They formed an equilateral triangle, all of them keeping a safe distance from the orb in the middle.

From Lenna's spot, she saw Ayla extending her arms in front of her, ready to wield her powers depending on what happened next. Lenna's own hands were half opened closer to her body, keeping the gravitational center stable. She didn't need to see Hope to know her hands were on her blades, the ever-present companions of the black-eyed and black-haired woman.

The orb cracked loudly, and three red-feathered arrows shot towards the three of them simultaneously.

Lenna closed her hand and Took the arrow away, making it vanish. Ayla opened her hand to Give an invisible wall, and the arrow hit against it, breaking before falling on the floor. Hope moved a step to the side and caught the arrow by the shaft mid-air and then Gave a spark of fire that combusted the whole thing in a few seconds.

"I doubt the Cardinals will appreciate the use of red feathers in arrows," Ayla said, not putting her hands down.

"I appreciate the appreciation. Our goddesses are welcome to come and complain." Lenna didn't need to look at Jake to know he couldn't care less about bothering the five red Cardinals who created Thyria.

The next crack of the orb was followed by ten arrows aimed at each of them, and Lenna was too fucking busy Taking the arrows away before they hit her to spare a glance at the others to see their strategies. Hope didn't have ten hands to catch so many arrows, that was for sure.

Lenna Took two arrows away before realizing their speed would make it difficult to vanish all of them in time. She Gave herself a metallic shield to hold which was painfully heavy but sufficient, so the eight remaining arrows collided against it.

Now she was safe until Jake Gave them another brilliant scenario, she saw Ayla protected behind the same invisible wall as before, more arrows spread on the surrounding floor.

Lenna turned around to see that Hope had taken matters into her own hands and—

"How the actual Fifth have you cut every single arrow in half?" Lenna frowned.

"With my daggers."

"Without magic?" Lenna asked. Hope nodded, swallowing and looking slightly disappointed. Was she disappointed in herself for not having used magic? As if she had remembered that the practice today was meant to be magic and not blades, Hope Took the twenty halves away, making them disappear.

"But *how*? They were fast," Lenna insisted.

Hope looked slightly puzzled, as if she found explaining something as basic was really complicated. Except there wasn't anything basic in what she had done, and there shouldn't be that much complication in explaining her steps.

"The arrows were aligned in two parallel lines and equally distant. I stepped forward a few steps to be in the middle of both lines and I cut them top to bottom when the time and distance were right."

Lenna's golden eyes widened. Every time she thought she got used to the extreme abilities the heir of the Organ House had, Hope proved they had yet to see so much more. "Cardinals fucking guide me," Lenna whispered. Ayla muttered something that sounded like agreement.

Lenna looked at Jake, wondering if that had been the whole display and they had been lucky that evening. Jake only said, "Eyes not on me, Brachyan."

Lenna snorted while turning around. She doubted he would say that line many other times.

The crystal orb made a gulping noise, and total darkness followed, then silence.

Lenna Gave an invisible shield around her, unable to see if anything came out of the orb but hearing a clear hiss on the ground.

Lenna inhaled sharply, her jaw tensing. If Jake had brought a slithering beast to the room, she was going to destroy him. Later. When and if they made sure the beast didn't destroy them first.

Red sparks floated across the room, coming from Hope's hands, illuminating it slightly. Lenna Gave her golden sparks, the same hue as the panom mark between her breasts, making them float around as well. Ayla's came after.

She wished she could stop and contemplate how beautiful the three colors looked together. Lenna's golden sunshine, Ayla's silver moonlight, and Hope's Cardinal-red sparks.

Especially as the hissing creature was nowhere to be seen and it had stopped dragging its body through the floor. Maybe it thrived in darkness alone.

The orb made another noise and Took every single spark away, as if it had swallowed them. Blackness surrounded them, and the three young women Gave another set of sparks, stronger and brighter this time, before the orb absorbed them again.

For a couple of minutes, the three of them Gave, and Gave, and Gave, only to be thrust back to darkness every time the orb ingested their lights.

Lenna could feel the balance of Giving so much without Taking tilting the inner magical balance that kept her safe. Giving and Taking were opposite poles of the same scale, as the North and South Petals, origins of said powers, also were direct opposites. The same happened with Healing and Harming, the powers of the West and East Petals, except these were harder to master and drained the panom wielder faster, in most cases.

Each panom reacted differently when their inner scale was uneven, and the slight blurriness in her mind, beginning of cold sweat on her forehead, and growing dizziness were signs that Lenna was pushing her inner scale more than she should.

There were only a few things she could Take to compensate her inner balance: the invisible shield, which she would only do over her dead fucking body until the hissing beast was gone; her own clothes, which she wouldn't mind if she didn't hope they were an extra layer of protection against the creature; and her own health, which was likely to happen sooner rather than later if she Gave much more, anyway.

The lights were swallowed by the orb again, and the last thing Lenna saw before the darkness and the hissing returned was Ayla pressing her palms against her eyes with a painful moan.

"Lenna, Ayla, please stop. You look unwell," Hope said.

Lenna would have made a comment about *unwell* being a very kind and generous description of their ridiculous condition, but she wasn't sure if she could talk and hold the content of her guts in at the same time.

Hope removed her shield. She Gave herself a sword and ran towards the orb, smashing it in pieces, all their sparks exploding into the room in a nebulous of red, golden, and silver light.

A hissing creature was cornered. Hope tilted her head. Was she considering letting it go?

"Out now. Please," Lenna begged.

"I'm thinking whether to Harm it, kill it the traditional way, or Take it away," Hope explained without taking her eyes away from her target.

Right. So many options.

After what seemed like an endless moment, Hope Harmed the beast, twisting its body over itself until it was a pile of pulp. Lenna was glad her sight was blurry. She Took away her invisible shield and felt the slightest improvement.

Hope walked towards Ayla, who was still covering her eyes with her hands with a grimace. She opened her hands until the room became a forest. Grass, moss, and flowers covered the ground, trees towering over bushes and plants. Only someone who had been raised in the woods could recreate one with magic with such precision. It was obvious Hope had lived and grown up in the woods of Verdania for twenty-four years.

Hope hovered her hands in circular motions atop Ayla's eyes. The green-eyed twin whispered her gratitude, her contorted features relaxing as Hope Healed the consequences of her inner scale being unbalanced. When Ayla could open her eyes slightly and finally take in the forest surrounding them, her body shook with the sudden change in the Badassery Suite.

Hope asked Lenna, "Do you need Healing, Lenna? Or do you think you can Take bits of the forest away until your inner scale is reestablished?"

"I can tidy up this beautiful mess, even though a part of me feels sorry. It's gorgeous."

Hope smiled with melancholy. "Thank you."

"But please Take away the hissing pulp, who thank fuck isn't hissing anymore. I will owe you a favor for the rest of my existence."

Hope closed her hand and the leftovers of the beast were gone.

Ciaran had stood all this time in the archway, analyzing everything as he always did. He walked towards a red rose and picked it up with his metallic arm. "We must start planning our next moves."

3

Hope

T he dining table in the living room of the Crystal Clear safehouse was full and busy. The fugitives seated around it were loud and hungry.

Plates clattered around as people served the delicacies Ayla had cooked for them, the way Hope had always cooked: with food, utensils, fire, and patience. Even if the starting ingredients had to be Given because they couldn't get them in any other way without risking being seen in the markets.

Jake and Lenna sat next to each other. Lenna's curly-haired best friend, Sasha, was chatting with Lenna in their usual profanity-full talks. Indianna, with her black bob and ever-so-stylish outfits, happily joined in the conversation.

Next to Indianna was Brendon, the blond, stunning man with green eyes who used to work for the most secretive organization of Thyria before becoming one of the most searched for beings on the island. He was next to Ciaran, the pair of them full of ink on their arms and upper bodies. Over the recent weeks, Hope had noticed Ciaran always seemed comfortable around Brendon, as if he could be his true self.

Hope and Ayla sat next to each other in an awkward silence since the cheerful white-haired female had left to check in on her brother next door. Hope would never understand how Nina could be so talkative and look like she enjoyed talking at the same time.

Hope found both things equally exhausting and totally draining, especially when she was in groups, which was often the case while they were secluded inside this house.

Living a quarter of a century in the peaceful woods of Verdania with the sole company and presence of her mother was not the best preparation for when one started living in wider society from one day to the other.

"This is delicious, Ayla," Hope said, putting the fork with cranberry tart on her plate. "I'm going to check if Nina is okay."

That was a good enough excuse to go get some air. It wasn't a lie. She would check in on Nina, right after taking a few deep breaths on the patio. She needed air and clarity of mind to recharge her social energy long enough to make it until the end of dinner without feeling overwhelmed.

The scent of jasmine hit her as soon as she stepped outside, and a smile spread across Hope's face. She walked to the jasmine plants covering the walls and stayed there, inhaling in the nature and exhaling the crap that her mind struggled with.

She could do this. Of course she could. Feeling overwhelmed had never stopped her before. *Nothing* had ever stopped her before, but she truly wanted to get to know these people. From the science-related obsessions of Sasha to Jake's sarcastic comments; from the intelligent yet quiet eyes of Ciaran to Lenna's wishes for an equal and just world, where all beings' lives are respected and valued fairly.

Hope gritted her teeth as a slicing pain made her arm twitch involuntarily.

She didn't need to look at her now blood-dripping inner forearm to know who had sent her an inked message.

Again.

At this point, Hope knew his handwriting by heart.

When panom beings sent inks, the words of their written messages had the color of their panom magic, the same color of their sparks and the panom mark on their skin.

But this wasn't the case.

Rhei Coralt, the Organ Mandor of the Organ House, and Hope and Jake's father, had been sending her *bleeding* inks. Inks that cut through her skin and didn't vanish for hours. The reason Hope did not wear short-sleeved tops anymore and only wore clothes that were between the range of very black and utterly dark.

For the sole purpose of not having a soaked shirt, she pulled her left sleeve up and patted the drops of blood with one of the black tissues she now always carried with her.

She had tried not to read his ink messages while cleaning them, but that proved to be very messy and not as easy as she might have expected. Right now, the bleeding ink on her arm read:

Your mother would be heartbroken if her daughter hid for the rest of her life.

Her daughter, as if Hope wasn't also his own daughter. Bastard daughter, perhaps, but daughter all the same.

Ironic, that he who had broken her mother's heart twice dared to mention it.

Rhei Coralt didn't have the slightest idea of the many ways Hope was planning to slice him.

Impatience riled Hope as she and her not-dripping-anymore-but-still-sore arm walked to Raoul's room.

Of course, her father wanted to bait her to come out of hiding and confront him now. But she would not be hiding for the rest of her life. She only needed to get the Fifth Power first to stand a chance against her father.

The young man with ocean-blue eyes standing next to Nina resembled her so much that no one could miss they were brother and sister. Raoul was taller than Nina, and his white hair had a couple of black streaks coming from his temple.

"You're looking good, Raoul," Hope said, walking towards his side to offer an arm as Nina was helping support him from the other. "First time standing?"

"First time, indeed." His voice was less weak than the last time Hope heard him.

"Are you coming to join dinner?"

"If I make it that far," his voice lacked the confidence that Nina's encouraging nod had.

Hope surreptitiously moved her spare hand to send her red ink to Ciaran, Indianna, and Ayla, the ones more likely to act quickly and without making the fuss that Raoul surely wanted to avoid.

*Please make space for Raoul.
We're coming.*

The chatter coming from the living room stopped for long enough to let Hope murmur, "Shit."

Of course, making three out of seven people look at their inked forearms at the same time hadn't been the best strategic decision of her life. Of course, the short-lived silence was followed by multiple chairs dragged in a rush, and a louder, more energetic and approaching chatter.

And, in a matter of seconds, multiple people appeared at the doorway simultaneously. Mainly people standing, with Lenna already sitting on Jake's shoulders to get a better view, Sasha pushing Brendon to the side with a bit too much elbow, and Ciaran not lasting long inside the tight crowd before he moured next to Raoul and supported him from behind.

Raoul wasn't walking anymore. He was looking at the diverse emotions of the multitude of people staring at him. There were grins, half-tears, and reassuring smiles. There was empathy, excitement, affection, and joy.

"This is not a safehouse. This is a madhouse," he chuckled, a single tear leaving the corner of his eye.

"Says the man who spent the last few months unconscious, muttering random, unintelligible stuff while mysteriously traveling across the world," Lenna grinned. "You fit right in, R."

Raoul tilted his head back with a roaring laugh. "You lot are nuts. I missed you too, L."

4

Lenna

Sat at the table amongst them, Raoul couldn't stop smiling, and Lenna couldn't take her golden eyes away from him. She couldn't remember the last time they had seen each other in such normal circumstances. As "normal" as being fugitives chased by the damned Roix was. But well, oh well, wasn't that their new normal? No big drama.

"Do you remember when your father found us playing in the flowery bit by the servant rooms when you were around nine?" Raoul said.

Lenna snorted. "He got so pissed when he couldn't find us for five hours."

"Five hours?! Where did you hide, in the gardens?" Ayla asked.

Lenna shook her head, cocking an eyebrow. "We sneaked into his chambers while he was out desperately looking for us around the house."

"Shut. Up." Ayla's eyes widened, her mouth twitching as if she was considering hiding a smile.

"We put on tons of his North Ruler's clothes and jewels and pretended to be him until we got bored and went back outside," Lenna continued, enjoying seeing the smile that definitely won Ayla's inner battle.

"We left behind a disgraceful mess for him," Raoul added.

"Sorry, not sorry, asshole." Lenna felt a tinge of proudness at her younger self not standing and conforming with societal barriers. Being a member of the North House and only being allowed to have relationships with other panoms and the members of the Elite had never stopped her from talking to anyone she wanted to. Especially when most Elite beings won their bullshit status by paying disgraceful amounts of money to the Houses. Sums of money that could feed entire homeless families for a century, if not more.

Elite members who won their privileged status by having certain unique skills, intelligence, or abilities were rare. Hence why Sasha, Brendon, and Indianna were one of a kind, each excelling at their own fields. Sasha had an amazing scientific mind. Brendon was unique at intercepting and hacking the systems, analyzing and manipulating information, and Indianna was one of the best non-magical healers in Thyria.

The proud feeling of her younger self for pissing off her father came accompanied by the constant anger any thoughts or memories about her family came with.

One would think that her panom parents would have sent her one damned ink to ask if she was still alive and breathing. They hadn't. Not that they had cared when she was tortured by the Organ Mandor right in front of their fucking faces, or that they did anything to avoid it.

Lenna had little doubt that their parents were communicating with her twin sister, Ayla. For succession of the North House purposes and all that crap. Lenna didn't miss being the heir of the North House. Not that she'd had any say in the decision when the Organ Mandor passed her heirloom of the Northern Petal to Ayla.

All because Lenna had refused to apologize to him and swear absolute royalty. No, Lenna hadn't very much not done that. Instead, she called the Organ Mandor a piece of shit with powers.

Her parents surely had felt nothing but relief when Lenna told them it was their dutiful daughter who would become the North Ruler. Instead of the daughter that rebelled against the stupid political system since she had memory.

The only good thing about having parents who didn't give a shit about her was that Lenna had learned the lesson years ago. Now, it didn't hurt nearly as much. Plus, who cared if her official family didn't love her well when she had a real family surrounding her? The officiality could go to the Fifth hell for all Lenna cared.

Her real family was an unusual group of people. If that didn't make life more interesting and entertaining, she didn't know what would. *A bunch of badass bitches and extremely good-looking men,* Sasha said the other day. A pretty accurate description.

The black-haired man next to her stroked her bare arm, invisible sparkles immediately trailing up her nerves. Lenna was going to demand explanations for the snake-looking-whatever creature Jake had summoned earlier, but despite her annoyance, there was no denying he was the most unlawfully handsome at the table, and very likely from all of Thyria. He was also the one who had earned more than her physical affection by not giving up on her and somehow seeing past the multiple self-imposed barriers that had protected her for over twenty-five years.

"Have you been sleeping better lately, Raoul?" Ayla asked.

He blinked. "Some nights I don't sweat or scream. I guess that's a good sign?"

"You haven't had a really bad night for a few days now," Nina added. "Since the second black streak appeared in your hair."

Which, like the first time it happened, hadn't gone away, painting his pure white permanently.

"That attack wasn't fun," he whispered, his unfocused eyes on the table, as if the memories were back in his mind.

"Attack?" Hope asked, narrowing her almost-dark eyes.

Raoul slowly dragged his eyesight from the table to the people surrounding it. "I haven't found a better description for those dreams. I've had nightmares before, but these . . ." He inhaled deeply before continuing, "They feel like a personal attack against my mind and my life. There is no escape. The only freedom is waking up." Raoul swallowed.

Lenna didn't need to ask why his voice trembled in the last sentence. Raoul had to be absolutely terrified of not waking up again. How could he not? He had been stuck in an unconscious state for months before they rescued him and managed to wake him up. *His best description for that time was an unconscious limbo full of blackness and whispers.*

He sometimes still said random shit no one understood the meaning of, which was worrying and disconcerting in equal parts. But at least he hadn't become aggressive again. Not since the first time he opened his eyes after taking one of the multiple drugs Indianna and Sasha had created for him.

According to the people who were there, that had been as scary as the worst panomquake. His pupils had been incredibly dilated, maybe from the drug's side effects or from his eyes being closed for months, and *he looked manic.* Surely Raoul grabbing Nina by the neck and saying something about a Crown of Death rising hadn't helped with his crazed look.

When Lenna and Jake had moured into the Crystal Clear Safehouse after that, Nina's bruises were visible around her throat and sore to look at, despite the Healing she had received.

Lenna held her multiple questions about the content of Raoul's mental attacks for another time. Tonight was about celebrating his improvement and the efforts he had put into making all this progress. She was so freaking proud of him.

"At this pace you'll be able to join us when we go get the Fifth." She nudged him gently enough to not make him fall from his seat but strongly enough for him to stop dwelling on his fears and bring him back to reality.

His eyes widened. "Is that what you lot plan on doing?"

Lenna frowned. "I mean, no shame for mundane fugitives, but I'd go up the damned walls if I had to hide here for eternity. Especially because of him."

Him being the father of the man Lenna shared her nights with—Jake.

And the father of the woman who Lenna had seen in full killing action and knew she could become death incarnate if she wanted to—Hope.

Shame the Organ Mandor wouldn't have much hope against any of them once they got the Fifth Power.

Because, yes, they hated him enough that they were willing to risk their lives to hunt the Fifth Power. The power no one in living history had possessed. The power that, according to Jake's lessons, was both a blessing and a curse. The power that would allow them to stand a chance against Rhei Coralt and kill him once and for all. Please and fucking thank you.

"So, how do we get the Fifth?" Hope asked, folding her arms.

Jake's silver eyes glittered with amusement. "I have done some research over time."

"*Decades* type of time or last-five-minutes time?" Lenna couldn't resist grinning at his unashamed self-importance.

"Centuries, more so. Is that good enough for you?" The corner of his lips tugged upwards at the same time as Lenna's heart skipped a beat.

"Fuck."

Jake turned his head towards the man with smooth, shoulder-long dark hair that never missed a word. "And so have you, Ciaran. Haven't you?"

"Perhaps." The index of Ciaran's metallic hand tapped the ring on his bottom lip distractedly.

"Or perhaps the *Origins of Cardinals and Other Gods* and Goddesses disappeared from the library at the West House by accident?" Jake asked, tilting his head.

"I figured it was worth hiding in case the rat who stole *Battle of Petals* and *Of Cardinals, Powers and Death* might want to steal it too."

"Clever chasing cat," Jake said, a mischievous side-smile on his lips.

"Is that what you truly did during your discarding visits around Thyria? Steal books?" Lenna asked. "Other than discard beings, I mean."

Jake purposely ignored the discarding part. "It's called research. For the preservation of the future and the land I was meant to rule if my father ever dies."

"Oh, he *will* definitely die." Hope's voice was calm and definite. A patient promise of death. "When can we go get the Fifth?"

Okay, maybe it was an *impatient* promise of death.

"Remind me why are we wanting to go on a death hunt to get the Fifth Power? Are our four panom powers not enough?" Ayla asked, her green eyes barely visible as she narrowed them.

"Not if you want to get rid of the disgrace of a man that kills innocent beings without remorse or consequence. The man who killed Ciaran's and Hope's mothers, who amputated Ciaran's arm in a failed attempt at removing his courtrade blood, who took my panom powers away and who would kill me if he knew I regained my powers, thanks to you all. And no, our four powers are not enough to kill the man who discarded Hope for existing when she was a baby, and her mother for giving birth to her. The man who is surely planning a slow and painful death for all of us," Lenna spat, the blood in her veins racing as her rage flourished to the surface. "If you're happy to be in a country where such a being rules, and don't mind living in a totally broken and corrupt society, then of course there is no need whatsoever to go on a death hunt. You can totally stay here waiting for him to hunt you to death instead."

The silence that followed could be cut into pieces. The green eyes of her twin didn't move from her amber ones.

"The sooner we get the Fifth, the sooner we get him." The determination in Hope's voice was undeniable.

"Jake and I will discuss our findings about the Fifth. Let's see if our theories align," Ciaran said, looking at Hope. "When we have a clear plan, we will move."

5

Hope

The steady banging music at the Sweetgum Beech kept the girls busy dancing and drinking myster. *The girls* being the regular night dancers: Lenna, Indianna, and Sasha.

Of the nocturnal shows in the busiest square of Corentre, Hope's favorite part was the colored water fountains surrounding whoever was performing.

The height of the safehouse was a privileged spot to enjoy these concerts. The girls were now jumping in a close circle, shouting some lyrics at the top of their throats while pointing to the red-tinged moon in the sky.

Hope chuckled from the rail of the balcony. Her head didn't pound as hard as the first time she had heard such loud music. It wasn't bad at all, in fact.

As for dancing, she doubted she would ever be relaxed enough to move her body at ease for any reason that wasn't fighting. It was amusing to see other beings living it so much.

The song finished its high, and the girls had a laughing fit as they hugged each other in a tangle of arms and heads.

Lenna filled a glass with myster and walked next to Hope, offering it to her with the confident grin of someone who wasn't used to being refused, or who didn't mind being refused.

"They didn't take long to fix the Cardinals Temple, did they?" Lenna snorted, looking at the crystal dome crowning the Organ House in the middle of Corentre. The dome Hope had unintentionally destroyed in a thousand pieces during her Fifth Ceremony.

"I guess more panoms-to-be will need their ceremonies, and it cannot be good for the Organ House's reputation."

Lenna shook her head. "As much as it pains me to admit, I think I love this city." Her mass of red waves flew to the side as Lenna snapped her head to look at Hope. The golden tone of her eyes was unnervingly similar to that of her golden magic sparks and her ink. "Have you ever been in love, Hope?"

Hope's eyebrows shot up, a knot automatically sitting in her chest as if she had received a kick between her lungs.

How to tell a woman who probably was in love with Jake that love was a trap, and one of the most dangerous ones?

"I haven't, and I don't want to. I don't need to. Love can kill and drown." The knot tightened at some very vivid memories of her childhood. Love had certainly drowned her mother.

Lenna narrowed her eyes. "Love can uplift and heal, too. It can transform."

"There are other ways to do those things that don't involve putting one's heart at risk of utter destruction," Hope said.

She respected Lenna's opinions, but she was not going to change her mind. Not when her mother's love had killed her, and Hope had been a witness.

"Are you in love, Lenna?"

The red-haired woman took her time drinking some myster before answering. "I would kill anybody who would harm Jake in any way. I would kill him when he makes my blood boil for all the wrong reasons." Lenna bit her bottom lip before saying, "I feel safe with him as I have never felt. I want to know him more and I am afraid of not having enough days to do so, even with our never-ending long panom lifespans."

"Do you trust him?" Hope asked.

Lenna's lips tightened in a thin line. "I have come to the conclusion that I will never fully trust anyone. Which is very sad, but . . . It's true. There is always a part of me holding back. A part of me expecting abandonment, betrayal or lies. As if not giving my full trust is the only way to protect myself from being hurt. I don't think I even know how to fully trust someone, because I have never done so. Jake is no exception to this."

Lenna exhaled deeply. Her eyes had a glassy look when she turned to face Hope. "Please don't tell your brother," she begged, her voice low as if she was ashamed of herself and what she had just admitted out loud.

"I won't," Hope promised.

It was way past ante meridiem, and Hope couldn't sleep.

The inner constant trail of questions and need for information was threatening to outburst her mind. She had lived with unanswered questions for decades, yet now that answers were a thing, she didn't seem to know how to wait.

Maybe that was a good thing. A sign that life didn't have to be a continuous mystery that slapped her face when she least expected it, even if it made her more impatient.

There was only one person who she dared talk to about her current worry. One person who could understand what she was talking about and not judge her for it.

Hope followed the scent of night and pine through the safehouse, down the extremely dark corridor that left her slamming her head against the intended door.

A rush of air was the only sign that Ciaran opened his door. "Very glamorous knocking."

Both the corridor and his bedroom were pitch black. He must have realized or remembered not everyone could see in the shadows, like his courtrade blood allowed him to. The next and first thing Hope saw were his blue eyes glittering on his pale face, followed by the shiny reflection of his metallic arm moving before dark green sparks illuminated his bedroom.

Another couple of movements of his arms reigned the black shadows to nothing. A bedroom full of packed bookshelves and weapons appeared in front of her eyes.

"Isn't it a bit late to be playing with weapons?" Hope asked.

"It's never too late for that," he said, and Hope couldn't have agreed more. "May I help you?"

"I . . . I have a question. About my magic."

Ciaran nodded. "Do you want to come in, or would you rather talk on the patio?"

Hope hesitated for the long span of half a second. She had never been in his bedroom before, and it felt like an intrusion of privacy. Even if this man had licked her blood to find out about her heritage, had helped her become a full panom by having a Fifth Ceremony, and had protected her after she semi-destroyed the island when her magic unleashed.

"Here is fine," she said entering his bedroom and heading towards one of the armchairs before she could reconsider her decision.

She was surprised to find Ciaran closing the door with a slight smile on his lips. Green sparks flickered intensely, rearranging themselves around the seating area as Ciaran sat in front of her.

"I'm all ears," he said, placing his muscled and metallic arms comfortable on the armrests.

"You told me about the inner balance of the magics. Of Giving and Taking, and Healing and Harming, and how opposite powers must be used warily to not tilt the magical scales. You said different panoms react differently when their scales are unbalanced."

His blue eyes were patient, and Hope was perfectly aware that she hadn't asked her question yet.

"I have tried pushing the use of one of the powers of each scale to see what happens. And that's the problem: nothing happens." Hope exhaled.

"Why is that a problem?" Ciaran asked.

"Well, it doesn't make sense. The other day, for example. When Jake Gave us something to practice with. After a while, Ayla was half blind, Lenna was very dizzy, and . . . What? I felt just *normal*?"

"I wouldn't say you are normal, Hope. Quite the opposite. I think that, amongst many other things, makes you extraordinary," Ciaran said, interlacing his fingers in front of his broad chest.

Hope blinked. Being dumped as a baby on an island where unwanted beings were discarded by Thyrian society was *extraordinarily* wrong. But she got his point, or a part of it.

"Is it common to not feel the inner balance tilting? Do you feel anything when you use one power without its opposite?"

"Panoms don't share their weaknesses widely. But, in cases like Ayla and Lenna, their symptoms are visible," he said. "My guess is every panom in Thyria feels something. You must be amongst the exceptions. If not *the* exception."

"Why?" Hope asked, playing with the loose strands of her braid as a theory grew in her mind.

Ciaran moved his eyes from the spot of dark hair she was holding to her black eyes. "You are the first female in centuries with panom blood that belongs to the Core. Your blood is linked to the strongest part of Thyria, the Organ House that rules over the others. And . . . The panom mark at the back of your neck and your magic is red. *Red*, Hope."

Hope inhaled sharply. The redness of her magic was in line with her new theory.

Ciaran continued, "The goddesses who created our land are red Cardinals. Red is a sacred color, and they have blessed you with it. Perhaps not suffering from an inner balance is another blessing."

"Only the Fifth knows," her voice was graver than she intended to. "You haven't answered my other question. Do you feel anything?"

"I do, and I've never told anyone," he said.

Hope nodded in silence. She wouldn't ask him for details. They barely knew each other, at the end of the day. It was none of her business to know his deepest, most guarded secrets.

For her own sake and self-preservation, she was going to keep quiet about her balance circumstances too.

6

Lenna

L enna knew she was being selfish as well as she knew she should feel remorse for what she was about to do.

She would make sure to find her remorse later. For now, she was too busy finding a silver-eyed man.

The last place she had left to check was where she least expected to find Jake.

Her knuckles knocked on Ciaran's door. A male voice invited her to come in, and there they were.

There, in the middle of a horrendously disorganized mess of parchments, notes, ink pots, quills, and books. *Lots* of books.

Considering Jake and Ciaran were meant to be studying and putting together their years of findings about the Fifth Power, this wasn't the least expected place to find him, after all.

"Good boys, doing all this hard work." Lenna walked towards the wide bed and moved a pile of books to the side to have enough space to sit. "Any progress?"

Ciaran nodded distractedly from the floor, underlining something on one of the books and adding a note next to a paragraph before putting the quill behind his ear. He passed the page and continued reading.

"I think we're finally getting somewhere." Jake turned around in his chair to face her, and as he looked at her, a side smile spread on his gorgeous lips. He didn't need to scan her from top to bottom for her to know it had been worth changing her outfit.

You clearly also want to get somewhere, *don't you, Brachyan?*

Jake's voice echoed in her mind, and she cocked an eyebrow. She didn't know how to speak to his mind, but her white, fresh clothes were answer enough.

"I'll be right back, Ciaran," Jake said standing up, before reconsidering and correcting himself, "Probably not *right back*, but I'll see you soon. I think we've got this, anyway. We're just getting to the same conclusion over and over."

Well, if she wasn't interrupting any ground-breaking revelation, there was definitely no need to go looking for her remorse for disturbing their task.

Ciaran hummed in response, passing another page and not seeming too concerned about Jake abandoning him to their mess.

As soon as Jake and Lenna were out of Ciaran's bedroom and the door closed, he pulled her back against the wall.

"Someone is looking dangerously attractive," he whispered in her ear. A shiver rushing up her spine.

"Someone better make up for the time lost studying," Lenna said. "I miss you."

Jake pulled his head backwards enough to look at her golden eyes. He put a finger down her chin, lifting it slightly until her gaze met his. The silver in his eyes was so clear and calm that Lenna wanted to get lost in them.

Lenna was ready to tell him off if he said that it was stupid to miss someone who was right next to her. If he argued they saw each other every day and slept in the same bed every night. If he asked her how could she miss him when they were together more than they had ever been.

But instead, he sighed.

"I miss you too, Lenna."

She was not ready for the slow and deep touch of his lips on hers. For the caring and the tenderness that their lips colliding transpired.

She, who had kissed countless men in what seemed another life, would never grow accustomed to being kissed with such an emotional connection. Jake stroked her red waves behind her ear, caressing her cheek with a soft yet callused hand. Lenna didn't need to open her eyes to guess his silver eyes were probably open, drinking her in.

Their lips broke open, leaving space for their tongues to dance with each other, and damn every Cardinal one by one if the built-up warmth didn't suddenly escalate to a live combustion.

Lenna grabbed his insanely terse biceps with her hands as if she was holding on to them for dear life. Jake grabbed her fire-colored hair with his fists, making her tilt her head backwards while he devoured her mouth. Lenna pulled her arm backwards to touch his luscious abdomen, her elbow loudly banging against the wall.

Ciaran appeared in his now open doorway, mere inches away from their tangled bodies and faces. His long, sleek dark hair flowed to one side as he tilted his head sideways.

"I would be grateful if you two don't fuck at my doorstep." His voice was serious, with an almost negligible hint of hidden amusement.

"What sort of disgraceful guests would do that?" Lenna asked with a grin.

"*We* would very much do that." The mischief in Jake's voice was enough to make Lenna stop talking and start taking clothes off. "I said it once before, Ciaran, but you're welcome to join us, if you want." Jake winked at the man now rolling his blue eyes. "Only if my woman doesn't mind, of course."

"Oh, I don't share," she declared. "Not when I'm starving in this house full of interrupting and nosy beings." Lenna lifted her eyebrows, looking at Ciaran with intent.

Maybe the heir of the West House decided he had made his point, and they would behave. Or maybe he didn't want to witness what would happen if they didn't want to listen, because he walked towards the end of the corridor and disappeared from sight.

And that right there was why Lenna had been missing the very man she was touching right now.

"I know you have to research and all of that, but maybe we could escape for a few hours," she said, putting her head against his chest. "It would be nice to be alone. Just you and me. Without others, without distractions, without noise."

"But I love the sounds you make when I make you come, sweet fire," Jake said, placing his arms around her body in a hug that brought her even closer to his chest. The beating rhythm of his heart was as comforting as his muscles next to her cheek. "Let's moure away from here. Do you want to do the honors?"

Lenna looked at him. Cardinals, he was stunning when he towered above her like this.

She hadn't moured anyone with her before. She had practiced how to move from one place to another by herself, and that had been challenging and exciting

Still, it was probably better to try now than in an emergency, like Hope and Ayla had been forced to do to escape the Beftac Center for Injured Beings not that long ago.

"Don't blame me if we end up hanging from the top of a tree."

Jake grinned, his eyes darkening to a light grey. "Then I will fuck you at the top of a tree."

Lenna put her palm on the back of Jake's neck, concentrating on the hideaway beach house that Jake had only ever shared with her.

The guarded place somewhere in the South Petal where the sand was white and the ocean water blue. The place where they had spent some time together before coming to the Crystal Clear Safehouse. There, the bright sun was a given and the heat a constant. Lenna felt like wearing anything but white clothes in such a pure place was outrageous. So it was that, or nothing at all.

She had the conviction that the golden panom mark between her breasts would allow her magic to moure Jake with her. So, she took a mental step towards her destination, and the world started spinning around them.

7

Hope

H ope had finally decided to talk to Lenna about a recurring worry she had. Shame she had been unable to find her today. Jake hadn't been around, either. They must have moured outside the safehouse, as they sometimes did.

The risk of someone intercepting them in the middle of a guarded mouring was very low, according to Ciaran and Jake. But that was the thing with risks—the possibility of error was always there.

Not that risks had ever stopped Hope before.

She had been considering for a while what would happen when Rhei Coralt died. Because everyone in the house seemed to think that because Hope was the heir, she would take on the role of the Organ Mandor. But she had no clue about how Thyria and its society full of human beings, Elite, and panoms worked. She was not the appropriate person to rule anyone, let alone a whole country.

Sometimes Jake and Lenna came back in a few hours, sometimes in a few days. Since Jake and Ciaran were meant to be discussing strategies to get the Fifth, the former was the likely option in this case. But in case, it wasn't, Hope sent her red ink to Lenna:

Can you come to the Badassery Suite?

There wasn't an answer straight away, but eventually the golden letters of Lenna's handwriting inked Hope's forearm:

When the biggest badass is calling?
Coming.

Hope snorted. The amount of fuss Sasha and Lenna made when Hope did anything with her blades was something unheard of.

Not that long ago, they had interrupted her daily throwing practice, right after she aimed at the head of a mannequin she had Given the room and knocked it backwards, by squealing, clapping, and cheering. She had patiently waited for them to leave, talking about their books, before she Gave another mannequin and aimed at its heart from a bigger distance.

Another golden ink followed not long after:

Apologies for the delay. I'm nearly there.
I was coming in many ways.

Hope heard the confident steps of the high heels before a smiling Lenna walked through the door.

"Hi there. Brendon just told me the roixers are busy following some fake clues leading to us in the South Petal. The amount of work that man can do in the span of a few hours is admirable."

Hope nodded vigorously. "He's very good." Years working at the Invisible Grand, the most secretive organization of Thyria, had made the blond and green-eyed man a dangerous, misleading tool. Hope sometimes doubted if he was doing it purely to help them not be caught, or because he was delighted messing around with the military roixers and making them waste their time.

Lenna looked at her expectantly.

Hope inhaled. "So, I've been thinking about what will happen when the current Mandor is dead. And I thought . . . Would you do it?"

"Do what?" Lenna raised an eyebrow.

"Rule Thyria."

Lenna's eyes widened and the look she gave Hope made her hear her thoughts out loud. Lenna thought Hope had lost her mind. The tinge of worry in her frown might have been a sign that the red-haired thought Hope's brain damage would be irreversible.

Hope continued before the red-haired woman could add any ironic retort. "You know how things work here well enough to fight against the injustices of the system and speak up for the voices of the beings that panoms don't want to hear."

Lenna shrugged. "That doesn't mean the Cardinals have blessed me with the blood of the Core. They would be royally pissed if you just pass your heirloom like you're passing a lipstick. Plus, I don't think it's doable. Your father took my heirloom and passed it to my sister because being twins makes us similar enough that the change in duties didn't make the land collapse." Lenna bit her bottom lip in an unsuccessful attempt at keeping her side smile in. "Seeing how your Fifth Ceremony went in terms of breaking half the city, I can guess how refusing to become the Organ Mandor would go."

A panomquake caused by that would leave no one and nothing left to rule.

Hope swallowed. "I can't do it, though. I mean, if I have no choice, I will do it. I'm not going to let people die because of me." Not *again*. Not if she could avoid it. The desperate cries and the bodies spread on the Beftac Center for Injured Beings after her Fifth Ceremony still chased her dreams. "But I want to do it properly, and I cannot do that by myself."

She couldn't remember the last time she had asked for help. So openly, and most importantly, without being ashamed of admitting out loud that she couldn't do something by herself. Maybe there wasn't a *last time* because this was her *first time*. Ever.

Lenna passed a hand through her fire-colored waves, the ends of her hair moving against the white, revealing stripes of her top. Her golden eyes were fixed on a spot on the opposite wall.

"I could be your First Hand, if you want," Lenna said.

"Excuse me?"

"Some Rulers in the past had a panom that gave them advice and supported them when making decisions and that sort of stuff." Lenna chuckled before adding, "My mentor would be proud to know I remember some facts from his history lessons."

"Why *Hand*, though?" Hope asked.

"The Fifth only knows. But it's boring, right? I wouldn't sign up to be called body parts of anyone. But if you call me something cooler, I would consider it."

Hope lifted her eyebrows. She was not the right person to think in terms of coolness. "Is First Feather a better fit?"

Lenna put a finger on her chin. "I can work with that."

The sudden sharp pain in Hope's arm woke her up as the door of her bedroom opened with a bang.

Ciaran stormed inside, panting and gasping.

As soon as his blue eyes locked with Hope's, he covered his face with both hands. "I'm going to kill him even if it's the last thing I do," he muttered through clenched teeth.

Shadows trembled on his wrists and ankles as if they held so much tension and rage that they could kill someone there and then.

She could feel the deep frown on her face. She had never seen him like this. Ciaran always was the embodiment of self-control and serenity.

"Are you hurt?" His voice was urging.

"Me?" Hope shook her head, the adrenaline of the feeling that something was very wrong building up in her veins. "I was sleeping. What's wr—?"

Before Hope could finish her sentence, Nina screamed, horrified, at the other end of the apartment. Hope jumped out of the bed and started running towards the location of the scream.

They collided in a corridor, Nina shaking while touching Hope's face over and over to make sure she was real. Her ocean-blue eyes were tinged with red broken little capillaries. Nina hugged her, crying while she repeated, "Thank the blessed Cardinals. Thank the blessed Cardinals."

Ciaran's steps had followed Hope closely from her bedroom, and while Nina cried, Hope asked Ciaran, "What happened?" Her face tensed with worry at whatever danger Ciaran and Nina had encountered.

Ciaran looked at the crystal ceiling, shadows still curling around his ankles. Dark green sparks jumped from his metallic arm as if it was electrified. "Come and see."

He guided her to the balcony facing the Sweetgum Beech. Hope only stopped briefly to leave Nina in the kitchen with Ayla, who started preparing her a hot drink straightaway. Whatever had caused Nina to be so distressed, she didn't need to see again.

Hope let out a broken gasp when she saw the water fountains.

The water wasn't clear as usual. It was red. And there, in the middle of the platform, surrounded by water where the artists used to perform, lay a dead woman.

A black-haired woman with two braids, a muscular and fit complexion, taller than average and wearing the same dark clothes Hope usually wore.

A chill ran through her veins, placating the warm adrenaline rush into an icy fury. The eyes of the dead woman were closed, but Hope had a feeling they were black like hers.

The Organ Mandor had done a public mock assassination of his daughter.

"Does he know we are here?" Hope asked, her voice steady despite the tumultuous emotions cascading inside her.

"He can't know that. The house is invisible to unwanted eyes." Ciaran didn't falter, his clenched teeth marking his strong jaw. "He has chosen the busiest part of his city to make a public threat."

Even if the beings looking at the corpse, covering their mouths and whispering, had no idea who the threat was for, and what it was for.

"You're bleeding," he said, his voice tense, on edge like his shadows and his temper.

Hope knew all too well who had sent her bleeding ink. Her bleeding arm was nothing compared to the innocent, lifeless woman left on display for the citizens of Corentre to see. For the citizens of Corentre to *fear*.

She read his ink with a devastating repulsion and hatred towards the sender, and a nauseating frustration at not being able to stop his words on her flesh.

Until I can end your life, I will end others. The longer you hide, the higher the deaths. All of them are on you.

Her blood froze.

It was wrong.

It was so wrong that he could invade her body like that. It felt almost like a violation. It was a wicked, disgraceful intrusion.

Ciaran's eyes widened as he read the ink before Hope Gave herself a bandage. He looked at her, an angry and concerned frown making his eyebrows get closer. "This is not the first time he's sent you ink."

It wasn't a question. It was an affirmation.

"It's not," Hope confirmed.

Ciaran's blue eyes darkened with the promise of the painful and long death Hope was planning on giving the Organ Mandor.

Until now, she had found the bleeding inks unnerving but useful to keep track of how lost and desperate Rhei Coralt was to find them. To find *her*. But this . . . This sadistic exhibit of wickedness and barbarity was too much.

"Is there any way to stop his inks from coming?"

Ciaran grabbed the rail of the balcony, the muscles of his biological arm tensing. "He is very powerful. I can show you how to block incoming inks, but he might still break the glass."

"It's worth trying," she said. "We can do that another day." She wasn't in the mood for any lessons right now.

"Please come with me," he said, as he moved his hand, and dark green sparks went flying through the door in different directions.

Hope had seen him use that trick to gather people a few times before. Each spark would find a person and lead them towards where Ciaran was.

Shortly after, his sparks had gathered everyone in the living room.

Ayla had a gentle hand on Nina's shoulders. Nina's eyes were still red, but she wasn't crying anymore.

Raoul had walked by himself, Indianna hovering next to him in case he needed an extra hand.

Lenna sat on Jake's legs, her lips tight in a line that promised serious trouble if required. Jake's hands were laced around her waist, and Hope didn't miss the dark cloth covering his forearm. It looked like she wasn't the only one receiving bleeding inks from their father.

Brendon and Sasha sat in the same chair, both using half the seat and looking surprisingly comfortable considering half their legs were unsupported.

From the empathetic stares around the room, Hope knew the word must have spread about what happened at the Sweetgum Beech.

Ciaran looked around the room, his jaw set firmly, and his blue eyes narrowed. When he finally spoke, his words were a declaration.

"Enough researching and planning. There is a man who needs to be killed, and it better be soon, or I will lose my fucking mind. We're going to get the Fifth Power."

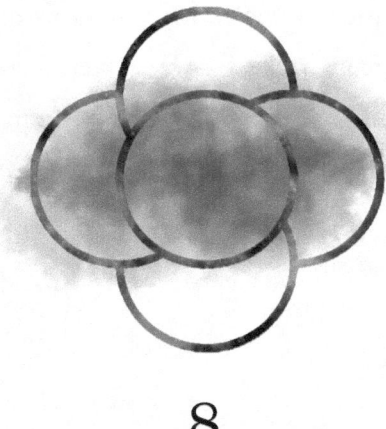

8

Lenna

Lenna was grateful the explanations about how to get the Fifth didn't involve the dozens of piles of books and endless notes she had seen Jake and Ciaran going through.

No, there wasn't any of that.

What Ciaran had drawn atop the table of the living room was the same panom mark that so many of them bore on different parts of their bodies.

The four-petal flower that represented each of their powers. The same flower where the different cardinal points of Thyria correlated to each petal: the North House in the North Petal, the East House in the East Petal, the South House in the South Petal, and the West House in the West Petal. At the circular-shaped center of the flower was the Organ House, in the Core of the panom.

Every person in the safehouse was expectantly waiting for Ciaran and Jake to reveal the big mystery they had been studying independently for years and collaboratively for days.

Ciaran and Jake looked at each other, as if there was an internal silent debate to decide who was to start the explanation. After a few tense seconds, Jake nodded slightly and started speaking.

"We know no one alive owns the Fifth Power. Probably no one in the past few centuries owned it, either. This could be because the Cardinals are extremely protective of it and there have only been vague mentions and references to what exactly the Fifth Power is and how to get it, or because no one is as dumb or desperate as we are to be willing to risk their lives to get it."

"Do you know what the Fifth Power actually is?" Ayla asked, her green eyes fixed on the middle of the panom shape.

"It is the greatest power a panom can ever possess. A power that is a blessing and a curse, and it can't be rivaled," Ciaran said. "A magical power granted by the Cardinals themselves after an aspirant has proved to be worthy."

"Cardinals fucking guide us. *Proved to be worthy* sounds as risky as the Fifth," Lenna spat. "How exactly are we expected to prove we're good enough?"

Ciaran exhaled deeply before frowning. "The Cardinals created the Fifth crusade. Aspirants—or *strivers*, as all literature talks about—must prove their worthiness in five ordeals." He lifted his blue eyes, scanning the people around the room. "Each Cardinal hid a crystal-red feather in an ordeal related to their power."

"The North Cardinal's ordeal needs a striver who has full control of the Giving power. The South Cardinal's ordeal demands that the striver masters Taking. The striver for the West Cardinal's ordeal has to dominate Healing, and the one for the East Cardinal's ordeal must be an adept at Harming. As for the Core Cardinal . . ." Ciaran looked at Jake.

The silver-eyed man shook his head slowly. "We have not the slightest clue of what the ordeal of the Core Cardinal will demand of its striver."

Lenna swallowed. "Delightful."

"And each . . . *striver* has the potential of dying during these ordeals?" Hope crossed her arms in front of her chest.

"Yes, basically." Jake nodded sharply.

Brendon snorted. "How very kind of them."

"How many ordeals does each striver have to survive?" Hope asked.

Lenna's eyes widened, and she saw Nina's eyebrows shooting to the roof. If Hope was nervous, Lenna couldn't tell. But what was this woman made of? As if she was even considering one single person would risk their lives over and over, up to five times.

The corner of Ciaran's lips twisted upwards. "Five Cardinals. Five crystal feathers to seize. Five ordeals—"

"Five strivers. Got it," Hope finished for him. "And once we get the five crystal feathers, what do we do with them? What happens next?"

To her surprise, Lenna found herself not feeling half as hesitant or freaking-the-absolute-fuck-out about the whole Fifth crusade. It surely helped that the woman next to her was talking about their forthcoming *death hunt*—as Ayla had described it—as chill as if she was talking about the weather forecast.

"This is where our theories don't align," Jake said.

"And the lack of references in literature doesn't help," Ciaran added.

"Well, surely you must have *some* idea of what we have to do if we're still alive after the five ordeals?" Lenna put her hand on her waist. Silence followed, and Lenna's jaw dropped. "No idea whatsoever?"

Ciaran scratched his chin with his metallic thumb. "Only one tome mentions that the Fifth comes together where the light meets the darkness. Whatever that means." He shrugged, then added, "If we're still alive after the ordeals, I believe the Cardinals will guide us to the next step." He looked at Hope and opened his mouth to continue but closed it again. Lenna had no doubt that Hope hadn't missed that brief but clear hesitancy.

"The Cardinals who, by then, would have tried to kill us five times, would *then* be willing to help?" Ayla's green eyes were wide-eyed and amused in equal parts. "Lucky us."

Jake chuckled. "I think that once the five crystal feathers are put together, something will happen. The Cardinals will appear from them, or the feathers will be pieces of a map where the Fifth is waiting, or something along those lines."

Speculations. That's what awaited them if they survived the five ordeals.

Lenna wasn't even sure she was ready to start thinking about who the striver for each ordeal would be, let alone what they would do with the crystal feathers if they never found the next step. At least they would probably make nice decorations.

Even with all the doubts, Lenna didn't need convincing that it was still worth risking their lives if getting the Fifth was the only way to get rid of the Organ Mandor once and for all.

"Where are the ordeals?" Lenna asked.

Jake smirked. "Well, that's a separate issue altogether."

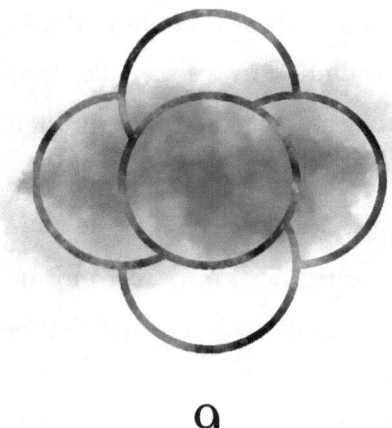

9

Hope

Hope was glad that her half-brother and Ciaran had finally arrived at some conclusions.

Five strivers, one for each of the five ordeals, to get a crystal feather from each Cardinal. All so the strivers could prove their worthiness to the goddesses, in the hopes that they would be granted the Fifth Power.

Yes, there were unanswered questions. And yes, she didn't care that much about them. Hope had lived with a lack of clear answers for almost a quarter of a century. It was not the end of the world.

The red-haired woman with golden eyes stole Hope's next question. "Where are the ordeals?"

"Well, that's a separate issue altogether," Jake said.

Ciaran continued, "We couldn't find a single book that said exactly where the ordeals take place. Maybe no one ever wrote about this. Personally, I think the Cardinals made sure no written word was on Terrha."

"Shady bitches," Brendon muttered, earning a stare from Lenna that could very possibly kill, and a nod from Jake.

Ciaran walked to the table and put his metallic palm flat in the center of the Core. "Everything begins in the Cardinals Temple. The crusade seems to be a recreation of how the Cardinals created Thyria. They want the strivers to understand what each of them went through, how each goddess channeled her unique power into the world. Only by experiencing what they suffered and truly owning each magic, can an ordeal be survived."

Hope bit her tongue to keep from interrupting. She walked towards the panom shape on the table, her biceps accidentally brushing Ciaran's metal arm and sending a trail of goosebumps up her shoulders and neck. His night and pine scent inundated her nostrils, and she fought to keep from closing her eyes. He smelled like home, and she missed the pine woods of Verdania so much.

"If everything begins with the Cardinals Temple as the pivotal reference of the land they created, it makes sense for the ordeals to be in equivalent latitudes and longitudes," she said.

"Did anyone understand a single word?" Sasha asked, her brown, wild curls shaping her pretty face with dark eyes.

Lenna laughed out loud, some people muttered some words, and next to Hope, there was silence. She lifted her stare to meet Ciaran's. He was looking at her as if it was the first time he had seen her.

Luckily, this time, she was not throwing one dagger after another at him.

"Imagine parallel lines that circle our planet, Terrha, running horizontally." Hope looked at Sasha and Lenna and waited for them to nod before continuing. "Now imagine the main latitude line crossed the Cardinals Temple, as if it was slicing it from the East to the West. If I were the East Cardinal, I would put my ordeal right in that line, towards the East."

"Like slicing a cake in four pieces," Nina said with a bright smile that reached her ocean-blue eyes. "Except the cake is the Cardinals Temple, and the two cutting lines go from North to South, and East to West."

Hope nodded. She took a step backwards from the table and asked, "Do you know if the ordeals are on land or water?"

Jake answered this time. "That is the issue—the ordeals clearly are not *in* Thyria, but outside."

"What do you mean, *outside*?" Lenna spat. "There is nothing outside."

"Oh, there very much is," Jake bit his bottom lip, as if he was enjoying seeing Lenna riled up and about to arrive to the same conclusion that Hope just had.

"Please, no." Lenna covered her eyes with a hand. "Not the fucking Radel Sea."

"Very much the fucking Radel Sea," Jake confirmed.

"*On* the Radel Sea, or *in* the Radel Sea?" Hope frowned.

She had spent way too many weeks in the underwater tunneled Vessels traveling in a cellholt vehicle from Verdania to Thyria. The end of that trip had ended with lots of deaths. She didn't care about the tons of roixers they had killed, but the memory of the six dead courtrades gave her a painful sting in her chest. She hadn't known them personally. Not like Nina, who didn't struggle to socialize, and Hope had no doubt remembered all their names. All Hope remembered were the words of the leading courtrade, Marcus Olanett.

"*May the stars not hinder their darkness. May Llunal shade them all,*" he'd prayed. Llunal, the god who gave courtrades their shadows and their whispers of night.

Whenever she thought about it, she was still shocked to know being dual-powered was a possibility. But there was Ciaran, in front of her, blessed by Llunal and the Cardinals and their panom and courtrade magics, ready to answer her question.

"Not in the vessels," he said.

"Thank the Fifth," Hope exhaled, without realizing she had been holding her breath in.

"We'll have to swim, then? Does that already count as an ordeal?" Ayla asked, pressing her lips.

Sasha snorted. "No fucking chance. Swim North in a straight line until something happens? We'll be dead before we know it." Indianna, Nina, and Lenna nodded in agreement. Hope didn't miss Lenna's amber eyes narrowing when Sasha said *we*.

They still had to talk about who was going on this crusade. Hope had total conviction that said conversation would come with *a lot* of drama and verbal fights.

"We could use a courtrade navia," said Ciaran.

"A *what*?" Ayla cocked an eyebrow above her emerald-green eyes.

"A vehicle that transports people above the waves of the sea."

"How, floating? You can't be serious," Hope said, struggling to keep a smile in despite the seriousness on Ciaran's beautiful features. Out of all the things she had heard and seen before, this was amongst the funniest.

"I think good old Ciaran here is fucking joking," Lenna said.

"Does he even know what a joke is?" Jake asked. "If such a vehicle exists, and it belongs to the courtrades, how come it moves without panom blood? Or do they steal panom blood?"

"Not everything in the world functions thanks to panom blood," Ciaran said, examining the unbelieving faces staring at him. "I know it's hard to believe in a place where everything is ruled by panoms. A navia moves at night, with Llunal's shadows pushing it through. I am no expert, though. I know they exist, but I have never seen one, let alone traveled in it."

"There is a courtrade who owes me a life-saving debt that surely knows all about these things," Hope said, turning to Ciaran. "Is it safe to bring Marcus here?"

Ciaran tucked a long strand of his dark hair behind his ear. "If we are going to ask him about using a courtrade vehicle, bringing him to our safehouse is an initial sign of trust."

Hope appreciated him using the plural ownership in regard to *his* safehouse. She had never owned anything other than her now-abandoned treehouse in Verdania, and her daggers. Subtle remarks like that made her feel less isolated, as if she truly was a part of something that mattered.

10

Lenna

It didn't take Ciaran long to moure to the courtrades' Thyrian quarters and convince their leader to come to the Crystal Clear Safehouse.

Funny, that shadow-wielders were real, and Lenna had never known of their existence until a few weeks ago. Not funny, that the courtrades somehow managed to stay under the radar of the military Roix and the Houses' Rulers. Except when Brendon regularly informed the courtrades had attacked certain areas in different Petals. None of them had failed to notice the courtrades' attacks were more frequent as days passed by.

Lenna followed the dark green sparks back to the living room. The man talking to Ciaran was dressed in utter black, his dark eyes focused, and a beard covering his face. It was not hard to imagine him wielding shadows. Even the way he moved, the way he *walked* . . . It looked as if the shadows of the room were dancing with him.

"Lenna Brachyan." She offered her hand, tilting her head slightly back-wards, and shook his vigorously. "And you are?"

"Marcus Olanett from Orizane. Honored to meet you."

Hope entered the room, and Lenna noticed she was wearing two thin daggers in belts around her thighs. Lenna suppressed a chuckle. She was now used to seeing Hope without her blades, but she would never forget the first time she had seen Hope, wearing fifteen of them, nor how she had thrown two daggers at Jake after introducing herself as the sister he had never heard of.

Marcus walked towards her and bowed his head, grabbing Hope's hand and placing a kiss on her palm. The middle-aged man looked at the dark-haired young woman as if he owed her his breath and his life. Cardinals, the *intensity*.

Hope bowed her head and said, "I didn't think I would see you so early, Marcus. How's life in Thyria?"

"All fun and games." His narrowed eyes followed Jake, who paced as if he owned the safehouse until he was behind Lenna. She liked it when Jake held her from behind. Whatever the reason, the courtrade leader didn't look pleased to be in the same room as the son of the Organ Mandor.

It didn't take long to get into the thick of why Marcus was here. In fact, it took exactly two sentences from Hope.

"We were wondering how your floating vehicles work. We need to use them."

Marcus looked at Ciaran with a furrowed brow. "Spilling courtrades' secrets, are we, now?" Ciaran didn't reply, and his marked jaw was warning enough. Marcus faced Hope as he said, "My *floating vehicles* are blessed by Llunal and all his stars, therefore his shadows move them only at night."

"Can we travel in them?" Hope asked.

Marcus looked around the table, taking in the ten beings waiting for his answer. "Whether Llunal will allow so many panoms on his navia, I'm not sure. I guess if one of his courtrades is on board, our god won't sink the bloody thing."

Hope was not going to give him a break. "Can the shadows of one courtrade move it?"

"The navia?" Marcus's lips twisted as he considered it. "One courtrade could do it, I guess."

"And during the day? How will we hide in plain sight?" Lenna asked.

"We could Give it an invisible barrier," Ayla suggested.

Marcus hummed. "You could. Courtrades usually cover the navia with shadows and push by quick enough when they are closer to Thyria. That way, they are out of the visible safe zone for only one night."

"When the shadows and the night keep them safe," Ciaran added.

"When *Llunal* keeps them safe."

"Can we not do that, then?" Lenna asked.

"Cover that distance in one night with only one courtrade aboard? Not unless you want to kill them." Marcus crossed his arms.

"Panom invisible barrier it is."

"But we will still need some other courtrades, to be safe. If something happens to me, you don't want to be stuck in the middle of the sea for the rest of your existence," said Ciaran.

"Nothing will happen to you," Hope snapped. Ciaran swallowed and avoided her black-eyed, pinning stare. "Could you come with us, Marcus?" she asked.

Marcus shook his head slowly, his shoulder-long hair moving from side to side. "I can't, sadly. There is an awful lot of work to be done here. But I am sure I will find some courtrades willing to go on an adventure."

Exactly what work was he and all the other courtrades working on in Thyria, Lenna would like to know. Considering the tightening of Jake's grip on her waist, she was not the only one.

"Why did we not use these navias to come from Verdania? They sound much easier than the cellholt and the Vessels."

Marcus chuckled. "The location of Verdania didn't allow for navias to reach there safely without being noticed, hence why they were all in Orizane. But don't be fooled by apparent simplicity, dear Hope. Nothing is ever *easy* in courtrade life. Navias are made for and by us. They will take you where you want, but their commodities are not to everyone's taste."

Hope nodded, not seeming very concerned about what exactly the commodities of the navias were. "How long will it take to prepare two navias and some courtrades in each?"

"Let me see what I can do," Marcus said, and turned to Ciaran. "Expect a whisper of night shortly."

Right. Whatever the Cardinal's fuck that was. Lenna leaned backwards to press her back against Jake's muscled chest, his hands tightening his hold on her waist.

Marcus said a brief, general goodbye and did a *very* intense bow to Hope that had Lenna lifting her eyebrows. As soon as Ciaran put his metallic hand on the back of Marcus's neck, they moured away.

11

Hope

Everyone had agreed to continue planning for their Fifth crusade the following day.

It was a lot of information to digest, they said. It would be difficult to decide who would be the striver for each of the five ordeals, they thought. It would take time to pack whatever they needed for however long they were going to be on their navial trip, they claimed.

Everyone had agreed, except Hope. She could understand people benefiting from time to mentally prepare, though. Allowing them a brief pause before they were ready to risk their lives was a reasonable request. Hence why she had shut her mouth.

She had finished packing as soon as she lined up her fifteen blades on the table. Next to the beautiful and lethal array of her favorite weapons was a small pile of dark leathers and belts to hang those daggers from. That was all she needed. That was all she had ever needed to survive.

Compared to a few months ago, when she had packed before leaving the island of Verdania, the major difference was that her leathers were made of a sturdier, more protective material. And, of course, she now had her panom magic.

The magic that caused a panomquake that almost destroyed the world when she became a panom and left her unconscious. The warning of the Core Cardinal in the conversation they had while Hope didn't know whether she was dead or alive never fully left her mind.

She who remains in the deep sleep we forced her to is awaking. She who should be contained for many more years might rise before it's time.

She. The Cardinal Queen.

Sometimes Hope wished she were unconscious again even if it was just to speak to the Core Cardinal in her mind. There was so much more she needed to know.

In the emptiness of her bedroom, she sighed. Accepting that the impatience would not let her sleep anytime soon, and refusing to sit in her room looking at the wall until the sunlight made an appearance, Hope headed towards the balcony of the safehouse.

There was someone already there, looking at the body still hanging from the fountain of the Sweetgum Beech. Courtesy of her father, there hadn't been any live music at night since the woman's corpse had appeared there.

Hope walked towards the rail, looking at the red moon illuminating Corentre.

"Hi," Jake said. His arms were crossed, and his silver stare went from the dome of the Cardinals Temple in the Organ House to the water fountain.

"Hi," Hope replied.

They stood in silence for long minutes, taking in the unusual silence of the square. Hope didn't need to ask what—or more precisely, *who*—was Jake thinking about.

"Did you know my mother?" Hope asked.

Jake looked at her, his pale features tinged red from the moonlight.

"Us panoms live long lives, and your mother was a human being. I knew Aurora Nevada when she was the Roix Reigner, yes."

The sharp, invisible shard that seemed to be permanently stuck in Hope's heart was sorer than usual. She clenched her jaw, holding in the tears that she had only allowed out when her mother had been stabbed in front of her eyes.

"Did you know that your father—*our* father—and her were . . ." She swallowed. She felt the bile threaten to go up her throat at the thought of the Organ Mandor and her mother being together. Even if Hope's life had been the very outcome of that union. "Did you know she was pregnant?"

Jake shook his head slowly. "I didn't. I wouldn't be surprised if only he did. One day, your mother was commanding the roixers as she did for many years. The next, she was gone."

"Did nobody wonder what had happened to her? Did nobody wonder why she disappeared?" Hope bit her lip, the pain she caused herself helping keep her devastation in. How could nobody care enough about a woman to wonder whether she was dead or alive, discarded or not?

"The Organ Mandor does not give explanations." His voice was low. "I'm sorry for your loss."

Hope nodded in silence, the invisible shard seeming to slice her up and down with an unbearable amount of sorrow. No biting of her lips would keep her from crying if she acknowledged his condolences, so instead, she waited until she found her words again.

"Is your mother . . . present in your life?" she asked.

"She is, and I miss her." His brief look at his forearm made Hope think she was not the only one having ink interchanges with family members. For a moment, Hope thought he would not add anything else, but after a few seconds, Jake continued, "I love her dearly, and it is very painful to see—to *know*—she means nothing to my father. She has never meant anything to him."

The memory of Rhei Coralt laughing out loud when Hope asked him for answers echoed in her ears.

I damn the Cardinals every single day for letting women believe they have a say in life, he had said. How could a male like this *ever* care about any female?

"What does she look like?" Hope asked.

Jake swallowed. "When she is not bruised, she is very beautiful."

Hope snapped her head towards him, her dark eyes wide with urgency and worry. She could feel the blood in her veins rushing, her pulse speeding at what that woman had to endure.

The silver in Jake's eyes glittered with rage or heartbreak, Hope couldn't tell. "Sometimes she lets me Heal her, sometimes she prefers to let her body take her time. She says the wounds make it easier to remember why she hates my father and why she must never drop her facade."

"Can't she stop him? Can't *you* stop him?" Hope asked, only half-regretting such an inquisitive and personal question. She wouldn't be surprised if he told her to fuck off, as she had heard him say so many times to other people.

"She can't. I could. I did, many years ago. And what came after was worse. He almost killed her, and I wasn't there to avoid it when he did. She . . . She asked me to never mention it again. To never stop him again."

Jake exhaled, and for the span of a second, Hope saw the weight of the years he had lived on his drained expression. He finally added, as if it was a self-consolation, "I don't think she feels the pain anymore."

"Can pain not be felt?" Hope frowned. She was used to pain. Fighting always came with pain. She didn't mind it, not enough to let it stop her. But she always *felt* it.

"Yes," Jake's voice didn't have a trace of doubt. "When it's as common to you as breathing, you stop thinking about it. You stop realizing you are in pain."

The conclusion hit her hard and fast. "He's hurt you as well. Many times."

"Not all of us are lucky enough to own the power of his family blood but not have suffered the pain of his rage for centuries."

"I'm sorry," she said.

"So am I."

12

Lenna

T he Badassery Suite was in full bloom with all the badasses in town.

After Ciaran confirmed that Marcus would indeed provide them with the two navias Hope had requested, the ten habitants had arrived at some conclusions.

First, that they probably would need a hell of a lot of myster to drink in the navias, as well as dice and cards to play CoreCode while they were en route.

Second, that they didn't have to pack much, as they could Give themselves most of the things they needed.

Third, that they would leave for the seaside where the navias would meet them as soon as they agreed on the remaining key points: who would be the five strivers for the five ordeals, and who would travel in each navia.

"I will get the Core feather," Hope said, as if it was a decision already settled, and they were not in the middle of a debate.

"I can't think of anyone more suitable for the Core Cardinal's ordeal than the heir of the Organ House, to be honest," Ayla said. "Even if we have no clue about what that ordeal will ask from you."

Lenna looked at Jake, who believed for centuries that *he* was the heir of the Organ House—and he *was*, for however long the Fifth only knew—until Hope was born a quarter of a century ago. Lenna still didn't know exactly how old Jake was, and she wasn't sure it mattered much, anyway. Very fucking old, probably. He was very fucking sexy, ruthless, and sharp, too. *That* was what mattered, at the end of the day.

"Whatever it is. I will get that crystal feather." The confidence Hope spoke with would have sounded arrogant, were it not because Lenna couldn't imagine a situation the woman wouldn't survive. Hope *was* survival. In its purest, rawest, full-of-blades-and-braids form.

"The Healing ordeal is mine," Ciaran said. Of course it was.

"Being the heir of the West House, surely the West Cardinal has to give you some advantage in her ordeal," Sasha said, shrugging. "She would have to be a royal bitch to kill the heir of her own house."

"I don't know how tough the ordeals are actually going to be, but if they are as difficult as you two said . . ." Lenna lifted her eyebrows, looking between Ciaran and Jake before continuing, "The more leverage we have in the ordeals, the better our chance to tell the tale."

"Which is why I will do the Harming ordeal from the East," Jake said. "No one here dominates Harming as I do, both as a wielder and as a receiver."

No one argued with him. Except Raoul, who had still been unconscious, they had all seen Jake in action at the Beftac Center.

Lenna pursed her lips, reaching for his hand until his palm met hers. She squeezed it, hoping he would feel everything she wanted him to. The knot in her stomach didn't come from the memories of Jake creatively Harming dozens of roixers. No.

It came from knowing the Organ Mandor had tortured him countless times with the Red Lawful Stab. And from the fact that what Jake felt when his inner magical balance was tilted was precisely that: pain. Which is why it didn't stop him from using his Giving and Taking or Harming and Healing unevenly. Because pain was nothing to him.

As distressed and outraged as this made Lenna feel, if anyone in this room knew about Harming and being Harmed, it was Jake.

It was also Jake who stroked her skin, and Lenna just wanted to get this conversation done so she could talk to him, caress him, look at him. Even if all those stupid actions were fucking useless to protect him from being hurt again. She clenched her jaw to keep from cursing the Organ Mandor out loud, as that would sure as the Fifth deviate the conversation for even longer.

"The North ordeal should be mine, then," Ayla said. "Unless you want to do it, Lenna?"

Both twins belonged to the North House, and even if Lenna had been the heir before, the Mandor had taken her heirloom and passed it to Ayla.

"You're the Northern heir, Ayla. Plus . . . you donated your South Petal to me, so you wouldn't stand a chance in the South Cardinal's ordeal."

The green eyes of her twin were serious. "I wouldn't. I can't Take anymore."

"So, the Taking ordeal from the South Cardinal is mine, then," Lenna said. She had mastered Giving and Taking before the other two powers, and she felt comfortable using them. Out of the five ordeals, this would have been her second choice. She wanted to have a non-dead sister, though, especially now that Ayla wasn't a politically correct, ass-licking asshole anymore. She would have to be good enough at her second preferred option to survive.

"Five panoms for five ordeals. That's settled. Now, the other question: who must come on this crusade?" Hope asked.

"What do you mean?" Brendon frowned. "You panom lot are not leaving us boring mortals in this house to rot for weeks or months until you come back."

"Absolutely fucking not," Sasha agreed.

"It will not be safe for you," Hope said, looking at Nina.

Indianna shook her head. "Hiding in a safehouse with no panoms that can moure us in or out, without powers for us to bring supplies and food we need, is not safe either. This safehouse is not designed for beings who aren't panoms."

"We could leave you plenty of stock," Ciaran said. "And I could make adjustments to the mouring conditions to enter and leave the house, but then—"

"It wouldn't be safe," Hope finished.

Sasha smiled, happily nodding. "And we don't want to bore to death here, wondering all the fun you're having but unable to leave these four walls."

Brendon snorted with a grin. "Exactly. We would much rather end up dead with you."

"What about you, Raoul?" Hope asked.

"I'm not staying here by myself, that's for sure." His blue eyes flickered with amusement. "I would like to be with Nina and Indianna, if possible, as I still need treatments and healing every now and then."

Jake Gave two floating orbs in the middle of the Badassery Suite. Inside one of them, three miniature figures of Nina, Indianna, and Raoul appeared.

"I will go with you," Hope said. Lenna wasn't surprised to hear that. Hope always seemed both protective and caring towards Nina, as if she was her own sister. Considering how concerned she was about the safety of certain non-panoms during the crusade, the closer Hope was to them, the better protected they'd be.

Hope turned to look at Ciaran, and he seemed puzzled even before the dark-haired woman opened her mouth again. "Are you coming with us, Ciaran?"

He put his metallic hand above his heart as he inhaled deeply and nodded. "Always."

Hope and Ciaran's miniatures appeared inside the orb with Nina, Raoul, and Indianna's.

"That's a very fair split," Lenna laughed. "Jake and I go to the other navia. Sasha and Brendon, are you coming?"

Sasha squealed, running towards Lenna and holding her arm. Lenna grinned, kissing her friend on her tanned cheek. This would be fun. Perhaps deathly-as-fuck too, but still fun.

Jake Gave the four miniatures inside the other orb, and Lenna didn't miss the mini Jake touching the ass of the mini Lenna.

"Well, I don't want to hear Jake and Lenna fucking all day," Ayla said.

"And night," Jake clarified.

Ayla Gave her own miniature to the other orb.

Lenna sighed. "Definitely not very fair split. Six of you, four of us."

"But you will have more courtrades on board than us," Ciaran reminded her. He was one of the courtrades needed to move the navia and hide it from plain sight.

"And I will bring another reinforcement to our navia," Jake said. Lenna looked at him, cocking an eyebrow. Jake gave her a reassuring nod. Whatever.

"Ayla, Nina, Raoul, Indianna, Ciaran: we will find our navia at ante meridiem in the North Petal meeting point," Hope said. "Jake, Lenna, Sasha, Brendon: your navia will be waiting for you at the East Petal. Do you mind letting Marcus know, Ciaran? Or I can send him an ink."

Ciaran closed his eyes briefly, twirls of shadows spiraling up his ankles before they vanished. "My whispers are on their way."

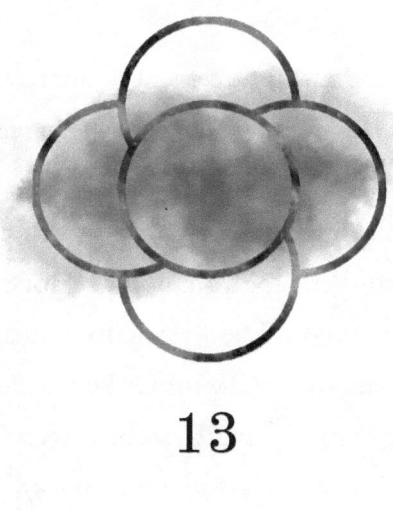

13

Hope

There were more nerves than people in the safehouse.

Almost everyone seemed either very excited, very nervous, or very on edge. The combination of those nerve-wracking feelings in an already-explosive mix of people was dangerous. Even if they were about to split into two groups for however long the Fifth crusade would be.

Hope unconsciously caressed the hilt of the daggers on her waist, an ever-familiar movement that comforted her. She was more impatient than she would have wanted.

The jasmine scent of the patio made her smile. She would miss this space, especially at night. She missed nature and the woods so much already. In a navia in the middle of the Radel Sea, there would be none of that.

Hope walked towards the bench where Lenna and Indianna were talking at a speed that was difficult to follow. "May I speak to you?" she asked the fire-haired young woman with golden eyes.

Indianna stood up, squeezing Lenna in a tight hug and giving her a kiss somewhere between her hair and her cheek. "Ciaran is mouring me and Ayla next, so this is me saying goodbye. Take care of Sasha and Brendon, please."

"I will." Lenna grinned, kissing Indianna's black bob back. Then she headed towards Ciaran, who was already waiting for her next to Ayla.

The snappy yet intense words between Ayla and Lenna a few minutes earlier had been unpredictable. There had been a few *don't you dare die without me, you better survive or I'll kill you*, and *for Cardinal's sakes*. There had also been extremely long hugs, unexpected tears, and love. The type of love that only two people who were born together could feel. A love that hates and breaks but is there when it matters most.

Lenna waited until Ciaran's hands were on the back of Ayla and Indianna's necks and the three of them vanished, before she turned to Hope. The unusual shine in Lenna's eyes was the only proof of what was truly happening underneath the surface.

"I don't need to wish you luck. You will survive this," Lenna said.

"I don't believe in luck. But yes, *we* will survive this."

"We shall see." Lenna's usually confident and authoritative voice trembled a bit.

"Do not die, Lenna. I will need a First Feather after I kill my father. Thyria will not rule itself."

Lenna's golden eyes widened. "Oh, fuck. I had forgotten about that." She shook her head while grinning. "No pressure, right? The Fifth crusade might as well be a walk in the park."

"Send me an ink if you need me," Hope said. "We'll be in two navias, but we are all still one team."

Lenna tilted her head, narrowing her eyes while looking at Hope. "You would be a great leader."

Hope felt a slight blush striking her cheeks. She was not used to compliments that mattered. Her lips tightened in a smile. "We shall see," she echoed Lenna's words.

The scent of pine and night reappeared in the patio of the safehouse, and Hope inhaled surreptitiously. She might not see any woods in a while, but at least Ciaran's scent would remind her of home while they travelled in the navia. That is precisely where they moured to, as soon as the metallic hand of the man touched her neck and sent goosebumps down her spine.

The navia floating on the dark waters was like nothing Hope could have ever imagined.

An immense crescent-shaped moon formed the main body. Its thicker part floated on the water, while the two sharp ends pointed towards the red moon in the sky. Two parallel platforms crossed the curved form horizontally.

A moon shape, crossed by two straight lines. Hope had seen that symbol before. It had been on the cloths the courtrades used in their quarters in Verdania. Even if this time, the symbol had become real and had such dimensions that she was surprised courtrades could hide from plain sight.

"It's splendid." Hope couldn't hide the awe in her voice. How did the courtrades keep this metal beast from sinking? "Its shape . . . It's the courtrade's symbol, isn't it?"

"Indeed."

The shape Ciaran had on his skin before Rhei Coralt tried to remove his courtrade blood from him by amputating the arm where the courtrade mark had been. Hope struggled to imagine him with two biological arms. His metallic, bionic arm made Ciaran so much more special, and sometimes Hope wondered if there wasn't anything at all said arm—and said man—wouldn't be able do.

From the thick shadows around them, two courtrades emerged.

The shortest woman Hope had ever seen wore a white eye patch, heavily contrasting against her dark brown skin. Next to her was a tall, old man with the straight composure of someone who had been muscled in his youth. His hair was short and white like ivory, his eyes dark blue.

If Hope had to guess, she would bet her daggers on them having hidden on the seashore since they moved the navia there.

"Do you like our baby?" the man asked Hope. His voice was slightly raspy, but his words were expressed with happiness.

She chuckled. Hope tilted her head backwards to see the navia at its fullest. "Your monumental baby? She's precious."

The smile of the man marked elegant wrinkles around his eyes and cheeks. She didn't know him, and yet his knowledgeable and peaceful smile filled Hope with calm and joy.

"Hope Nevada, nice to meet you. This is Ciaran Castel," she said.

The old man's smile didn't falter, and his eyes glittered under the moonlight. He inhaled deeply before replying, "It's my biggest pleasure meeting you. My name is Stevian, and this is Nyxara. We are honored to join you in this mission."

Ayla, Raoul, Indianna, and Nina joined them just when the woman with the eye-patch—Nyxara—said, "Is this everyone? We must leave now, or no shadows will keep the roixers from seeing us when the sun rises."

14

Lenna

Apparently, the courtrades were in such a fucking rush to depart from Thyria that there was no time for proper introductions.

There were three courtrades, that much she knew. Lenna had barely had the chance to even look at them before they disappeared somewhere in the navia to do whatever busy courtrades usually did in these floating vehicles.

She would admit it: she had not expected their transport method to be so humongous. It was very . . . black. And metallic.

Some beings often complained that the Cardinals were obsessed with red, crystal, and the four-petal panom mark. Well, Llunal and his black passion could give them a run for their money.

Lenna and Jake had Given an invisible barrier around the navia, and swirling shadows courtesy of the courtrades seemed to hover around the two horizontal, flat platforms and the two towering, curved peaks above. Hopefully, that would be enough to keep anyone from seeing them overnight. As for moving as far as they could from the shores of Thyria at the biggest speed possible . . . Whatever the courtrades or their god were doing, it was working. It was so awfully windy and cold on the top platform that they had decided to hide in the roofed cabins underneath.

And precisely here was the not-so-pleasant surprise Lenna hadn't counted on.

Apparently, the blond young woman, svelte and fit as the damned Fifth, was the *invited guest* that Jake had found necessary to bring on board.

"Reinforcements, my ass," Lenna spat, making Sasha chuckle next to her.

"Talking about asses, hers is top tier."

There was no point contradicting her friend. Everything in the strange blond woman seemed to be top tier. Including the passion with which her green eyes scrutinized Jake from the very top to the very damn bottom.

"Arabella D'Arcy," Jake greeted her. "Thanks for coming."

"I would never refuse a personal invitation from you, Jake." She grinned, biting her bottom lip with perfectly white, straight teeth. "It's been too long since the last time we deeply caught up."

Her red-haired high ponytail swung as Lenna and Sasha interchanged silent stares full of hatred. Cardinals give her fucking patience. Or a wall to slam that pretty face against.

"Arabella, is it? My name is Lenna. My sincere apologies for not knowing who you are. We were not expecting last minute guests on this trip."

"Oh, no worries at all." The pretty smile turned sharp and cold in no time. "I'm a member of the South House, and Jake and I have had the pleasure of knowing each other for many, many years. He asked if I could offer *you* help with the Taking power for some important challenge, and I could never say no to him."

Lenna's nostrils flared as she smiled tensely. The connotations of what this woman was implying between Jake and her shouldn't have hurt as much as they did. What in the Fifth world had made Jake—*her* Jake—think about bringing this being to the crusade was a good idea?

"Of course you couldn't. My man is irresistible."

Jake's grave voice whispered in Lenna's ear, loud enough for the others to hear as well. "Our bed awaits, sweet fire." The firm hand on her lower back was reassuring in a way that she was too annoyed to admit right now. She let him guide her towards the corridor, and she wasn't out of the room yet when the last words of the blond bitch sent that reassurance out of the fucking navia.

"Lenna," Arabella said, waiting until she twisted her head backwards to look at her green eyes before she continued, "You should let your hair loose. He really enjoys pulling it when fucking."

Her words felt like an ice-full bucket on Lenna's body. She felt Jake's arm tensing, his muscles marking in more than their usual places. Why the actual Cardinals' fuck did he think it was a good idea to bring this woman to *help* her? If Lenna didn't end up killing her, it would be a goddesses' damned miracle.

"I know *everything* he likes, sweetheart. Worry fucking not." Lenna winked. "Have a lovely, peaceful and *soundless* night."

Without looking back again, Lenna let Jake guide her to a very black, very metallic door that led to the place they would share during their stay in the navia. Arabella was going to be in for a treat.

Their cabin was bigger than Lenna had thought, including a private en-suite. A four-post double bed with no sheets was in front of the window facing the waves of the Radel Sea outside. Black curtains with a minuscule pattern of white stars framed the window. A big couch with a high back and rolled, thick arms covered one side of the room. There were multi-ple pillows of different-but-equally-dark patterns on the bed and on the couch. A few desks covered the other side of the room.

The only unusual thing seemed to be the lack of any source of light, but Lenna sent golden sparks across the room as soon as she shut the curtains. Just in case the invisibility barrier hiding them from sight, and the shadows doing the same, weren't enough to keep unwanted, curious roixers at bay.

"You can see your guest and I are not going to get along, correct?" Lenna's hands were on her hips.

Jake leaned against the doorway, his arms crossed. The blackness of the room allowed the silver of his eyes to shine, as if his eyes were the brightest stars in the room. His face was grave, lacking the usual amusement that was, in some measure, always present.

"I decided to bring someone from the South House to help you prepare for the Taking ordeal. You should use her."

"You *decided*?"

"I am not willing to lose you, and if someone can help you increase your chances of not dying, I will fucking take any help. You should as well."

"Except the Cardinals-damned help is stunning, blond, with green eyes, tall and spectacularly fit?"

He walked towards the desk where Lenna sat and put a finger under her chin, forcing her to look into his eyes. Silver eyes full of anger and . . . Was that fear?

"Do you realize that out of the five strivers, you are the one who is at most risk?"

"Thanks for believing in me, Jake. It's great for my self-esteem."

"Leave your cockiness aside for one fucking second, Brachyan, and listen to me." *That* was definitely fear in his eyes. "Ayla, Ciaran, and Hope are doing the ordeals of the Houses they are heirs to. I might as well be the heir of the West House, for how familiar I am with Harming in every damned sense of the power. Passing my ordeal should be a fucking breeze." He inhaled sharply, exhaling deeply before continuing. "Whether you admit it or not, you are not in a preferable position here. Or do you think I don't know you would have wanted to do the North Cardinal's ordeal instead? I was your Panom Guidor, Lenna. I saw you dominating the Giving power before any others. That's who you are. Where your blood and your magic belong."

"I was not going to send my sister to death," Lenna said.

Jake looked at the ceiling, biting his bottom lip. "I know. I *know*, okay? But I am not going to let you walk to your death either. So, please. *Please*, Lenna, use the help I could find you. I'm begging you."

Lenna sighed, caressing his cheek while he closed his eyes. She didn't want to acknowledge how worried he had to be. Exactly how desperate was he for her to use the help of this person? And what could Arabella teach her about the Taking power that Jake himself couldn't?

"Okay, I will."

The immediate side smile on Jake's face caught her off-guard, sending waves of desire up her thighs. "Do you know what I think?" he asked, looking at the room.

"That this room is very monotone?" she said, closing her hand to Take her clothes off, leaving her just with a very suggestive, fire-red underwear full of laces and straps. Sasha and Brendon would have to understand why she couldn't put a sound barrier on this cabin. Not tonight.

His eyes roamed from hers to her half-open lips, to her breasts, trailing down to her core as his leather and ginger scent intensified. He looked at her as if he had been deprived of air and she was a very welcome tornado. "You playful little thing."

"Who, me?" Lenna said, unlacing one of her straps to reveal a peaked nipple. She was surprised his hands were not on her yet. She doubted that would last long, though. This man was not one to be satiated by looking. "Kneel down for me, Jake."

His eyes darkened to a duskier grey, his voice low as he said, "Your wish is my command." He kneeled, putting her thighs behind his shoulder blades so fast that the next thing she knew was—

Was the world upside down?

Yes. Jake stood up with her hanging upside down in front of him, as if she weighed no more than a handful of sand. His firm hands gripping her thighs as he inhaled deeply, the tip of his nose so close to being buried where it belonged—between her legs.

Lenna felt the front part of her thong being pushed to the side by his firm fingers.

She gasped. "How dare you? Put me back on the—"

Her deep and loud moan filled the air as his tongue penetrated her deeply. Without warning. Without stopping.

"*You wanted me to obey, didn't you, sweet fire?*" His voice echoed in her mind.

Fuck, yes. She would have replied, were she not too busy enjoying every damn lick from his masterful tongue on her clit.

Her mind blurred, maybe from the effect of going from zero to delightfully tongue deep, maybe from being upside down. Her only grip was on Jake's muscled and firm legs. Legs that were still clothed, and that was absolutely not okay. A movement of her hand and she Took his clothes off. Her ass felt the muscles tensing on his broad chest as he devoured her without reign. His hardened cock pressed against her upper back.

Then his hand joined in the feasting party and massaged her clit, and Lenna would have begged every fucking Cardinal to stop time and let her stay there forever. Maybe she didn't mind seeing the world upside down, if that meant she had to hold onto his body for dear life, and that Jake would keep her on him.

Lenna arched her back, and the movement let his cock spring free next to her face.

She grinned between moans. Daring to remove one hand from the grip on his legs, she grabbed Jake's preciously long cock until her mouth was full. It was so easy to be full of him when he was so damned big, thick and perfect. Even when the tip of his cock touched the back of her throat and made her gag.

His deep, low groan was followed by his tongue and lips, working her core harder. The hand across her chest gripped her peaked nipples.

"I can't lick your masterpiece properly like this, Jake," Lenna said between ragged breaths.

She felt the exhale of his chuckle against her clit, the warm and sharp breath making her roll her eyes unconsciously.

He pulled her body up until she was sitting on his shoulders, her core right in his gorgeous face, his disheveled dark hair brushing her lower abdomen. He placed her on the floor with all the gentleness, lightly pushing her shoulders down until her knees were on the floor and her face had the most beautiful view one could imagine.

His hardened cock awaited in front of her, the tense muscles of his chest, arms, and legs with a thin coat of the sweat holding her upside down had required, and his dark grey eyes pinned her down from above.

She cocked an eyebrow. "You're unusually gentle today. Don't be too worried about me dying to stop you from enjoying."

"Stop me from what, exactly?" he said, grabbing her ponytail and pulling it backwards, keeping her from touching his cock. "I was about to fuck your mouth as if the world ended tomorrow."

Lenna couldn't nod while his grasp controlled her head. Instead, she grinned and opened her mouth wide open, exposing her very ready tongue. Jake bit his bottom lip and pushed her face forwards until his incredible length filled her in.

Fuck, if this man wasn't delicious.

She couldn't move her head backwards. She couldn't move her head at all. Not as he fixed it with his hand on her ponytail, staring at her from above as he moved his hips and filled her mouth in and out. Again and again. She couldn't take her eyes off him. He looked between the heated golden eyes threatening to burn her alive and her wide-open mouth, taking in his hardened cock as he fucked it over and over.

"You take my cock so fucking well," he praised between cut breaths. His hand moved and navy sparks floated in the air, grouping in a curved shape that headed towards—

Lenna's eyes widened when his shaped sparks reached the spot where her hand had been adding to the already increased levels of pleasure. He wouldn't do anything to hurt her. No, quite the opposite.

The moment his sparks touched her raw, exposed clit, Lenna gasped, the sound muffled against the cock in her mouth. She didn't know if the feeling was hot or cold, sharp or soft. She only knew that it felt like Jake licking and touching her. She only knew that she wanted it again. She *needed* it again. She wanted it all the time.

The muscles in Jake's clavicles tensed further and he must have seen the begging in her eyes because he obliged. He very much obliged, a display of navy sparks feasting on her core, on her inner lips and her clit, while she massaged her breasts, and he kept pushing her head back and forth on his cock masterfully. He went from allowing her to lick his length to slamming his cock against the inner part of her cheek, to—

She gagged when he pushed his length too far back, and yet she didn't want him to stop. Thank all the Cardinals, he didn't stop. Instead, he went faster, harder. Her gagging sounds as he fucked her mouth were his undoing.

His eyes rolled back with pleasure as he continued moving her head forwards and backwards with his hands. The sound of his orgasm, the taste of his cum on her throat, and his navy sparks on her core sent Lenna spiraling head-first towards her own.

15

Hope

It had taken Hope all of five hours to realize that her daggers and her panom magic were pretty useless in the navia.

These five hours, Ciaran, Stevian, and Nyxara had been moving their hands with complex movements, creating twirls of shadows of different sizes to guide the massive vehicle across the Radel Sea. Ayla, Hope, and Ciaran had Given an invisibility barrier earlier, and now it was all a matter of moving far away from Thyria so that, when the sun appeared on the horizon, no one could see them floating on the waters.

Nina, Raoul, Indianna, and Ayla had gone to their respective cabins hours ago, but Hope knew she wouldn't be able to sleep. Not while knowing the three courtrades were working as hard as they could to beat time and sunlight. Not only would she not be able to, but she didn't *want* to.

Even if standing on the deck meant she was going to end up with the lowest body temperature she had ever experienced. The unstoppable wind was angry; the strong waves seemed to speak in an ancient language that sounded threatening and final. How the courtrades were managing to stay in a straight line towards the North, that was a Cardinals-blessed miracle. She wouldn't even blame them if, come day, they realized they had gone completely the wrong way.

She was glad that her two long, dark braids kept her hair—except a few strands here and there—somehow controlled amongst said wind. But Ciaran's long, usually smooth hair . . . It was almost unrecognizable.

The chaotic look combined with the permanent, incessant focus of his blue stare on the dark sky above them, and the shadows dancing around his body at his order was mesmerizing. Hope couldn't be able to say how long she had been staring at the movements of his arms, at the way he fixed his feet on the floor when the air currents were too wild, at how he seemed to pull the shadows from nowhere at times. At other times it looked like Llunal was sending them straight from the clouds above.

He briefly switched his attention from the sky to Hope, and she couldn't take her almost black eyes from his as her heart jumped. His blue eyes peeked through a disarray of dark hair covering his face, the metal ring of his bottom lip and his metallic arm shining despite the darkness that seemed to have swallowed the navia whole. The same darkness that was pushing the navia across the sea.

Hope's arm tickled as she felt ink incoming and, for a change, it didn't come with the sting of pain the Organ Mandor always sent his inks with. No. She knew who had sent this ink before she looked at her forearm and saw Ciaran's handwriting in dark green.

*It's cold outside.
Us courtrades don't have body
temperature, but you will freeze.*

She hadn't failed to notice it. During her five-hour-long, thorough observation of Ciaran and his interaction with the night, she hadn't seen him sweat. Not one drop, despite the exhausting, muscle-draining effort he was enduring. Stevian and Nyraxa didn't have a single drop of sweat, either. The white-haired old man had started to look slightly tired over the past hour, but he was relentless, and so were his shadows.

At one point, hours ago, Hope had tried to Give herself a blanket, thicker clothes, and a windproof coat. They had been useless despite having put all of them on. The navia either didn't allow items that helped with body temperature, or didn't care about them, since the courtrades didn't require said items.

She hoped the cabins were not as cold, or she didn't rule out the risk of finding the other passengers frozen by the time the sun shone above. Surely the sun would warm them up.

The sound of Ciaran's steps was indistinguishable but they didn't falter. If he was going to tell Hope off, she was ready to tell him to focus on his duties.

"You are not going inside, are you?" he asked, getting closer to her ear so that she could hear him. The thunderous sound of a wave crashing against the navia synchronized with the loud whistle of the wind.

"I'm not." She almost had to shout to make herself heard.

His lips tensed and Hope couldn't tell if it was from frustrated amusement or desperation. "Thought so," he said. "You're shaking. May I help?"

Hope frowned, unsure if she had heard him properly, or exactly what he meant.

"I can help you, if you let me," he repeated.

"I'm okay."

The slight bob of his throat was the only sign that he had chuckled. "Sure. You will not be okay in a few minutes. Let me help you." Even through the now roaring sound of the waves and the wind, Hope felt the urgency in his voice.

He was not going to let this go. Hope sighed and nodded. "If it makes you go back to shadow business and not be distracted."

Ciaran walked behind her and kneeled. She felt both his hands around her ankles, circling her legs in steady and rhythmic movements as his hands trailed upwards. And upwards.

Hope's eyes widened. She could feel warmth where his hands had barely touched her, as if a thin coat of protection against the wind was being created. Maybe the source of warmth was not solely the layer of protection he was building for her, which Hope now saw was made of shadows.

His hands continued trailing upwards, and when he reached the height of her waist, there was an inch between his hands and her leather clothes as he kept circling her body. The sudden need for him to cover such a small distance was overwhelming, as it was the closeness of his pine and night scent and the warmth, the warmth, the warmth. The warmth definitely *not* caused by his protective layer alone.

She never thought her teeth could be clattering and her head and hands shaking, and yet the lower part of her body felt so . . . *Not* cold. So *very* not cold at all.

Bless the Cardinals for ensuring Ciaran was behind her and not in front of her, because the look on her face would have revealed more than she wanted. More than she should. Even if his circling touch on her lower abdomen made her inhale as deeply as if she could swallow all the air in the Radel Sea at once.

Now that he was finally standing, she felt the strands of his hair flying and slamming against the back of her neck, right where her red panom mark was. She felt his metallic hand across her thin, tight clothes around her breasts, and the tension between the distance of his touch and her body seemed to be electrical and as dangerous as the most fatal wave. A wave that could crash lands and worlds at once.

A rational part of Hope seemed to want to remember why she was not allowed to have his touch on her. Something about being forbidden, but every time she tried to grab the thought, it slipped from her mind again, replaced by his hands now touching her neck in steady circles. When his metallic hand touched her panom mark, her eyes rolled backwards, her head tilting slightly upwards and colliding against the curvature of his neck. She thanked the Fifth for the loud noise of their surroundings for the first time that night. The loud noise that covered her own, not-as-loud-but-still-very-loud noise. Her *moan*.

She inhaled deeply and took a step forwards, spinning around to face Ciaran. His eyes were glazed, and he breathed as if this had been as much effort as controlling the hefty shadows he had reined to cover and move the navia.

"Last bit, I promise," he said, stepping towards her, lifting his hands. If she thought her heart couldn't beat any faster, she was wrong.

He placed his palms on top of her head, moving them down to her chin with a slow caress that sent shivers down her spine when his biological and metallic indexes touched the sides of her lips at the same time.

"Th—" she started, unsuccessfully. She swallowed before trying again. "Thank you, I feel much . . . warmer."

Warm to the point of boiling, in fact. Ciaran smiled, his eyes pinning her down as if he was absorbing her, and without further ado, he went back to where Stevian and Nyxara were still reigning the power of darkness.

16

Lenna

By the time the sun shone through the curtains of their cabin in the navia, Lenna had a pounding headache and surely blueish lips from trying to sleep in such cold.

She had stacked blankets on top of her and Jake until somewhere around the fifteenth she had assumed that Giving them any sort of cover was as useful as a pile of rotten feathers.

"Is fucking our brains out the only way to survive this place at night?" Jake said, echoing her own, still-defrosting thoughts. "It is a question, not a complaint."

Lenna would have chuckled, were her cheeks not rigid as the metal door. "Llunal is a dirty bastard." Lenna didn't find the god of the courtrades one damned bit funny. "If we have to be kept so busy at night, we might as well sleep when the sun is out. Actually . . . It would make sense that the god of shadows wants us to give nights a better use, don't you think?"

"The Fifth only knows why these gods and goddesses do what they do." Jake turned his tense body towards her on the bed, casually leaning his head on his hand. "Do you think your friends are still alive?"

Lenna's facial and arm muscles seemed to find enough strength to elbow Jake while she pursed her lips. He didn't flinch at her not-so-candid touch, and her elbow was almost sore by how his abdomen muscles appeared to be made of the same steel as the door. "For Cardinals' sake, Jake. They better be."

She wasn't shocked that Jake didn't consider Sasha and Brendon *his* friends. Why would he? Jake had made it clear that the only reason he was in this group of people was to get the Fifth. He wanted it to avenge his father torturing Lenna, stabbing her until she was unconscious, and taking her panom powers away.

It still shocked her that such a male, ruthless and unforgiving, gave a shit about her. According to Jake, he gave much more than a shit. Those weren't his exact words, actually. They had been more like . . .

I chose you, Lenna Brachyan, because you have the fearless heart of those who change worlds. I chose you, because I can see who you are behind the walls you insist on putting for everyone to see. I chose you because even if you have accepted that everyone who should love you has given up on you, I know you are worth fighting for. I chose you because I know you can be as powerful as I am, if not even more. And I chose you, sweet fire, because you are absolutely insufferable, and I can't get you out of my mind.

It didn't make sense that he cared so much, that he saw her *so* much. Of course, Jake Coralt of the Organ House wasn't here for friendships. He didn't seem to care for anything or anyone other than himself and the red-haired woman lying with him in bed.

Did this man, consumed by a centuries-long life of pain and vicious orders under his wicked father, have *any* friends?

The thought was depressing and solitary, and a piece of Lenna's heart wanted to hide it away to make it less real. She didn't dare ask him the question. She didn't dare want to hear the devastating answer and hurt him by making him say it aloud. Maybe not having anyone at all in the world was not even a hurtful thought for him.

Her golden eyes threatened to fill with sudden, unstoppable tears born from the need to protect a man that didn't need protection.

"What's wrong?" he asked, his silver eyes narrowing as his full lips tightened in a line. He caressed her slightly-less-cold cheek.

"I am lucky to have you. In whatever way I have you, if I have you at all. I hope you know that you have me as well, in whatever capacity you want me, if you want me at all."

Jake's eyes narrowed even further, his pupils barely two visible slits.

"I know that didn't make any fucking sense." Lenna wanted to hide under the fifteen blankets and perhaps add a few more until her blood circulated to her brain in a way that didn't make her seem totally stupid and totally overthinking. Which was *precisely* what she was doing.

Shame hiding away and being sensible were as unknown to Lenna as the bastard god who would freeze them to death. She closed her eyes, taking a breath in before saying, "You have me, Jake. You had me yesterday, you have me today, and you will have me tomorrow."

"Don't think I missed the part where you said if *I want you*, Brachyan." His tone was chastising and severe. "I donated you petals to help you regain your panom mark; I threw my previous life and my old responsibilities away; I became a fugitive. I joined a crusade that I have only read in books because it's too risky to attempt in real life; I distanced myself from the only member of my family that I care about, and the Fifth knows that is only half of what I've done for you, and to be close to you. Just so I have it absolutely fucking clear. What part of this makes you even think that I might *not* want you?"

Her golden eyes were not teary anymore. They were full of utter passion for this male. She didn't deserve him. "You didn't need to do any of those things for me."

"I very much know that, sweet fire. And yet, I would still do them five hundred times again."

The intensity of his lips on hers could have consumed her life, the navia, the whole Radel Sea, and perhaps the Cardinals themselves. She grabbed his face with both hands, answering his kiss with the same devotion. Devotion that spoke of raw desperation, excruciating need, and longing to feel each other closer forever more.

Eventually, perhaps hours later, Lenna let go of him. "Right. My friends. I must see if they became ice cubes overnight." She widened her eyes, suddenly remembering why she hadn't bothered putting a sound barrier in their cabin the previous night. "And your special guest? Maybe poor Arabella whatever-fancy-second-name isn't alive."

The side smile on Jake's handsome face matched his chuckle. "That would definitely make your day."

Not only were Sasha, Brendon, and Arabella fucking D'Arcy very alive and very not frozen, but also, they were enjoying a delightfully complete breakfast under deck.

"Morning, morning." Lenna took a seat next to Sasha, giving her a quick but firm hug. "You all look very well." Jake sat at the end of the table, next to a still-sleepy Brendon.

"Not as well as you, surely." Sasha snorted. "By the second or third time you guys came, I was glad the sound of the waves was that loud."

Lenna served herself some of the nuts and pastries mix. "Was your night peaceful and quiet, Arabella?"

"It was, when I finished touching myself with you two moaning in the background." Arabella nodded distractedly. "It was very enjoyable, actually. To the point that I might request my cabin to be moved closer to yours. It helped me keep warm."

Brendon had a coughing fit, and Jake patted him on the back so intensely that Lenna wouldn't have been shocked if a rib or two had broken.

"How did you two keep warm?" Lenna turned to Sasha and Brendon to avoid showering Arabella with some aggressively thrown nuts. She didn't know if Arabella masturbating to the sound of her and Jake eating each other made her jealous, or hot. Because whichever way it was, Lenna had purposely forced her to listen to them having sex. And either way, it was ridiculous if Lenna was pissed off by the consequences of her own Cardinals-damned actions.

"Brendon went to find the courtrades and asked them if Llunal preferred to bury our dead bodies or throw them into the sea."

"Savage." Lenna laughed.

Brendon grinned, the green of his eyes shining with pride and delight. "It worked. One of them—I think he's mute—threw a weird thing at me. I think he might have made it for us, actually. It was like a thick, static shadow that I could move around."

"This cheek blackmailed me into accepting him in my bed or *dying the coldest death ever*." Sasha's voice was grave in a weak attempt at imitating Brendon's voice. "He was all smug smiles and retorts until we fell asleep."

"Hold. On. A. Minute." Lenna lifted both palms in the air, her jaw dropping dramatically. "Did you two sleep together? And you didn't tell me? When were you going to tell me?"

Sasha's eyebrows shot upwards. "When you stopped fucking, perhaps?"

"And remembered other beings cohabitate in the same world as you two?" Brendon added.

"Shut up. Tell me everything. Every single damn thing." Lenna filled her mouth with another spoonful of nut mix, and crossed her arms, awaiting nothing but a proper response.

"Nothing happened. We used the shadow cloak thing; we laid down, closed our eyes, and woke up this morning. Ready for a new day." Sasha smiled wickedly, already knowing how boring Lenna was going to find reality.

Lenna rolled her eyes, turning her face to the side. "Nothing happened *yet*, you mean. Clearly, not all of us know how to enjoy life in bed."

"Other than talks about beds and fucks, do you do any work around here?" Arabella asked, shoving a bunch of perfect blond waves behind her shoulder.

"Give us a break, will you?" Jake said. "It was an exhausting night."

"I know. I *heard*. But I thought you brought me here to show this woman how to dominate Taking like a professional."

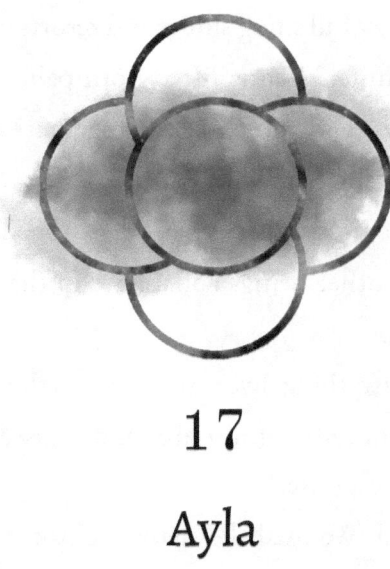

17

Ayla

From the couch in a cabin that was not hers, Ayla looked through the curtainless window to the unrealistic view in front of her.

Surely the courtrades couldn't have traveled that far in one night.

Surely the Cardinals had to give the heir of the North House a better chance than this.

Surely the perfectly smooth ramp emerging from the sea waves into the clouds above was a mirage and not the North Cardinal's ordeal of the Fifth crusade. Because if it was, then the transparent crystal hill reflecting the colors of the rainbow as the sunlight hit the water underneath was there for her. And only her.

Ayla felt set up and absolutely doomed. She was not ready to be the striver of anything today, not after a night without sleep. Definitely not the striver of an ordeal that would put her life at risk. She had been at risk of freezing to death all night.

And what a night that had been. At first, she had been Giving animals made of silver sparks, hoping—in vain—that the cats and dogs around her legs and trunk would give her some warmth. Then, after so much Giving her inner scale tilted and her green eyes started to feel sore, Ayla somehow stripped the night-patterned curtains from the windows of her cabin bare and wrapped them around her body. Whatever material they were made of was better than before.

Later, in a semi-awake doze between exhaustion, concern, and blindness, she had walked towards the rooms of Indianna, Raoul, and Nina, covering them with the curtains that she also ripped off their rods. Finally, she must have lost the last thread of consciousness while falling asleep, because she had just awoken on the couch in Nina's cabin.

She didn't even care if the white-haired, stunning woman thought she was creepy for walking into her room in the middle of the night and covering her trembling, curled body with destroyed curtains. Ayla cared that at least they were still alive, now that the sun had appeared blasting through the windows that had never lacked curtains so much.

The sight of the ramp emanating from the Radel Sea up into the sky was a nightmare not nearly as bad as the one she had just woken up from.

That nightmare was about her twin sister being tortured by the Organ Mandor in front of all the panoms of Thyria, because Lenna had been stubborn and hopeful enough to try to protect Raoul from being killed after the Mandor finished experimenting with his psychic state.

That wasn't the true nature of her nightmare. It was a memory, and Ayla welcomed it to her mind on certain nights as a form of penitence for the devotional obedience and belief on the system she had for over two decades. For thinking that somehow, her father or mother would step up and protect Lenna from being exposed, bleeding, begging, and sobbing.

Ayla would never forgive herself for allowing the Organ Mandor to publicly torture a twenty-five-year-old woman who lacked good manners but had good intentions at heart. Even if Ayla knew that, had she stood up and said anything, she would have been tortured as well.

But that wasn't what she had done. All Ayla had been capable of doing that night in the Cardinals Temple was stay rooted to the floor, clenching her fists so hard her nails cut through the skin on her palms, seeing each stab as if the speed had been slowed down so much it nearly halted. Her body shook every time the Red Lawful Stab had made contact with Lenna. Ayla's beliefs in the political system and how society worked sliced her own mind at the same time as the blade sliced the skin of her twin.

The unmitigated shock had kept Ayla from moving, from acting, from *helping*. Nothing would ever make her feel so powerless and paralyzed.

Ayla blinked twice to confirm what she already knew: that the crystal ramp in the sea was not going anywhere. If the North Cardinal truly wanted her ordeal to happen now, she might as well not make her wait.

After stretching her limbs, she folded the curtains and left them on the couch. Her silent steps stopped when Nina rolled her body quietly on the bed. Ayla stayed still, praying to the Cardinals that the ocean-eyed, snow-haired beauty wouldn't wake up. She didn't want to see the worry in her usually cheerful face. She didn't want to be the *cause* of her worry.

Nina didn't move further, and Ayla found her steps following the foolish impulse to get closer to her rather than to the door she needed to head to.

She shouldn't be here. She should totally not be staring at Nina's pale, smooth skin, listening to her steady breathing sounds, admiring what a precious soul she had in such a world of corrupt beings. Ayla pushed her own long, smooth red hair behind her neck. If she was honest with herself, she had never been able to stay away from Nina, not since their eyes crossed paths. But this? Was she a psycho? To be invading her privacy . . . Something was very, very wrong with her.

Ayla pulled her hand back from where it had been mere inches from caressing Nina's hair. No, she wouldn't be that creepy. She couldn't take advantage of someone who had only been pure, cleansing, and refreshing to her soul.

This moment—this very intrusive, forbidden and secret moment—had only happened because the North Cardinal's ordeal had every probability in the world of killing Ayla in usual circumstances. Even more in her unusually cold, shitty circumstances. Regardless of the circumstances, the ordeal was happening, and it was happening now.

Ayla wasn't surprised to not find anyone awake as she walked to the upper deck of the navia. The courtrades were probably sleeping after a busy night.

Gentle waves crashed against the navia, the sound peaceful and relaxing. She allowed herself a moment to close her eyes and breathe. She breathed in the motivation to get the red crystal feather of the North Cardinal's ordeal. She breathed out the mistakes of her past.

She breathed in as she Gave herself more suitable clothes for what she was about to do next; she breathed out every fear of not seeing anyone again if she didn't make it out alive.

Ayla climbed the rail, breathed in again, and jumped to the Radel Sea.

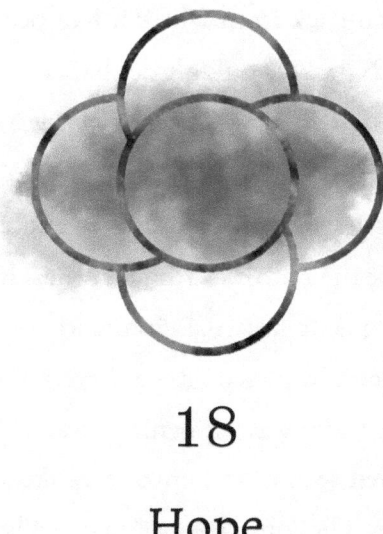

18

Hope

A sense of urgency woke up a startled Hope. She stood with a jump, grabbed her daggers by the hilt, and ran as fast as she could to the top deck.

Goosebumps covered her thighs and forearms as she spun around, taking in the sight around her.

The sea was still, as if it had tired from raging and fighting overnight. The horizon didn't show any land masses. However far Ciaran, Stevian, and Nyxara had moved the navia, it had been enough. They were safe. Safe from Thyria, the Roix, and her father, at least. Because the massive wall of crystal with a forty-five-degree inclination emerging from the water to the sky above was the opposite of safe.

Then she saw it. She saw *her*. Hope covered her mouth with the back of her hand, not letting go of the blade. She held her breath as the red mass of hair swam towards the crystal mass.

Ayla's body was small in the distance, and yet Hope could see she had reached some steps that were pulling her out of the water. A feminine voice spoke from the top of the wall, where it mixed with the lower white clouds covering its peak.

"Welcome to your ordeal, Ayla Brachyan of the North House. May you demonstrate your worthiness to possess the Fifth by securing my crystal feather. The Cardinals will not favor you. Striver, you stand alone."

Hope saw Ayla look up at the wall in front of her with more determination than fear.

Only a fearless woman would head towards a challenge that required one power without having access to the counterpart's power to balance her inner scale. If anyone thought that being the current heir of the North House would make anything easier for Ayla in the Giving ordeal, the voice of the Cardinal had just proved them wrong.

This was a losing game, and of all the things she could lose, Hope wished Ayla didn't lose her life.

Ayla kneeled, both palms touching the crystal wall at her feet, and looked up. Ayla Gave a thin red rug in the center of the inclined wall. Hope couldn't see the texture from the navia, but surely it had to be some rough material. Water and a smooth surface were never a good combination.

The next second, Ayla was running up, up, up the wall.

Behind Hope, there was a male gasp. "Is that—Of course she is. Fuck. Cardinals guide her." Raoul's voice sounded from behind. There was no point in Hope telling him that the Cardinals had made it clear that they *wouldn't* guide her. Not today.

The wall seemed to swallow the rug, vanishing under Ayla's feet and slamming her face against the crystal. She started slipping down all the way she had already climbed. She Gave two metal poles anchored to the crystal, that she used to propel herself upwards to keep from sliding down.

After a few minutes, Ayla regained some speed again. She kept repeating the same actions: Giving anchors, holding onto them and pushing herself up, until she Gave another two anchors to a higher area.

In an ideal world, Ayla would have been Taking the already used anchors, keeping her inner balance steady. In the real world, Ayla couldn't Take because she had no South Petal. She had no access to the Taking power.

She would have to continue Giving anchors, rugs, or whatever she needed until she reached the top. *Whenever* she reached the top, and that wouldn't be anytime soon.

"Do you think she will make it?" Raoul asked.

Hope nodded slowly. "She has to."

19

Lenna

"What exactly is so special about you or your magic that only you can teach me about Taking?" Lenna inhaled sharply, crossing her arms.

She had agreed to be in an empty room with Arabella D'Arcy, but she would not waste a second of her day giving the woman the benefit of the doubt. Miss Blond Bitch had made her points very clear about how *deeply* Jake and she knew each other and what a *pleasure* it had been to know him for Fifth knew how many years. But the advice about letting Lenna's hair loose because Jake liked it more when fucking? That gained her some extra points on the scale of nasty, vile bitchiness. Period.

Could Lenna be behaving quite immaturely? Probably. Did she give a royal fuck? Probably not.

"How does your inner scale react?" Arabella asked, unmoved.

"Excuse me?"

"You heard me."

"I don't want to tell you that." It wasn't even personal. Why would she want to share her biggest panom weakness with a stranger?

"Then we might as well finish now. From what Jake told me, you'll be expected to use the Taking power a lot on your ordeal. If your inner scale is unbalanced for a long time, you could die."

Lenna tried to find all her faith in Jake by making her learn from this woman. It could have been that, or the actual curiosity to know what was so unique about Arabella's approach that not even Jake could teach her. "When I use my powers unevenly, I get dizzy, my mind blurries, and I faint."

"Not one of the rarest symptoms by any means," Arabella said. Lenna couldn't decide if it was better not to be unique in this sense. Ayla's and Jake's symptoms seemed equally incapacitating.

"To Take without limit one must Give in the same capacity. Correct?" Arabella paced the empty room, the sound of her high heels breaking the silence.

"Yes. Unless I want the inner magical balance tilting to the point that I can't continue."

Arabella looked at her, narrowing her blue eyes. "What if you Took, and could Give at the same time?"

"Simultaneous use of opposite powers? Is that a thing?"

"That is *my* thing."

"Your thing as in . . . You invented it?" Lenna lifted an eyebrow. Surely Miss Nasty couldn't be some sort of magic prominence.

The eye roll that followed was completely unnecessary and completely annoying. "Of course not, you fool. Panom magic is so ancient that nothing is new anymore. This simultaneous use of powers is how *I* use my magic. My balance threshold is very low, so I cannot allow my inner scale to tilt even one bit. Ever."

"What would happen if you did?" Could it be truly that bad, or was Arabella exaggerating?

"I would be moured away against my will. Until I mastered how to use two sources of magic at the same time, it happens all the time, every single time. One day I was moured to the cave of some wild beast who wanted to feed me to her offspring. Another day, I appeared in a club between two men stabbing each other. I don't fancy disappearing from where I am meant to be to appear Cardinals know where."

"Fair play. How can I do it?"

Arabella smiled in a now-we're-talking kind of way, and Lenna tilted her chin slightly upwards. Maybe she even gave her the smallest smile. Now, she was interested and intrigued by what Arabella had to teach her.

"When you use two powers at once, each hand leads on one. One hand will Give, and therefore you will open as usual. The other hand will Take, and therefore you will close it at the same time. The opposite side of the brain will focus on pulling the respective petal of your panom mark. For example, if you use the right hand to Give, the left half of your brain will be leading on how the North Petal of your panom mark is used. If you use the left hand to Take, the right side of your brain will ensure that happens."

Lenna frowned, recapitulating on what she had just heard. "The brain part is confusing, but I think I get it."

"It is very interesting, that's what it is. It's easier to do if what you Give and Take is the same."

Arabella put her hands in front of her, one open and one closed. She Gave a drop of water into the air and at the same time she Took the drop away, making it visible for less time than it took Lenna to blink. She continued opening and closing her hands, and a drop of water appeared every time before vanishing and reappearing again.

"Taking a drop, Giving a drop. Same amount of magic required. If you Take a drop of water and Give a lake, your inner balance will still tilt. Which for you, is not the end of the world," Arabella said, and Lenna could have sworn there was a tinge of jealousy and frustration in her voice. "But you could Take a drop of water and Give a pinch of sand, and it would still be even. Different products, same amount of magic."

Lenna inhaled deeply. Cardinals guide her to the uneven tilt.

This use of magic sounded clever, useful, and *very* fucking complicated.

She wasn't sure she had ever seen two types of panom magic being used by the same wielder simultaneously. She wasn't even sure she would be able to do it herself, or if it would help her in her ordeal, but she was definitely going to give it a go. Or, most likely, a hundred goes.

Lenna placed her hands in front of her, ready to start the first of surely many attempts to master this synced use of powers. It was then, when her forearm tickled, and the red ink of Hope's handwriting threw all her plans out of the fucking navia.

Your sister has been doing her ordeal for hours. We can't see her anymore, but we think she's still fighting and alive.

Lenna read the ink, and reread it, and re-reread it, unable to process her rapid heartbeat and the whirl of fear overwhelming her.

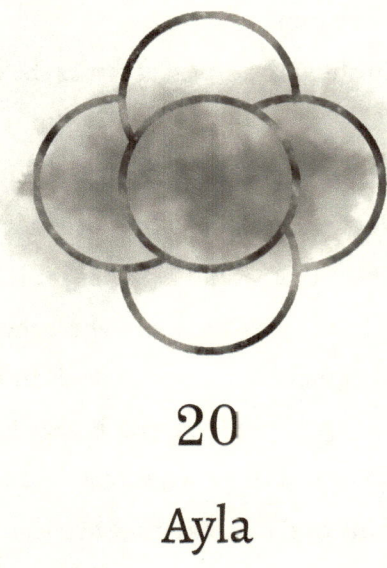

20

Ayla

The world was dark, smooth, and exhausting. So, so exhausting.

Whatever level of tiredness and mental drainage Ayla had felt in her life before this moment faded in comparison to *this*.

The North Cardinal's ordeal had made her give everything. The strength and physical force she didn't have, the resistance to stop pursuing the damned crystal feather that awaited her somewhere, the perseverance to not give up.

The world was dark because her eyes had stopped allowing her to see a long time ago. It was probably twilight, but she couldn't tell. The pain in her eyes was blinding and limiting. A pain she had never experienced before, but then she had never pushed her inner balance so much before. If by some blessed miracle she survived this ordeal, throwing her scale upside down would definitely not be in her future plans. Ever.

She had tried Healing her own pain, but then the horizontal scale between the East and West Petals of her own panom mark had tilted, and the ocular pain increased even more.

She had settled in finishing the ordeal as fast as she could, as alive as she could.

Her hands were sore from grabbing the metal anchors she pinned to the immense wall every two steps. She didn't need to see the wall to know where to Give the anchors that would help her push upwards. Each time she pressed the palm of her hand in the spots where the skin had lifted from her palms, she wished her hands were not so weak and sensible.

She had spent too much of her life gossiping, at Elite parties, dinners, and private meetings. None of those would save her now. She wished she could look back and think of the past as if she had learned something from those years. All she had learned was a waste of time and energy, and that most people had their own agenda and looked after their own asses and nobody else's.

What had sucked Ayla into the dynamics of Ciaran's safehouse in Corentre was the opposite of that empty pretense.

This group of people shared not only an enemy, but they also had a common goal. They wanted to make this world better. Even if their exact definitions of *better* varied.

And the first step towards that change was getting the Fifth, even if that left Ayla blind, sore, and with callused hands. But she was not going to give up. She would continue, however long she needed to climb, until she reached the end of this wall.

And if there was no end, then she would lose. Not only her life, but the hope to once more see the universe behind the blue eyes that struck her heart with lightning from the first time they crossed paths.

She didn't want to imagine what Nina would do if she didn't come back. Not because Ayla meant anything special to her, sadly, but because Nina was a generous and kind human being who cared and cried. It wouldn't be fair for such a kindred soul to suffer because Ayla couldn't climb a fucking wall.

The next metal pole she Gave clattered against the crystal, misplaced, tumbling down the wall with loud, scattered bangs.

Holding onto the current anchors, keeping her steady and standing, Ayla dared to lift her foot towards where the pole should have stood, and—there was nothing there. There wasn't a ramp anymore, because there was a floor. A marvelous, perfectly horizontal floor.

The tears of relief, pain, desperation, and exhaustion left her eyes before her second foot stepped on the floor. How under-appreciated were straight floors. She choked out a laugh that sounded manic between the sobs.

"Ayla Brachyan," the voice that had welcomed her before, now spoke in front of her. "You Gave what you had and what you didn't have."

"Are you the North Cardinal?" Ayla asked between shaky breaths.

"Who else would have been so patient for you?"

Ayla lifted her eyebrows. A part of her damned her useless eyes for not allowing her to see and admire the goddess in front of her. A part of her wanted to tell the goddess that if she was in a rush and didn't want to be patient, she shouldn't have made the damned wall so tediously tall. But Ayla kept her mouth shut and smiled. She knew when to keep quiet, and when she could throw her manners out the window. The Cardinal in front of her had something Ayla needed. Something she had fought for.

"Thank you for allowing me to be a striver for your ordeal. It was my pleasure to Give you everything and more."

"I don't tolerate liars," the North Cardinal said, and the floor under Ayla's feet trembled.

Ayla frowned. "I am no liar. I willingly became a striver, and I willingly chose your ordeal. The ordeal of the House I will one day rule. I knew my chances of not suffering were nonexistent. The moment I Give, the moment the pain and blindness start. And yet, it was a pleasure to demonstrate to you that I care about the Fifth enough to Give you not only my silver sparks but also my tenacity, my resolve, and my courage. This is who I am, this is what I have, and I willingly offer it to you to deem me worthy or not."

There were long moments of silence, and the only way Ayla knew the Cardinal was still there was because of her quiet steps walking towards her.

A soft, cold hand touched her cheek. "You are worthy, Ayla Brachyan."

Flapping wings sounded next to her, and the sound of crystal clattered at her feet. Ayla didn't even bother drying her tears, not as she grinned and kneeled, searching the surrounding floor until she found the crystal feather of the North Cardinal.

21

Hope

It had been hours since Ayla disappeared from their visual reach. The crystal wall was still fixed in the middle of the sea. Hope assumed that meant the ordeal wasn't over yet.

Raoul's stomach rumbled, and Nina side-eyed him in a way Hope had never seen her look at anyone before. In all honesty, all their stomachs were empty by now. After assuming Ayla's ordeal was going to be lengthy, Indianna had brought some bowls with breads, dips, and olives. Some of them had eaten more, some of them hadn't bothered at all. The Fifth only knew where the couple of olives Hope had ingested were at this point.

Dusk was fast approaching, and the concerns about visibility would then be a whole other issue.

One blink, the wall was there. Another blink, and it was gone. Gone as if it had never existed before. Which meant—

"Where is she?" Nina asked, putting a hand on her forehead, narrowing her blue eyes to focus on the waves.

It was too dark and the waves too strong to see anybody from such a distance. But . . . The thought hit Hope's mind before her frustration could dominate her feelings. She had coexisted in pitch-black darkness with Marcus and other courtrades while in the vessels.

Courtrades saw in the dark, because *they* were darkness.

"Can you see Ayla, Ciaran?"

"She's swimming to us. Wait, no. Where is she now?" He frowned. "Fuck, a wave drowned her for a bit. I see her now. She is swimming the wrong way."

"She can't see. Her eyes must be—" Nina said, panic in her blue eyes as she looked at Hope and Ciaran as if they were the answer to the equation. "She needs help."

"Can't she moure into the navia?" Raoul asked.

"Llunal's protection doesn't allow mouring. Otherwise, we would have intruders every minute of our nights," Nyraxa said, the patch-free eye focused on the same spot where Ciaran's blue eyes were fixed. "Your friend will have to swim."

Nina opened her mouth, ready to argue back, but held her opinions in as Ciaran walked towards the rail.

Hope would have been happy to help in daylight, but the red moon half-peeking through the clouds wouldn't be enough for her to guide Ayla safely to the black navia. If there was no other alternative, Hope would still do it. Her black eyes met Ciaran's blue ones before he removed his black shirt from over his head.

It required all the determination one could imagine *not* to look. Even without focusing her stare where her curiosity wanted her to, Hope could sense the marked muscles on his chest, abdomen, and arms. She could hint the intersection between his metallic arm and his shoulder that she so wanted to examine, and the inked dark patterns trailing from the upper part of his chest down his biological arm. His arm had more ink than many letters.

Ciaran turned to the waves and the night and jumped into the sea.

It was night by the time a dripping Ciaran climbed the ladder of the navia carrying a drained and blind, but definitely alive Ayla.

Ayla thanked him in a muttered, weak voice when her feet touched the floor. Hope walked to her other side, so she and Ciaran could guide Ayla to the common area under deck, where Raoul, Nina, and Indianna were waiting. It hadn't been easy to convince them to go inside, and Hope had promised to send them warning sparks as soon as Ayla arrived.

Nina brought a chair behind Ayla's legs. When the edge of the chair touched the spot behind her knees, she sat, tilting her head backwards as if it was the biggest pleasure this life could provide. Indianna had many ripped clothes piled up. No, not clothes. They were *curtains*. The shadow-powered curtains that protected from the cold.

"How are you?" Nina asked.

Ayla half-scoffed, a tear rolling down her still-closed eye. "Destroyed."

Hope kneeled in front of her and placed her hands over Ayla's eyes. The eyes she hadn't yet opened since Ciaran had brought her to safety. Ciaran joined her shortly after, kneeling next to Hope and Healing Ayla so that each of them could focus on one eye.

It took long, very worrying minutes from Ayla pressing her eyes shut, to her features easing slightly, to her blinking multiple times before she could open her emerald-green eyes.

"Thank you," she sighed. "I wasn't sure if I would ever see again, and that would have been very unfair, because I need to see—"

Ayla put her hand inside her tucked-in shirt and pulled out an object. A very red, very crystal, and very feather-shaped object.

"By the Cardinals," Hope whispered. "Congratulations, Ayla."

This was it. The first factual, tangible proof that they were on their journey to obtain the Fifth power.

The Fifth crusade was not a myth. It wasn't a made-up theory. The crystal feather of the North Cardinal was *real*, and Ayla was holding it as a mother would hold her newborn.

"I'm not sure if congratulations, condolences, or apologies are in order, but thanks. I'm too exhausted to think and too glad I won't have to do that ever again. I'm too fucking annoyed that, after everything, I couldn't see the North Cardinal with my own eyes."

"Talking about being annoyed . . . Your sister will kill me if I don't update her now," Hope said.

She sent her red ink to Lenna:

Ayla made it to the navia.
We are taking care of her.

A few seconds later, Ayla looked at her own forearm and the golden ink in Lenna's handwriting was on her skin for all to read:

*You couldn't be bothered to tell me,
dear sister?*

Ayla chuckled, silver sparks leaving her fingers, on the way to Lenna. Before Hope had time to figure out or ask what Ayla replied, Lenna's ink was back on the forearm of the redhead.

I don't give a shit about the feather, you moron. But I guess that's good news as well. It makes sense that you were too busy not dying to let me know. Rest and recover, Ayla. Love you.

Ayla swallowed, a smile spreading across her lips as her eyes fixed on the last two words of the ink from her twin.

22

Lenna

Where the Fifth hell was this man?

It was ante meridiem, and Jake still hadn't come to the cabin. Lenna had gone from pacing in the cabin, to pacing in the corridor, to pacing in the cabin again. The cabin was not *that* big.

She didn't want to pace any-fucking-more, thank you very much. She wanted to *talk*.

Lenna debated between sending him an ink threatening to cut his balls—an absolutely empty threat that she would never perform for her own sake—or getting out of her very comfortable, silk burgundy nightwear to go find him wherever he was in the navia. Even if the navia was *that* big.

The worst thing that would happen if she didn't change her clothes was that one of the three courtrades would see her in her very transparent trousers and shirt. Lenna stopped her too-high-to-count step, putting her hands on her hips, and concluded that she didn't care enough about how others saw her to be bothered to change. Especially when she cared even less about what others thought of her. They were lucky the navia was already becoming cold, or her clothing selection would have been definitely more revealing, and definitely less covering.

She stormed towards the black door, ready to find the silver-eyed man that was too late to bed. As she opened the door, her face crashed against a wall. A wall of flesh and muscle that towered above her.

"Why such a rush?" Jake asked.

"The Supreme Leader of the Ocean dared to appear. May the Fifth bless his slow ass." She grabbed a fistful of his shirt and pulled him inside the cabin. Luckily, he didn't offer resistance, because if he did, Lenna wouldn't have moved him in twenty-five years.

Jake widened his eyes, cracking a laugh. "The Sovereign Ruler of this cabin is in a mood."

Lenna opened her mouth. "I upgrade you to boss of the ocean and you make me ruler of this cold misery?" She lifted her arms, pointing to the place around them. "Gracious is the piss-taking Supreme Leader."

Jake grinned while chuckling, and *that* was a very gracious sight. He looked to the side, shaking his head slowly.

"No, what?" Lenna asked.

"I'm not saying it. You will tease me to death if I do, and I may end up dead right here, right now, cursed for calling you such a corny thing." He folded his arms.

It was Lenna's turn to grin. Was he trying to show determination in his decision? Because the amused glitter in his eyes showed the complete opposite.

"Jake Coralt of the Organ House calling me something corny? The Fifth crusade can fuck off. I offer my soul to the Cardinals for this."

He let go an exasperated sound. "Weren't you in a rush to find me? What did you want?"

Lenna pushed her tongue inside her cheek, lifting her eyebrows. "Don't you think for a minute that you're getting out of this conversation. Because it is not a debate. Tell me the cheesy thing. I will do whatever you want in exchange."

Jake's eyes darkened immediately, his head tilting upwards as his now grave voice said, "Careful there, sweet fire. You could ignite."

Lenna put her finger on her lips, tapping it a few times, reminding him of what she wanted.

"I will say it once, and I will never say it again. And if I survive saying those fucking words aloud, you will owe me a desire of my choice. Deal?"

Lenna nodded, biting her tongue now that he seemed to be about to tell her. Jake exhaled deeply. He was the loser of this battle, but the winner of a future one.

"I was going to call you the Sovereign Ruler of my heart."

Lenna's jaw dropped dramatically, and she covered her wide-opened mouth with both hands.

"Cardinals take me away. That is very over-the-top, but also very . . . Cute?" It seemed absolutely wrong and against the Laws to call Jake *cute*. A black-haired panom that towered over her, full of inks and muscle, that fucked her like there was no tomorrow, and with such an unethical and troubled past? She had never cared about the Laws before, and she was not going to start now.

Lenna grinned. "*Very* cute, Jake. And you were right. You have no idea how many times I will tease you with this. Now that I will never become the Ruler of the North House, I will very happily take on the responsibility of ruling your heart." Her lips curled upwards. "And that is as much sentimental sappy bullshit as we can both tolerate."

She walked towards him and placed a kiss precisely on that part of his chest. "I was looking for you because Ayla got the North Cardinal's feather."

"One ordeal done, four to go," he said, holding her hand and pulling it until he was sitting on the bed. "How is she?"

It warmed a deep part of her that the man who never cared about anyone other than himself and Lenna was asking about her sister's wellbeing. Lenna knew it wasn't common courtesy. There was nothing about Jake that was common, and he lacked all courtesy.

She smiled, letting him guide her to his lap on the bed. "She was well enough to send me ink."

"Did she tell you anything about the ordeal?" he asked, and then quickly added. "Actually, I prefer not to know."

Lenna looked at him in silence, swallowing. He preferred not to know, because Jake was going to be the next striver.

Lenna had barely seen the three courtrades guiding the navia. They seemed like pretty efficient and helpful beings, but they definitely liked to mind their own business. There was a mute male, a bald male, and a short-haired, lanky female. According to them, the navia had been traveling in a straight line towards the East since they left Thyria.

Which meant that any minute of any hour, and any hour of any day, the East Cardinal's ordeal could start, and Jake would have to demonstrate his dominance of the Harming power.

23

Hope

The curtains of the navia were nowhere near as warm as the shadow outfit Ciaran had tailored for Hope, but at least they didn't come with waves of all sorts of feelings that she wasn't sure she was ready to experience again.

She'd have to tread carefully with him. He was dangerous. *Truly* dangerous. Not in the sense of physical danger. He had never hurt her, and Hope had no reason to believe he ever would. Even if he did, she wasn't afraid of that.

What was truly frightening, *absolutely* terrifying, were the thoughts.

Her thoughts.

How she found herself looking at him when she didn't mean to. How she seemed to know when he was entering a room before he even set a foot in it. How his scent made her close her eyes against her will. How she saw him swallowing and looking at her mouth when she spoke. How time didn't seem to pass when they looked at each other. How she wished to know him more.

She didn't *want* to wish to know him more, but she did. There was no point in lying to herself or pretending this wasn't the case. She wanted to know him, to talk to him, to look at him.

She wasn't as scared of the Core ordeal as she was from *this*.

She was used to being in control of her body, her emotions, her thoughts. When it came to Ciaran, all that vanished. The unavoidable physical reaction her body had when he was near, the undeniable *desire* to spend time with him, the impending need for time to stop . . . It didn't matter how many times she repeated herself this—he—could end her. The more she saw, the more she heard, the harder it became.

It wasn't that realization that made her open her eyes. It was the bleeding ink on her arm.

I've lost count of the women hanged on your behalf. They all scream like cowards until hope leaves their fearful eyes. If you don't come to me, I will come for you.

The first bleeding ink from her father in weeks. Hope doubted he had forgotten about her. Maybe the Organ Mandor hadn't bothered to send her any inks for a while or, more likely, she had been so distracted that she hadn't been able to block his ink, exactly how the dual-powered man that invaded her dreams and her mind had taught her.

The dripping blood on the floor seemed to mock her.

Drip, danger, drip. Drip, danger, drip.

The price of allowing herself to be distracted by a man was wet and red.

Her white-haired friend greeted her with a cheerful hug that squeezed Hope's ribs and made her smile.

"Morning to you, too, Nina. Morning, Indianna, Ayla." Hope sat at the head of the table, between the women who had almost finished breakfast. "Is Raoul okay?"

Nina sighed. "Sort of. He's been having more nightmares."

"More black strands in his hair?" Hope asked, lifting her eyebrows.

"A few more," Indianna replied. "We tried washing the color away, but it doesn't fade."

"Like permanent ink," Hope muttered.

Nina pressed her lips in a straight line. "I'm worried," she said quietly, like a secret declaration she didn't want her brother to know.

"So am I," Indianna agreed, scratching her forehead distractedly.

They had good reason to, but Hope knew saying this aloud was neither helpful nor useful. They ate in silence for a while, the pieces of thick bread with tomato spread melting in Hope's mouth.

Indianna spoke first. "Do we know if we're heading towards the next ordeal?"

"Nyraxa said we're heading West, yes," Ayla said. Toward Ciaran's ordeal. "She also asked if we know where we are meant to go after that, but you don't know yet, do you, Hope?" Her eyebrows lifted, her emerald-green eyes focusing on Hope.

"I haven't got a clue about where my ordeal will be."

Indianna shrugged. "Sometimes not knowing is better than knowing too much." She turned to Nina, crossing her arms. "I might ask Nyraxa if she wants me to look at her patched eye."

Nina chuckled. "I already offered our help. She said she *hadn't needed the bloody eye in decades,* and *it would be a nuisance to get used to having two again*. Oh, and that she liked her patch more than an actual eye."

Indianna snorted, and Hope laughed. Courtrades and their easy ways of living.

The door to the deck was half-open, the sound of gentle rain falling on the wooden surface, calming and well-known. Hope was about to walk outside when Stevian opened the door and entered.

"Beware of the rain if you don't want to get wet."

Hope chuckled. The man had been soaked the first night while pushing the shadows to move the navia away from Thyria.

"I don't mind getting wet every now and then," she said.

His smile was pure, his blue eyes shining with wisdom and something that resembled understanding. "You are not the only one, then. He just said he likes the rain."

Hope's stomach reacted as if she had just dropped from the top of the navia. She didn't need to ask to know exactly who *he* was. She didn't *dare* ask anything else.

Stevian bowed his head, still smiling, and disappeared behind her into the navia.

She could decide what to do. She could decide where to go. Hope swallowed, her breaths fastening as an array of questions, thoughts, and warnings filled her mind at the speed of beating wings.

She shouldn't. She totally shouldn't.

But she still did.

The raindrops fell on her face as she closed the door behind her. She closed her eyes, inhaling deeply, smiling at the pleasant touch. She lifted her hands, palms facing the clouds blessing them with precious water.

The smile became a grin, became laughter. Seconds became minutes, maybe hours. She could stay there until the rain stopped and the clouds left.

She could, but she didn't.

She opened her eyes, blinking a few times until the drops fell and allowed her to see clearly. And clearly, she saw.

She saw Ciaran, his back leaning on the rail, his face looking towards the sky, his eyes closed and peaceful, his wet, dark hair falling on his shoulders, his dark clothes shaping around the muscles on his body, the metal of his arm and the ring on his lip shining, the ink on his biological arm and the top of his chest fresh and clear.

Cardinals have mercy.

Hope didn't know how long she had been staring. But when he opened his eyes and his blue met her black ones, he half-smiled.

"It's raining," he said.

Hope chuckled. "Is it? I hadn't noticed."

"You caught me off guard. How long have you been here? I hadn't—"

He didn't finish his sentence, and Hope knew exactly what he meant. She hadn't scented him either, the smell of the rain covering any other scents.

"I'm not sure." It wasn't a lie, and it was better than *longer than I want to admit*. "Can I ask you a question?"

He walked towards her, closing the distance between them to a couple of steps. He nodded.

"What do the inks on your skin mean?" They were beautiful, intricate.

Ciaran inhaled deeply, letting go of a long exhale. "Do you want to ask any other question?"

Hope tilted her head to the side. "Of course I do, but why would I if you don't answer?"

"My inks . . . I can't tell you. I'm sorry." He sighed. "I promise to answer any other question I can."

"Have you ever been with a woman?"

No.

No.

No, no, no, *no*.

She couldn't have asked that. She was going to throw herself over the rail and hope the Cardinals were kind enough to drown her. She felt her cheeks flush, her heart fluttering in a way that couldn't be healthy.

"I have never been with anyone." His blue eyes were curious, assessing.

The next question slipped from Hope's mouth before she could stop it. The Cardinals didn't even know what mercy was.

"Why?"

His teeth racked his bottom lip. He took a long time to answer, but when he finally spoke, his words shook Hope in a way no panomquake could have.

"Why would I? I was waiting for you."

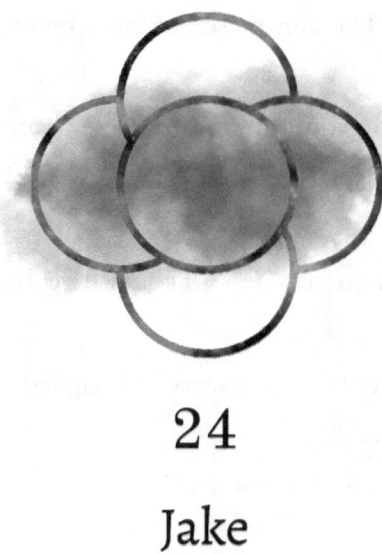

24

Jake

Here she comes, was his first thought when a tug in his chest claimed Jake out of bed.

He knew who was claiming his presence, but goddesses could wait when he had way more important matters in his hands—*on his body.* Nothing would ever be more important than his fire woman.

Cardinals, wasn't she beautiful when she was a sleeping naked fire.

He caressed the skin from Lenna's waist to the breast pressed against his exposed torso. Her red waves tickled his knuckles. He inhaled deeply, her scent of jasmine and ashes blurring any rational thoughts.

He definitely had time to lick her pretty pussy before his ordeal. His cock hardened at the thought of how delicious she was.

Another tug, rougher this time, wanted to pull him out of this paradise. *Impatient Cardinal.*

Lenna moved in her sleep, adjusting even more of her body to the shape of his, fitting *so* perfectly. It was a blessing.

If he woke her up with his tongue, she would see him going to his ordeal.

He was intrigued by what the East Cardinal would come up with to make him prove he was worthy of the Harming feather.

He had been Harmed since he had memory, and he had Harmed since he could. He was going to be fine in his ordeal. But Lenna . . . Her golden eyes had betrayed her these past few days, letting the silent worry speak for her.

His woman was going to be pissed if he left without telling her.

He could deal with her anger, but not with her suffering. It was unnecessary to make her suffer when there was no need to.

Carefully moving her, Jake gave Lenna a kiss in the soft spot between her closed eyes, another kiss barely touching the sensitive skin on the golden panom mark between her breasts. He covered her with multiple blankets and stood.

There would be time for making her scream his name later. Now, the Goddess of the East was waiting to give him hell, and he was going to give her hell back.

The invisible tug, constant now that he was finally answering his calling, guided him to the bottom of stairs he hadn't seen in the navia before. The stairs were dark like night, cold as ice, and steep as a pain in Llunal's ass.

The tug claimed his presence, and so Jake climbed up the windowless spiral staircase.

He climbed, and climbed, and climbed. There were only two parts of the vehicle that went that high. He knew he was at the top of one of the edges of the crescent shape of the navia before he opened the black door above him and pushed himself outside.

At the peak of the moon's shape was a small, circular, metallic platform. The vast expansion of the sea and the sky surrounded it from all sides. His eyes didn't take long to readjust from the pitch-black darkness to the clear light.

He would have been surprised if the courtrades had bothered to put rails. He walked to the edge of the platform, the breeze against his skin cool and pleasant. Jake tapped his foot on the corner of the precipice connecting the platform with the deck of the navia and the sea underneath.

What a simple and efficient way to kill someone.

"Some beings would think it was not clever to make the goddess of your ordeal wait, Jake Coralt of the Organ House."

Jake snorted lightly. "Some beings would think the goddess could have picked a place less than a thousand steps away to meet the striver." He turned around, his black waves moving with the air. "Long time no see, East Cardinal."

The Cardinal of the East stood taller than him in the middle of the platform, her red-feathered wings splayed proudly, her red eyes fixed on his silver ones, her red hair moving backwards as the wind hit her. Her countless scars crossed her beautiful, otherwise perfect face from side to side.

"Is it your bravery or your arrogance that made you think you would be a worthy striver of my feather?" Her eyes narrowed, her pursed lips showing that murderous anger he had met before.

"Very kind of you to ask, my dear. It is familiarity." He tilted his head to the side, the corner of his lips tugging upwards, daring the Cardinal to challenge his words.

"Do not disrespect me, Jake Coralt," her voice was a calm, lethal whisper.

"Do not forget I know your power like the palm of my hand, as the strings of my heart, as the words in my mind." His voice softened as his stare hardened. "Do not forget I know *you* know. I will not disrespect you, *my dear*, as long as you do *not* disrespect me."

The East Cardinal tilted her head back, her penetrating stare strong enough to throw him over the platform and into the sea, if she wanted.

"Some beings would think it is not clever to threaten the goddess that will oversee your ordeal before she deems you worthy, Jake Coralt."

"Those beings would be wrong to think I give a fuck about their opinion."

The nostrils of the East Cardinal flared, and his heart skipped a beat when she disappeared.

Nothing happened. Nothing *at all*. Could she deny him the opportunity to enter her ordeal? Could she *refuse* him as a striver?

They needed the East feather to get the Fifth Power. It was the only way to get rid of the male who destroyed his existence by making it agonizing; who dared touch his sweet fire and take her panom powers away, who hurt his Lenna into unconsciousness and assumed there would never be consequences. The Fifth power was the only way to kill his father.

Jake inhaled deeply, goosebumps trailing up his legs as his jaw clenched. There *were* going to be fucking consequences.

The Harming Cardinal couldn't ignore him. She *wouldn't* ignore him, because he was not going to let her.

"I am here to prove I'm worthy of your wickedness, East Cardinal. Harm me, bitch, or let me Harm." His voice faded without an answer. "What is it you want from me?"

From the air came a chuckle, followed by the East Cardinal's voice. "I want it all, *my dear*. I want your suffering, your pain, and your scars. I want you to regret breathing, to be ashamed of living. I want your torment and your torture."

He smiled; his goal achieved. His ordeal was happening.

"Then take it," he encouraged her.

One second, he stood on the platform. The next, he was free falling, his limbs out of his control, until his back was against the metallic side of the navia, his legs floating on the water, his hands—

Cardinals guide him. His hands were *pinned* to the metal, red crystal shards protruding from his palms—the palms he needed to use to perform any magic. The dripping blood diluted with the Radel Sea at the fast pace it dropped.

He looked up, the tall wall of the crescent side towering above him, and at the very top, barely visible, shone a small, red reflection.

It could only be one thing: the feather he'd claim.

With a grimace, he pulled his bleeding hand off the wall. His whole body hung dangerously from the hand still pinned. He lifted his free hand to his mouth, biting the crystal to take it out of his flesh. He couldn't.

Jake groaned at the pressure on the other hand. If the crystal broke, he would end up in the sea, and his ordeal would fail.

He slammed the free hand against the wall, above his head, the crystal secure in place before he pulled his other hand off the wall and pushed it upwards. Painful climbing, he could do.

Between forced groans and muttered curses at the shape of the fucking navia, Jake climbed. He pinned his right hand upwards. He let his left hand free and pinned it again.

He would lose a lot of blood—nothing he wasn't used to.

He would ignore the pain—his endless, always-present, most trustworthy friend.

He would persevere, like he always fucking did.

And then, while the pain didn't leave his breaking, perforated hands, while his knees hit against the metal wall of the navia . . . It was then when the visions hit his mind.

No, not visions. They were *memories*.

Memories he had buried so deep they never chased his conscious mind anymore. Memories that now lived in his nightmares.

He hadn't been more than ten when he found his mother hiding in a room in the Organ House. His father said she would come back soon, but he hadn't believed him. Jake never believed him. When his mother's eyes met his, her body shook vigorously. She was crying, and when Jake asked her why, she only shook her head. Her lips—the beautiful lips that kissed him to sleep, the soft lips that spoke words of strength—were sewn together.

His heart had seemed to stop when he got closer and saw black thread tracing the words *SHUT UP* over her lips. He couldn't take his eyes off them, his own body shaking as if the worst panomquake had shaken his world. As if a panomquake of rage, pain and frustration had hit his life.

The pain in his hands, the product of the ordeal, reminded him of his real, present surroundings. The East bitch was playing with his mind, but his body was still on the wall of the navia.

He wasn't in that room anymore, hugging his mother for hours while tears fell on the floor. No, his tears were now falling into the Radel Sea.

He didn't need to see to climb faster. His path was upwards. As he climbed, another memory solidified, courtesy of the Harming Cardinal. A memory that hurt so much it left him breathless.

The sarcastic, ready-for-trouble grin of a young man with dirty blond hair. Next to Evan was Atlas, her permanent raised eyebrow looking at him with a nostalgic side smile.

The first two people Jake had called friends. The first people without his blood that he had felt comfortable and safe with. The first people who seemed to care about what he felt, what he thought, what he wanted. Evan and Atlas were the first to make Jake feel like he was more than a piece of crap waiting to be thrown away. Like he was more than the heir of the Organ House. He was a *person*.

He hadn't been allowed to say goodbye to the first and last people he had called friends. One day, he was planning the next escapade with them. The following, their mutilated corpses had been left on the floor of his room for Jake to find as the ink from his father hit his skin.

It is dangerous for one's happiness to depend on others.

Jake roared against the wall of the navia, his fingers not curling as his hands were destroyed, the pain from this memory harming him more than any crystals could.

He wanted the ordeal to be over. He *needed* it to be over. He didn't stop climbing, but he couldn't see how far above he still had to ascend. He couldn't see reality yet.

He could only see images of moments of his life overlapping. Every time he had been Harmed, every time he had been hurt, every time he had felt hopeless, frustrated, or desperate. Every time he hadn't felt loved, every time he had cried, every time he had been lonely or frightened. Until . . .

There. The moment he understood he had to welcome pain to his life to continue living. The moment he greeted the pain instead of looking away from it.

It had been centuries since his tears had been dry, since he had been feared, since he had discarded, since his heart had hardened, since his hate had fueled him, since he had distanced himself from the world.

Endless images flashed in Jake's mind at the speed of panom powers, his breath jagged as he knew what came next. He had to climb to the top. He had to make it before the East Cardinal could make him relive *that*.

Between clenched teeth, he spoke. "Do you want to harm me? Harm away. Let's see if you can find the bottom of my well. I've dug deeper than any being could imagine. My pain is bottomless, my suffering immense. You, Cardinal, will not be my end."

His distraction was useless—red fire waves filled his mind as Jake let out a violent scream. He couldn't see again Lenna's exposed chest as his father brought the Red Lawful Stab to her skin five times. He couldn't relive it.

"Leave her alone! Get out of my fucking mind!"

His hands were soaked from the force and speed at which he pinned the crystals, crossing his flesh up and up the wall. How much fucking higher could a Cardinal-cursed wall be?

Lenna's screams and sobs from back in the throne room echoed in his mind, each painful sound hurting him more than if crystal shards went through his heart. He was going to lose his mind.

Faster he climbed, the regret of not having stopped his father from hurting Lenna threatening to kill him.

He *was* losing his mind. His woman hadn't been shouting his name in the throne room.

25

Lenna

"**J**ake!"

The courtrades had told her Jake was somewhere here. *Somewhere* being the smallest, shittiest platform Lenna had ever seen.

She was going to fucking kill him for not telling her he was going to his ordeal.

There was nowhere to hide here, and he very much *wasn't* here.

The absolutely terrified blood in her veins ran as fast as her heartbeat. What did that mean? Had his ordeal . . . finished? Fear, as she had never known, overtook her, tears flowing from her golden eyes before she had the guts to acknowledge what that could mean. Him *not* being successful was not a fucking allowed option—it simply *wasn't*.

"Jake!" she shouted again, her voice breaking with desperation. "I swear to the Five Cardinals, I will re-kill you if you are dead!"

A broken noise sounded closely, but Lenna couldn't see anything, anyone. Wait a fucking minut—

She ran towards the edge of the platform, gasping at the impressive drop to the deck of the navia. The very empty drop with no one there.

"Please, come to me," her voice was loud yet broken between sobs.

She heard a scraping noise and turned to look at the other end of the platform. A bloodied hand got hold of the floor by penetrating it with a red crystal.

A heartbroken gasp left her throat as her heart felt electrocuted with relief.

Thank the damned Fifth. Cardinals, bless the *fucking* Fifth.

She ran towards Jake, pulling from his slippery, blood-soaked wrist as his other hand followed.

His other hand was just as destroyed, another sharp crystal in the middle of his palm. Had the goddess made him *climb* the navia? If the East Cardinal hadn't flown away, Lenna was going to make her regret touching him.

When Jake managed to pull himself up with Lenna's help, his head rested on her lap. His silver eyes were closed, his face suffering and anguished, his body pained with exhaustion.

She wanted to say so many things. She wanted to *do* so many things. She caressed his pale face with shaking hands. "Jake, I'm here." He was so still it was unnerving. "You're not alone. I'm here for you."

He didn't react; his breaths didn't relax. When the silence of his pain was too much, Lenna spoke again. "Say something, please. Anything."

His silver eyes opened slowly, as if it was taking all his effort to even open an eyelid. The silver in his eyes was darker, moving, as if whatever was in his mind hadn't settled yet.

"I will always come to you, my love," Jake said, his voice barely audible.

Lenna's tears fell freely as her mouth tensed awkwardly between a sob and grin. "You better fucking do, because I will always be waiting for you."

She Gave herself a wet cloth, gently wiping his sweat from his face, attempting to clean the blood from his arms and wrists with little success because two royally damned, huge crystals were stabbed in his hands.

"We need to get these out of you."

He tried to prop himself up by leaning on his elbows, but Lenna put a hand on his chest and pushed him back on her lap.

"I'm not sure if my ordeal is finished," he said.

Lenna frowned, combing his black waves with her fingers. "What do you mean?"

He let out a shallow exhale. "I had to climb, so I climbed. There is no feather and no Cardinal. Either my ordeal isn't finished yet, or I was not deemed worthy."

"Do you think my most serious concern right now is the ordeal?" He had to be taking the piss. "You are the living image of someone Harmed, Jake. *Severely* Harmed. If that is not good enough for the bloody East Cardinal, then she can go ruin someone else."

"But I saw the feather. Before I—before I started seeing things, I saw the feather suspended in the air around the platform. That's why I climbed."

"There is nothing here, Jake." Lenna swallowed. "You saw . . . things?"

Jake shook his head slowly, frowning deeply, his eyes closed again. Lenna couldn't take her eyes off him, the pain of his expression shattering her heart as her worry increased exponentially.

He sighed. "She Harmed my mind with memories as she Harmed my body with crystals."

Lenna bit her bottom lip until it hurt, the taste of copper filling her mouth as unstoppable rage threatened to take control of her.

It was a blessing that the East Cardinal was not present. It was a fucking blessing, because Lenna would have attempted to rip her feathered wings off.

"You're hurt, Jake. Will you allow me to Heal you?"

He didn't move for what seemed like the longest pause, and then he nodded, his eyes still closed. "Only you can heal me."

Lenna carefully closed her hand above his, Taking away the crystal shard, making it vanish. It left a horrendous hole across his palm that moved her guts in a way she didn't enjoy. And despite that, she couldn't take her eyes off it.

A panom needed hands to perform any magic. How the actual hell was she going to fix *this*? Surely the East Cardinal wouldn't have Harmed him permanently, leaving him as good as panomless for the rest of his long life.

Surely. Fucking. Not.

Lenna was glad Jake's eyes were closed as she couldn't stop the tears, fueled by the biggest fear, from flowing again.

There was no way she could Heal his hands. She was not a good Healer, that was a shameful fucking fact. Maybe such damage, inflicted by the crystal of a Cardinal, was not able to be fixed at all.

Lenna lifted her hand over his other hand, the second and last red crystal protruding from his skin. She knew what she was going to see as soon as she Took it away. A second, perhaps also unrepairable hole.

She inhaled deeply and Took it.

A loud gasp of shock, fear, and hope left Lenna's mouth as a gasp of sudden relief left Jake's.

The crystal hadn't vanished.

The crystal had *transformed*.

It wasn't a sharp shard of red crystal anymore. It was a Cardinal-red crystal feather.

The feather, floating in front of Jake, waiting for him to pick it up.

His hands—magically repaired, full hands, completely unharmed, with no holes or missing flesh—lifted, wariness in his light silver eyes, and he held the feather of the East Cardinal. The feather of his ordeal.

Suddenly, his eyes opened wide, his jaw clenching as he swallowed. After a few seconds, his body relaxed, he lowered his hands and the feather on top of his chest.

"Did she speak to you?" Lenna asked, already knowing the answer.

Jake narrowed his eyes as he looked at the darkening sky above them. "She said a worthy striver can't have broken hands. And that I should consider killing everyone in the East Petal because no one in Terrha deserves being the Ruler of her Petal and her House as much as I do."

26

Hope

The red moon shone in the dark sky across the window when Hope's forearm tickled, and golden ink appeared:

Jake got the East feather.

Lenna's ink disappeared as soon as Hope read her words. It was a very factual, brief message, not like Lenna at all. Hope sent her red ink:

Is he okay? Are you okay?

A second later, golden words traced Hope's skin:

*Jake. . . I have no fucking clue.
I hope he'll be fine. I'm scared, and I would
be better if I could drown the East
Cardinal to the bottom of the sea.
Other than that, I am fine.*

The Fifth only knew what that ordeal entailed. Hope sighed, removing the daggers she had thrown against the opposite wall of her cabin and placing them carefully under her pillow, in the drawers, and behind the bathroom door.

She closed the door silently, waiting in the corridor, listening. Not a sound. Either most people were already asleep, or they were somewhere in the upper levels. The courtrades had been taking it in turns to push the navia towards the West, and Hope didn't know who of them was on duty tonight.

Still, she started walking, heading towards the stairs that led to the rooms they spent most of their time in. It was only when she slipped by Ayla's room that Nina's voice made her stop.

"It wasn't easy to assume I wasn't going to see or talk to them again. It was . . . painful." Nina's voice halted for long moments before she continued. "I didn't want to let them go. I couldn't let their *memories* go, because if I did, then there was going to be nothing keeping them alive."

Hope's black eyes fixed on a spot on the floor. Nina was talking about her and Raoul's parents. She had briefly explained to Hope that her parents, servants of the North House who ended up working at the West House, had disappeared years ago. Neither of the siblings found them in Verdania, so Nina thought they hadn't been discarded. The guess of the white-haired woman was they had been killed, even though their bodies were never found.

Hope doubted for half a second whether to knock and tell Ayla and Nina that the East ordeal had been successfully completed, but Ayla spoke before Hope could lift her hand—

The quiet sound of a hand caressing clothes was followed by Ayla's even quieter whisper. "Your parents . . . They are not dead, Nina."

"How do you know?"

Hope knew she was not meant to listen to this. Whatever *this* was, she was not part of their private conversation. She hadn't meant to eavesdrop, but her black eyes fixed on a spot on the floor, her feet refusing to move, the tight knot in her throat needing to hear what the answer was.

Until the answer came.

Ayla exhaled profoundly. "I—I have never told anyone. I wouldn't like to—Please don't judge me or be scared of me. Promise you won't."

Hope should have left as soon as she heard their voices.

"I can't think of anything that could make me fear you or judge you, Ayla," Nina replied.

Hope should leave right this very moment, but she couldn't. She *physically* couldn't.

"I see them. The long-gone, the beings who aren't here anymore . . . I see them." Hope's goosebumps trailed up her arms up her neck, but Ayla's voice continued, "If your parents were dead, I'm sure they would visit you and your brother, but I've never seen them."

Hope's body snapped out of the trance she had been suspended in. She scurried up the stairs, walking as fast and as far as she could away from the secret Ayla had been hiding for a quarter of a century. She felt her lungs tighten, the air struggling to come in as she couldn't take the image of her mother out of her mind. What if—

She needed air. She needed fresh air now.

She was not aware of her hands pushing the door to the deck of the navia open. She was not aware of her feet freezing, her head tilting backwards, her eyes closing, or the deep inhale that filled her lungs as if it was the first breath she had ever taken.

What. If.

She was not aware of how long she stood there, if she wasn't alone on the deck, or if the red moon had fallen from the sky.

Ayla was a necroseer.

Hope didn't know how long she had been lying on the comfortable bench that hadn't been at the deck before or how long she had been staring at the night sky.

The breathtaking smell of woods in the middle of the sea and the warm layer of shadows atop her body could only mean one thing.

"Thank you, Ciaran," she said as she sat.

"Not at all." He stood a few meters away, the shadows pushing the navia trailing from his arms and feet towards the darkness. "You seemed . . . affected."

"I was overwhelmed. *Very* overwhelmed." Their eyes met and Hope felt immediately at ease. "Sometimes life seems to be . . . excessive. Too sad, too loud, too risky, too hopeless. I lacked so many things living in Verdania."

Ciaran nodded slowly. He moved his hands and shadows stopped floating from him. He paced towards her and offered Hope his metallic hand.

Hope looked at it, admiring its beauty and strength, before she took it. Ciaran pulled her up, and when she stood in front of him, the touch of his fingers on hers lingered until he finally let go.

"What did you lack?" he said.

Hope looked towards the sea. There were so many things it was difficult to pick. She did not lack the worry about what food to eat the following day or attending Trading Day. She had missed friendship, truths, peace, trusting others, and not fighting to survive every day. But she had also missed smaller, insubstantial things. She had missed talking to people, deciding which game to play, and—

The memory of Sasha and Lenna jumping to the music on the balcony of the Crystal Clear safehouse, feeling it, singing it, was enough to make her pick.

"Music, having fun."

Ciaran's lips twitched. "We can kill two birds with one stone."

Hope laughed. "I thought bird-killing expressions were risky in a Cardinals-ruled world."

"What is life without risk?" Ciaran looked at her, and the way he spoke, as if it was a fact and a ruination, made her heart ache. He bowed his head slightly. "May I have a dance?"

Hope felt a rush of heat and shame jumping to her cheeks. "I have never danced."

His blue eyes glittered as he lifted his biological hand. An offer.

"Then it would be even a greater honor to be your first."

She couldn't deny him a dance. She didn't *want* to deny him a dance. She wanted to know what it would be like to dance, even if she felt more fear now than if she had twenty-five enemies waiting to kill her. She wanted to know what it was like to be close to him. She wanted to feel the touch of his hand on hers for as long as she could.

She could only pray the Cardinals didn't consider a dance between two heirs of the Houses a reason to cause a panomquake that could break Thyria in half.

It was *just* a dance.

She inhaled deeply, taking his hand with hers, her heart thumping wildly against her ribcage. Ciaran placed his metallic hand on her waist, above her leathers.

"Relax," he whispered, his thumb stroking hers. "You're safe."

She closed her eyes, hoping he didn't realize how much her hands were shaking as much as the waves in the surrounding sea. "I know," she said. "Don't we need music?"

Ciaran smiled and started singing.

He sang in a language she had never heard before. His eyes shone brightly while he guided her body, moving together around the deck.

It was a joyful song. A melody that reminded her of the things she loved, of a sunny day in a forest with the lightest breeze, surrounded by animals and flowers, of the happiness and innocence of childhood she had read about in books; of feeling full inside and knowing one's own path. The song went on, Ciaran's voice filling the night as his lips moved.

Hope couldn't stop grinning. She couldn't take her eyes off him, his eyes and lips the only firm things in the world as everything else appeared unfocused on a second plane. Ciaran made her spin around one more time as he sang the last note.

"I didn't know you could sing." The song had stopped, but her grin had not.

His eyebrows lifted. "I didn't know you could dance."

Hope swallowed, hoping the night covered her blush. "Can you sing another song?"

Ciaran smiled. "For you, always."

This time, he chose a haunting song, a melody about loneliness and sadness.

It wasn't a song to move as fast to as before; it wasn't one to spin around to.

Hope felt the need to be closer to him, to touch him as his voice trembled with all the words she didn't know, but all the feelings she knew too well.

She put her hands around his neck, moving in unison as his hands surrounded her hips. His mouth was all she could focus on as he sang with the emotion that came from the deepest of one's heart.

This was music about raw pain and solitude, hopelessness and devastation.

She felt wetness on her skin and Ciaran lifted his hand to dry a tear from her cheek.

She didn't smile. She *couldn't* smile.

Not as his song struck something buried deep inside her. Something she had spent years hiding under layers of self-convincing and not allowing herself to linger in the hurtful feelings that would stop her from moving forward. Feelings she knew were dangerous to acknowledge without letting them take over.

Yet here he was, singing about these exact feelings, without breaking on the outside.

But Hope knew the truth. Only someone could express these feelings, *sing* about these feelings, if he had been utterly broken by them where it mattered most: on the inside.

The song finished, and Hope was not ready to let go of this man who had opened his heart in such a devastating way without warning.

She placed her head on his shoulder, and Ciaran's arms embraced her while her silent tears fell.

He didn't need to ask.

She didn't need to explain.

They both embraced in silence for the Fifth knew how long, the only witnesses being the red moon, the Cardinals, and maybe even Llunal himself.

27

Lenna

Something wet woke Lenna up.

She covered her mouth to keep from waking Jake with a scream when she recognized the unforgettable handwriting and the bloody ink of the Organ Mandor on the arm he had over her stomach.

I am not as kind with the beings that need discarding as you were, boy. I don't bother sending them to Verdania. I send them to their graves.

Her nostrils flared as she read the message over and over again, fully aware that it was not going to vanish until the silver-eyed, black-haired recipient had read it, like any other inks. Except bleeding ink always remained for some time, even after that. Until then, Jake's blood would keep dripping where he rested on her skin.

Rhei fucking Coralt was a rotten shit of a man.

"You're shaking, sweet fire," Jake's voice was low against her hair.

"And you're *bleeding*, for Cardinals' sake." Lenna turned to face him; their noses so close they almost touched. "Tell me this is the first time he has sent you ink since we left Thyria."

Jake lifted an eyebrow. "But you don't like lies."

"When the Fifth damned hell were you going to tell me?"

He glimpsed at the ink and Lenna doubted any literate being could read that fast. Maybe it was a trick to make the ink-fading process start. As soon as his eyes left his forearm, they trailed to her naked breasts, his fingers following until they met his focus.

"I asked you a question, Jake." Her voice was meant to come out as pure rage, but it broke the tiniest bit when she said his name. The way he trailed his finger around her nipples without getting close enough to touch them was making her core ache.

I was not planning on telling you.

His voice in her mind made her jump, the hardening of his cock against her side making it very difficult to concentrate.

Lenna pursed her lips. "Also, will you ever tell me how you do your mind talking thing? Do you talk to everyone? Can I talk back to you? It's not fair, otherwise."

The corner of his lips tucked upwards as he covered her mouth with one hand while the other finally pinched her nipple, making her let out a muffled gasp.

I tried invading the minds of others, but it never worked. I guess I didn't want to fuck anyone as hard as I want to fuck you, sweet fire.

The tone of his glazed eyes as he spoke into her made her want to devour him a-fucking-live, but his hand covering her mouth made it physically impossible. She licked the palm of his hand, her tongue playing with the creases with the promise of how she wanted to lick every other part of him.

I love fucking your pussy, your mouth, and your mind. I love fucking all of you.

His other hand moved from her nipple to her core, but thank the five Cardinals, her hands—unlike her mouth—were not restrained. She went to grab his cock but found clothes in the way. Clothes that *hadn't* been there before.

She frowned deeply, demanding answers, and Jake laughed both in her mind and next to her.

He removed his hand, and Lenna inhaled sharply and loudly. Before she could recover her breath and speak, Jake stood up, the marvelous, muscled body of her real fantasies towering above her, his black waves a perfect mess, his teeth over his bottom lip as his darkened silver eyes admired her from above. The only piece of cloth was covering precisely what she wanted most, and she wanted it even more when she saw how fucking hard he was.

"What do you think you're doing?" she asked, annoyance and desire tracing her words.

He inhaled deeply, closing his eyes as if her smell alone was enough to make him leave this world. When he opened them, he lifted his palms.

When he spoke, his voice was a gravel that moved something deep inside her.

"I have plans for you."

Her golden eyes widened as he Gave petals the color of his magic onto her. The navy petals fell on her breasts and core, making her back arch as she realized these were not normal petals. They felt like *him*, like the pressure of his hands, like the warmth of his touch.

His nostrils flared, his chest moving up and down as he took deep breaths. "Do you want to play, sweet fire?"

"I'm all yours. Take me."

He grinned, moving his hands again and Giving more navy petals that floated to the bed, to her body—to her wrists and ankles. It was like having multiple Jakes pinning her down, the petals he created somehow being an extension of his wishes as the real hands Took away the piece of cloth, letting his beautiful, massive cock spring free. She moaned in anticipation and impatience as he grabbed his cock with one hand, pumping himself as he lifted the other hand.

"I will take you, but not so fast." His unhinged, lustful grin came with the words that were the beginning of her end. "Only when the petals have made you come a few times, my cock will make you scream. Until then, I will delight seeing you feel my touch all over you."

The pressure of his invisible touch on her wrists and ankles came as the petals over her core and her nipples trembled, sending waves of pleasure in her brain that sent her to the Fifth heaven in a matter of seconds.

Cardinals fucking guide h—

She screamed his name as her body shook, barely able to open her golden eyes enough to admire how fucking handsome he looked while pumping himself. The way his chin tilted upwards, the way his glazed eyes seemed to feed on her pleasure. She knew he was enjoying this as much as she was, and bless the feathers of all birds, she was intoxicated with ecstasy.

She lost count of how many orgasms she had by the time she begged him to fuck her.

"I need you inside me, Jake," she managed to say between ragged breaths.

She didn't need to beg twice. As if he couldn't wait a second longer either to fuck her until he left her in pieces, he Took the petals away, her arms and legs immediately freed, her core aching with pure need. She turned on the bed, bending her knees until her bare ass begged for mercy amongst the tip of his cock.

"Fuck, Brachyan. Is this how you want me to take you?"

She looked backward and found him looking at her ass as if it was the Fifth Power itself. Lenna winked, grinning. "Enjoy the view."

A brief slap sounded in the room, and she didn't need to see her butt cheek to know her skin was red. She bit her bottom lip as his hands grabbed the sides of her hips, and then he buried his cock into her core.

28

Hope

Hope hadn't slept at all.

She could blame the cold of the navia, the worry about the next ordeals, the knowledge that they owned two of the five Cardinal feathers, or the revelation that Ayla possessed a power even historians didn't know when it last existed.

She could blame all of it, and she would be lying to herself. She knew exactly what—exactly *who*—had kept her awake.

Cardinals guide her away from him, she was knee-deep in putrid eggs.

She adjusted her body on the seat in front of the window facing the Radel Sea. She had been staring at the waves for hours, and her eyes adjusting as the sun rose on this part of Terrha were playing tricks on her.

She blinked, willing the red sparks that had appeared atop the waves away.

Her sight didn't improve but worsened. Maybe it was the sleep depriva-
tion, or the turbulence of thoughts and feelings roaming wildly inside her.

She placed her hands on her temples, blinking a few times.

No, the red sparks were not vanishing—they were taking the form of a
thin bridge. A Cardinal-red bridge that grew from the sea to her *feet*. Hope
hadn't noticed the window disappearing until the breeze pushed her braids
to her back.

The arterial-red sparks that became the thinnest walkway one could
imagine were the exact color of Hope's ink, panom mark, and magic. Yet
she wasn't the source of this creation, which meant another being was
claiming her presence. A superior being.

She hadn't expected it to happen like this, or at this time, under these
circumstances, but the truth was she hadn't known what to expect at all.

Hope stood up, inhaling deeply as her foot tapped the crystal surface of
the bridge she was about to step on.

If the Core Cardinal was calling Hope to her ordeal, she was ready to
answer.

The moment her cautious feet—one in front of the other, the width of
the bridge not allowing for more—stepped outside the navia, everything
around her ceased to exist.

She could see no navia, no sky, no sea. She could only see the bridge,
her body, and the white, absolute nothingness she had experienced once
before.

After her Fifth Ceremony, she had met the Core Cardinal here, where
the line between life and death had barely existed.

This time, instead of stepping on a white floor, her feet were frozen on
the red crystal bridge suspended in the air, and underneath it, miles and

miles away, perhaps there was a floor she could not identify. Perhaps there was not.

Hope continued walking towards the middle of the walkway, her arms extended at both sides, to avoid any possibility of losing her balance. Her stare was fixed in the white void in front of her.

It was after long minutes when her foot touched the very center of the bridge, and an equally thin, equally red bar appeared, crossing it perpendicularly from her right to her left. No—from her *West* to her *East*.

She was balancing herself in the middle of a perfect cross. She was at the *core* of the cardinal points.

The sound of flapping wings made her look upwards, one of her feet losing its grip on the bar and making her body tilt dangerously.

"Daughter of Red," the Core Cardinal called.

Hope frowned. She had no idea what the Cardinal meant or what she was talking about, so Hope kept her mouth shut.

The goddess landed with grace; her red dress made of feathers covering her. Her flawless skin framed her crimson lips and her flaming eyes.

"My dearest Hope." Her voice was quiet, her eyebrows knitting as her lips tensed.

"Core Cardinal," Hope said. "You are not happy to see me." Was she disappointed she was the striver? Did she expect someone else?

The goddess of the Core sighed, her expression pained, and for a second Hope saw the centuries of history she bore on her shoulders.

"You came to prove your worth." It wasn't a question but still Hope nodded. When the Core Cardinal lifted her palms, her eyes shone brighter, determined. "Fate was written that you would make it here, yet I always wished it was mistaken."

"Why?" she managed to ask.

"Because after this conversation, I can never see what happens next. There are too many variants, too many risks, too many causes to lose."

The voice of the Core Cardinal echoed in the nothingness. "You may die five times, Hope Nevada. You may rise from each death stronger than before, or you may not rise at all."

Hope was pretty sure she only half understood, and what little she could make out was enough to make her ribs feel squeezed inside her chest. She had so many questions, so many doubts, but before she could ask any, the goddess spoke again.

"You could die today, you could die tomorrow, you could die in centuries. You survived the first death after your Fifth Ceremony. Four more deaths to go."

Four more deaths to come *back from*. That could take ages, and they needed the crystal feather *now*.

"Is that my ordeal? Dying four more times?"

"No, my dearest. That's your future."

Hope's eyebrows lifted, and she had to restrain a chuckle.

Well, that was promising.

"As for the reason you are here . . . I must confess, I am biased. I have been waiting for you for a long time. The *world* was waiting for you. My ordeal is simple: I have five questions for you."

Hope's eyes narrowed. Nothing of worth was ever given easily.

Without further warning, the first question came.

"If you obtain the Fifth Power, you could become the Organ Mandor of the land we Cardinals created. Would you protect the lives of the citizens of Thyria?"

The citizens of Thyria, who didn't even know of Hope's existence. She nodded. "I would protect the citizens who deserve protecting. With my life."

"Would you Rule with fairness and justice?"

"To the best of my capacities."

"Would you allow deserving others to assist you?"

The golden eyes and red hair of the Brachyan twin flashed in her mind. "A nation shouldn't be ruled single-handedly."

"Would you ensure the Cardinal Queen can't harm innocent beings?"

Hope frowned. "Where is she?"

"It is me who asks the questions," the Core Cardinal reminded her.

"I would do my best to ensure *no one* can harm innocent beings. A title or a crown on someone's head wouldn't stop me from fighting against them. Titles can be revoked; crowns can be destroyed."

Thrones can be usurped.

The crimson eyes stared straight into Hope's black ones. "Think carefully about your fifth answer, dearest Hope, for there is nothing more valuable than truth." The Core Cardinal looked at her for a long time before she fired her last question. "A true protector of Thyria would never risk the land breaking in any way or form. Would you always keep your feelings and needs aside to ensure the preservation of the land?"

Images of dead people inside the Beftac Center appeared in her mind. The number of innocents who died due to the panomquake after her Fifth Ceremony chased her nightmares very often.

The following image hurt even more. A flash of blue eyes, of shadows and night, of pine woods and dark green sparks. It flooded her with fear, with nerves and need and longing, with an urge to cry and scream and kill anyone who wasn't *him*.

Ciaran.

Ciaran.

It was a blessing and a curse that she was the heir to the Organ House, and he was the heir to the West House. It was a blessing and a curse that the heirs of the Houses couldn't be together without destroying the four-petal island where balance ruled.

She swallowed. Being forced to avoid panomquakes would protect Thyria. Being forced to keep her distance—and *her* feelings—from him would protect her heart.

"I will never risk a panomquake that can be avoided. I will never allow my feelings and needs to be the cause of one."

No. Her feelings and needs would cause destruction. *Her* destruction.

The Core Cardinal pursed her lips, her wings moving as a crystal feather appeared in front of Hope.

"If any answer turns out to be dishonest or untrue, my feather will break. Oh, and my dearest, blessed quarter of a century to you."

And with that, the Core Cardinal vanished, the whiteness disappeared, the red cross under her feet ceased to exist.

Hope was back in her seat, with a red crystal feather in her hands, and a devastating, forbidden tangle in her heart.

29

Lenna

"Y ou two are not so loud now, are you?" Arabella's smirk had the same effect as a bucket of iced water on Lenna.

The painfully pretty blond held her winning CoreCard up: a Cardinals-damned 55 of *Leafs*. The two dice the woman had thrown shone bright on the table, the inner part of the glass cubes filled with red liquid, the symbols facing up mocking everyone else on the table: a number 5, and a Floret. A bloody, cursed Floret.

"Shut the fuck up," Sasha exclaimed, her jaw dropping as her angry, dark eyes demanded explanations.

Brendon threw his cards on the table, his green eyes narrowing to slits as he threw visual daggers at Arabella. "Either you have weirdly awesome good luck, or you're an extremely good scammer."

Arabella lifted her eyebrow, her smirk not faltering as she held her palms up, waiting for what she was owed. The noise of clattering grolls and valers filled the room as the players emptied their pockets for the fifth time in a row.

When her hands were full, Arabella's eyelashes fluttered, her expression a pretty unbelievable portrayal of innocence. "You expect so little of me?"

"Cheating bitch," Lenna said with a forced smile, fluttering her eyelashes back at her.

She had been suspicious from the first round, but it had taken all her pride to keep from asking Arabella D'Arcy, from admitting that she couldn't find out the trick of the blue-eyed beauty.

At this point, Lenna's pride was as lost as the remaining valers and grolls she had just handed in.

Jake snorted from a couch, his hands behind his head pushing his black hair towards his face. He hadn't bothered joining the game. Beings could have thought he was just chilling, and then those beings would be *fools*.

Relaxing was not an option for a man like him, for a mind like his. The Fifth only knew what he was thinking about, what Jake was planning, where his head truly was. Other than the lacy, white tights gripping Lenna's legs and the small black bodysuit marking her cleavage. She had noticed many times how well he was inspecting *that*.

When his silver eyes met her golden ones, the corner of his lips tucked upwards.

Jake purred into her mind. Fucking *purred*.

Lenna's eyes widened, biting her bottom lip as she realized she wanted to hear him again. She *needed* to hear him again.

Sasha stepped into her vision, frowning. "Have you had too much myster, love?"

Lenna cleared her throat, putting a few rebel red strands behind her ear. She handed her empty glass to Sasha. "I could do with some more."

"Of course you could." Sasha laughed, pouring the liquid into Lenna's glass and refilling everyone else's at the same time. "Jake?"

"If I drink anymore, I will lose the little control that's keeping me from fucking Lenna on your playing table."

Lenna cracked a laugh, tilting her head back as Brendon choked on his drink. He latter coughed twice before he managed to say, "Your navia, your home, Jake. Do as you wish."

"Excuse me?" Sasha tilted her head, a mass of brown curls dropping to one side. Her dark eyes gleamed with something difficult to identify.

Brendon's eyebrows lifted. "Jealous, Sasha?"

The brunette pursed her lips. "Maybe I'm the one who'd like to be fucked on the table."

"Excuse-fucking-*me*?" Lenna's nostrils flared, her hands immediately on her hips, facing Sasha.

"For the love of all the feathers, Lenna, I didn't mean I'd like to be fucked by *Jake*," Sasha exclaimed, frowning. "Thanks, but no thanks—he's all yours."

A proud grin escaped Brendon's mouth. "Fucked on the table, huh?"

Sasha stared back at him, not opening her full lips again.

Arabella crossed her arms as she put her high heel on the edge of the table. "You're so dramatic. You could share. It's way more fun that way."

Brendon scratched his chin, considering. "Would you want to join?" Sasha elbowed him in the ribs.

"What a stupid question." Arabella said matter-of-factly. "What about you, Jake?"

"I don't share." Jake's growl did something to Lenna's cores—the one in her chest and the one at the apex of her legs.

The blond sighed. "You mean you don't share *anymore*."

Lenna's jaw clenched, her golden, raging eyes not moving from the blue eyes of the teasing bitch. The sudden silence of the room could be cut with a blade.

The past was the past, and of course Jake had his. A multitudinous, centuries-long past. As she had her twenty-five-years-long past, that she had put to good use with half the men of Borealia. So why did this bother her so much?

Jake's shoulders tensed, as if he knew everything Lenna was feeling and didn't approve. He stood, pacing until he was behind her, his hand resting on the top of her chest. Could he feel her jealous heart racing?

"Of course, Arabella. I didn't mind others playing with toys I didn't care about." His voice was a shard of glass. "Lenna is *my* woman. She is *my* fire. She is mine, as I'm hers. And yes, I don't fucking share what's mine."

The knot in Lenna's throat eased, her fingers stroking his strong hand, the back of her head resting on his muscled abdomen.

Arabella inhaled sharply, opening her mouth to bicker back—

"Do you miss home, Arabella?" Lenna asked.

The blond snapped her head, looking at Lenna the way a predator would her prey before decapitating it. "Careful," her voice was a warning whisper.

Lenna didn't take her eyes off her. It hadn't been difficult to guess what the soft spot of someone with such bile would be. Someone who had learned how to use her magic in a way that didn't make her feel ashamed and lacking control every time she moved to a different part of the land, someone who didn't mind making the rest of the world uncomfortable. Someone with such revulsion, with such hatred, had issues. Big fucking issues Lenna knew all too well.

It would be so easy to make Arabella jump now. So damned easy to make her angry, *truly* angry. But there were two small things in the way.

The first one, that Lenna knew exactly what it was for home to be one's soft spot, the trigger that resurrected what needn't reviving. The second, that Lenna didn't care enough about her to want to *truly* hurt her, to open a box that she herself struggled to close with a mental lock every so often. So she didn't open the box. Instead, she stood up, Jake's hand moving along her side until he held her close by the waist.

"Mind your own damned business, then."

30

Hope

Hours passed while staring out the window, and Hope only knew because the sky was darkening, and the impulse of throwing the crystal feather through the glass was fading.

Of course, she wouldn't have thrown the feather of the Core ordeal, regardless of how much she wished the conditions—the *restrictions*—that came with it didn't exist. If she'd learned anything from over two decades living with her mother, over two decades learning to use her body and her weapons to fight, it was to master her self-control.

Two and a half decades.

If the Core Cardinal hadn't mentioned it, Hope wouldn't have remembered. She knew the date of her own and her mother's birthdays, but they had never marked them.

Her birth had ruined her mother's life. Hope's arrival in this world was what got them discarded. Was a birth like that a reason for celebration? For acknowledgment? She doubted it.

The fifth time the door knocked since past meridiem, she decided to go, rather than dismiss Nina with excuses from her seat.

She opened the metallic black door. "I'm oka—"

"Cardinals above," Nina shouted. "Is that *the* feather?"

Hope looked at the red crystal in her hand. "Oh—yes, it is."

Nina gasped, a tight hug following that almost knocked Hope backwards. "May the Fifth have mercy. I have *so* many questions. Like so, *so* many, but everyone needs to know. Cardinals spare me. Come, quick."

Nina took Hope's free hand and pulled her upstairs, half-walking, half-running.

When they entered the room in such a rush, everyone turned to face them. It was Ciaran who spotted the red crystal shining in Hope's hand first. His eyes widened with alarm as he trotted towards her.

"Llunal shade me, Hope. Are you—" He swallowed, his eyebrows knitted as he examined her body, her face, her hands as if he was trying to find any sign of harm. His metallic hand lifted to caress her cheek, the tip of his fingers sending goosebumps to all her fibers, as she couldn't take her eyes off the worry on his face.

"I'm okay," Hope repeated for the Fifth knew how many times. She followed Ciaran towards the couch, sitting next to him, Nina joining her other side. Indianna, Raoul, and Ayla sat in front of them.

"You've been telling me *I'm okay,* and you were in your ordeal?" Nina sounded disappointed. "I'm never trusting you again when you tell me you need some alone time."

Hope chuckled apologetically. "But I *was* okay, and I needed time to think. My ordeal finished many hours ago."

"You could have mentioned that." Nina looked at her, her ocean-blue eyes shining as she sighed. "Sorry, it's just—I get it. I truly do. I only wished I'd have known to . . . I don't know—help, somehow."

"Thank you." Hope smiled. She felt lucky to have Nina in her life.

"Where was your ordeal? In your *room*?" Ayla asked.

Hope put her braids over her shoulders distractedly. "Sort of. I walked over the water but then . . . went somewhere else."

Ciaran readjusted in his spot next to her, the black leather of his leg brushing her own, as if he didn't miss the broad description of where she'd gone. It didn't get less specific than *somewhere else*.

Raoul cocked his white eyebrow. "And what was the actual ordeal? Climbing, like Ayla's?"

"Talking."

Hope's word caused different reactions across the room. Raoul exclaimed, "*What?*" Ayla and Nina swapped utterly confused stares. Indianna narrowed her eyes as if reconsidering whether Hope was *okay* in a mental sense, and Ciaran . . . Ciaran tensed, still as the dead.

"We should tell the others," Ciaran said, cutting whatever question was about to leave Raoul's mouth. "Do you want to do the honors?" he asked Hope, and when her black eyes met his blue ones, she saw what his steady voice had hidden. There was tension, worry, uneasiness, fear, and more. There was a lot more behind Ciaran's apparently collected expression.

Hope lifted her hand, willing her red sparks to send written ink to Lenna.

I have the Core feather.
Not long left until we meet again.

Lenna's golden ink tickled her arm a few seconds later:

Fuck yes, Badass Queen.
So proud of you.

Ciaran's biceps brushed against Hope's arm as he moved to read the golden ink he had received. Hope read Lenna's handwriting on his forearm and inhaled sharply.

Only us left to kick some Cardinal ass.
You better put those shadows, metal,
and green sparks to good use.

Ciaran didn't move for a while, and when he finally lifted his hand, dark green sparks left with his reply.

It was almost ante meridiem when Hope climbed the stairs to the deck of the navia. She needed fresh air, and she really enjoyed admiring the shadows of the courtrades pushing the massive vehicle across the Radel Sea.

At first, the shadows of Stevian, Nyraxa, and Ciaran seemed all the same. By now, Hope had observed—analyzed—them so much that she was able to differentiate them.

Nyraxa's shadows were lighter, less dense, to the point that sometimes one could see through them, but they were also faster, more agile. Stevian's were sturdy and elegant, their shapes always whole, never a loose streak. And Ciaran's . . .

Ciaran's shadows were pure, lethal night, the darkest shade of black, and they never faltered.

Hope stepped outside, the red-tinged moon welcoming her. She inhaled the night deeply, the salty smell of the sea breeze filling her nostrils.

Stevian smiled when he saw her, the deep wrinkles around his blue eyes warming Hope's heart. "Good darkness, young lady."

"Stevian." She bowed her head, smiling. "Is the wind behaving?"

He chuckled. "Behaving badly, if we let it do as it pleases."

"Good blessing you have it under control." Hope sighed, looking at the indistinguishable horizon. "Are you doing all the hard work by yourself?" She had offered her help many times before, but the courtrade always declined politely, with the deepest gratitude.

"Ciaran was here a moment ago. Llunal allowing, I'm sure he'll be back shortly." His hands moved, and trails of shadows flew towards the peaks of the crescent shape. "I was thinking, right before you came, how cruel your goddesses are."

Hope looked at him, expecting disapproval, judgment, or disgust towards the Cardinals, but she found none. Stevian looked at the sky, his white hair bright in the night, as if he was talking to Hope but also to Llunal's stars.

"Do you know how Thyria and panom magic works?" Hope asked.

Stevian tensed his lips, his blue eyes glittering so vividly, to the point Hope thought she'd seen a tear.

"I had to learn many years ago," he whispered. "It's beautiful and powerful, the way your magic works. It's unique and devastating, that panoms live and die for balance, and *because of* balance. It's tragic and unfair that your goddesses built a nation where something as precious as love doesn't prevail above balance."

She had managed to rein in her tears in since her ordeal, and that had been an achievement.

Now, Hope bit her bottom lip to keep from crying, but it wasn't enough. She buried her nails in her skin, clenching her fists.

"No one should ever be ashamed or guilty of feeling," Stevian said.

She clenched her jaw harder, her inner castle of self-discipline threatening to go down with her.

"Have you ever been in love?" Her voice left her lips before she could stop it. The weakest question she had ever asked.

The tears from his blue eyes fell freely on his wrinkled skin. "I fell in love, and my life changed. We lived, we loved, we suffered, we laughed. We built a family, we grew, we learned. Then the darkness took her away." Stevian didn't take his blue eyes away from the starry night, his smile widening. "I've never stopped loving her and I never will. For as long as I breathe, I will love her in this world, and when Llunal claims me, I will rejoin my love in the stars."

Hope covered her mouth with a hand, her cheeks wet as her body shook. Stevian looked at her, dire sadness in his eyes and voice.

"There is nothing more heartless than your Cardinals forbidding love between panoms because of the blood in their veins. They will find balance in the land, but nowhere else."

31

Lenna

Nothing and no one could change Lenna's mind about five things.

The first, it had been a terrible idea to sign up as the striver of the Taking ordeal.

The second, that she progressively worried more as each day passed, and she now was officially in a freaking-the-royal-shit-out permanent state.

The third, that Jake being possessive had been an unexpected, massive turn-on.

The fourth, that she had missed the golden lynx who was scratching the walls of the room so much.

And last, but very-fucking-much not least, that if Arabella D'Arcy told her once more that she was doing the simultaneous magic wrong, Lenna was going to strangle her.

"Simultaneous Giving and Taking. Si-mul-ta-neous. As in, at the same time," Miss Nasty insisted.

The lynx cub hissed, and Lenna felt like a proud mom. She couldn't decide what she hated more. Arabella's patronizing, high-pitched tone, or the way her fingers interlaced under her perfect chin. "I know what it means, for Cardinals' sake," Lenna spat.

Arabella smirked. "Then do it. Two hands, two powers. It's not that hard."

Asshole. "Remind me how long it took you to master this again?"

The blond woman huffed. "Decades. But I can guarantee that if it takes you that long, you won't survive whatever ordeal the South Cardinal has prepared for you."

Lenna snorted. As if she wasn't well aware of how risky it was to let her inner scale be unbalanced. Unless the Taking ordeal didn't involve an insane amount of Taking—and that would be a Cardinals-blessed miracle she was definitely not relying on—there was no chance she wouldn't end up collapsing with dizziness. Fan-bloody-tastic.

"You're in a mood today," Arabella said.

Lenna cracked a laugh. "That's putting it lightly."

Arabella examined her, considering. When she next spoke, the nasty high pitch was gone. "We can practice tomorrow."

Was that pity in her voice? Compassion? It didn't matter if it was, or it had been Lenna's imagination.

Lenna lifted her hands again, a fist ready to open and Give, and a palm ready to close and Take.

"There may be no tomorrow."

The sound of Sasha's laughter filled her ears before Lenna stepped out to the deck of the navia, and it automatically made her smile.

Her curly-haired friend was surrounded by the three courtrades in charge of the vehicle, a grin on her beautiful face when she spotted her.

"Here you are," Lenna said, hugging Sasha.

"Here I am, talking to the poor guys in charge of keeping us afloat."

The bald, tall courtrade—Nevan—chuckled. "Not poor at all. This is a once in a lifetime opportunity for us."

"Don't you courtrades pilot these things all the time?" Lenna asked.

"Navias?" The eyebrows of the short-haired woman called Annie lifted. "In Orizane, where most of our society lives, maybe. But in Thyria? I'd never seen one of these in my life. Whatever favor Marcus owed you, it must have been a big one."

"He didn't owe *me* any favors." Lenna smiled, the proud feeling when she'd found out Hope got her feather still lingering.

"What exactly is Orizane? An island?" Sasha asked.

The mute courtrade, Franklin, nodded. Lifting his hand, shadows solidified on the palm of his other hand. Shadows in the shape of a thick crescent, with two straight lines crossing it.

"That's your symbol, right? Looks like the navia," Lenna said.

"Like the mark on our skins, and the shape of the island Llunal created for us and our magic," Annie said.

Sasha put a finger on her top lip. "Is it far? It must be."

"From where we are now, almost in line with the South of the Organ House, it's a few days away. It would depend on how fast we travel," Nevan said.

"And how little we sleep," finished Annie.

Cardinals only knew exactly where they would go once they got the five crystal feathers—*if* they managed to get the five feathers. Lenna had no doubt Ciaran would get his.

One moment, the sea around them was peaceful and quiet, the waves hitting gently against the navia. The next, a massive wave, the height of the navia, was heading towards them from a close distance. A wave that would hit them in less than a minute and would likely throw them into the sea.

The three courtrades regrouped and stood next to each other, their hands lifted, shadows interconnecting, building a thick wall for the wave to crash against.

Lenna ran towards the rail facing the gigantic wave, her golden sparks flying in the form of ink towards Jake.

Help.

He wasn't anywhere she could see, but Jake's words invaded her mind nonetheless: *I'm coming.*

"Sasha, run inside," Lenna shouted, hoping she wasn't hurt from the fall and would do as she said. Lenna's hands were in front of her, but she didn't know what to do, if the shadow wall was enough to hold such force. "What the fuck is that?"

"Nature at its worst," Nevan shouted, his face straining as he pushed shadows faster and harder. The wave was going to hit them any moment now, and there were many holes in their shadow wall. Many, many holes.

Lenna opened her hands, Giving electric sparks to fill each gap within the growing wall. Golden streaks formed between the shadows, the fiery, energetic sparks waiting impatiently to react against the water.

The door to the deck banged open with running footsteps Lenna knew too well stopping between her and the courtrades.

"This won't be enough," Jake muttered. Lenna couldn't take the eyes off the approaching mass of water, now towering above them. Their shadow and golden electricity wall was barely high enough to reach its mid-height.

"Courtrades, seek cover," Jake shouted, his silver eyes focused on the mass of water, his palms in front of him, sharp, navy sparks jumping around him. "Lenna, behind me."

Lenna didn't have time to question him, to wonder why Jake wanted to *be* her cover. She ran behind him, not daring to touch him in case he lost the focus on his target.

He clenched his jaw, the muscles on his broad back tense, and when the wave hit against the wall of shadows and golden sparks—

Jake roared, closing his fists with more strength than was needed to kill a man. Lenna inhaled sharply, the blood in her veins freezing with panic as she realized what he was attempting.

Jake wanted to *Take* the massive force of water that was going to drown them all. He wanted to make it disappear with his magic. With his hands.

And he fucking *did*.

The terrifying wave disappeared, and the wall they built with it. The navia stayed ashore, only rocking a bit harsher than before.

Jake didn't move, looking to the horizon, to the Radel Sea and every single wave in it. Lenna couldn't take her eyes off him, his brutality and his violence. She couldn't resist the need to hand him her heart.

"Jake," she prayed, pulling his face towards hers, kissing him as if it was the last time she'd ever do.

He answered her kiss with the same fervor, their lips and tongues clashing as if they were the wave and the navia. He pulled her up, her legs hooking around his middle, his fists filled with red hair, her hands unable to get enough of this man.

When she managed to speak, her lips were tender. "I can't believe you Took a Cardinal-cursed force of nature."

Jake didn't take his hands from underneath her thighs. He didn't set Lenna on the ground.

His silver eyes only moved from hers to the Radel Sea. "Whatever that was, it was not nature."

32

Hope

Her naked limbs were tangled with those of someone else, the touch of an arm in particular cooler than the rest. Shadows surrounded her body, her breasts, her bare, aching core. Everything was dark, save for eyes the color of the waters, the shine of a finger that pushed her chin down, her lips parting for—

Hope woke up sweating in her lonely, disarrayed bed. She wasn't naked, but her core . . . Her core ached as much as in her dream. She closed her eyes, refusing to let the fantasy leave her mind, trying to hold onto the shadows and the metallic arm as much as she could—It was useless. Her cheeks were flushed, her heartbeat fast, realization sinking in.

Fantasies were allowed.

Fantasies. Were. Allowed.

Fantasies didn't cause panomquakes, they didn't risk the land. It was Hope and her imagination, nothing for the Cardinals to worry about. Nothing tangible that mattered.

Hope closed her eyes, her hand sinking under her pants, finding the part that desired more, and let her mind loose.

They weren't her fingers anymore, they were Ciaran's.

Hard and smooth against her clit, rubbing against it as he breathed in her neck, her mouth, her breasts. Her second hand—*his* second hand—found her entrance, diving deep with two fingers as she was ready for him. He pumped her gloriously, his metallic hand not ceasing on her clit, not faltering despite her jagged breaths, until she reached the peak, a loud moan filling the room as she found release.

Hope laid in bed, her throat extended as she tried to recover. She didn't want to open her eyes, to face reality.

But reality knocked firmly on her door.

Hope's black eyes widened, her pupils readjusting to the sudden light. A girl couldn't even touch herself in peace in this place.

The second time around, the knock was more insistent.

Hope dragged herself to the door, opening it, ready to reassure Nin—

"Hi, Ciaran," she gasped, swallowing. She felt a sudden rush of heat on her cheeks, unable to stop it.

Ciaran examined her from top to bottom, apparently lost for words. Hope was suddenly aware of her black, long hair falling loose over her white shirt, her pants still wet, her bare legs, the flush in her bright cheeks, her hands—Cardinals hide her, *her hands*.

Ciaran leaned on the doorway with his metal arm—the arm that had been masturbating her in her mind a minute ago—holding it as if he was holding on to dear life. His other hand covered his mouth, but Hope could have sworn he was biting his bottom lip and the metal ring in it.

"I—I heard something. I thought you needed help." His voice was low, his blue eyes glittering with something desperate and raw.

Hope lifted her eyebrows, inhaling sharply. Needed *help*? Ciaran had not the slightest clue how much of his *help* she needed. And how none of his *help* she'd ever be allowed.

She bit the side of her mouth to keep from chuckling at his choice of words. "Everything is . . . fine, thanks for checking."

And with that, and before she could do or say anything she would totally, irreversibly regret, she closed the door.

The sun lowered toward the horizon when Ciaran interrupted Nina and Hope.

"May I steal your time?" he asked. His face was unreadable.

Hope straightened in her seat, clearing her throat. He hadn't specified whose time he wanted, but she knew. "Sure."

He led her towards corridors she hadn't seen before, and then they were going up. With each set of stairs, the dim light coming from the navia faded more. Light—that unnecessary thing in the eyes of a courtrade, in the eyes of their god.

She opened her hand, summoning Cardinal-red sparks that waited on her palm for direction. Hope looked up, the sparks illuminating her face from underneath. Ciaran was two steps above her, his eyes sparkling, his biological hand extended towards her.

An offer.

Hope took his hand, his cold touch sending goosebumps up her shoulder and down her spine. His eyes met hers, the tension in the air sharper than any dagger in her belt.

She could ask where they were going to confirm her guess. She could ask if there was much longer, or what they'd do there. She could have asked, but she didn't, because she didn't care.

She didn't care about anything other than his touch and the familiar night and pine scent guiding her to the darkness upstairs, her red sparks forgotten, unneeded.

"We're here," Ciaran warned her before he halted, right when she'd have slammed against him. His fingers didn't let go of hers. "You're not afraid of heights."

It wasn't a question. "I'm not."

There were few things she was scared about, and the man in front of her was the worst of all.

"Close your eyes." His voice was low, and it touched something deep inside her. "Or let me close them for you."

Hope's heart thundered inside her ribcage. "Do it." Her voice was a whisper and a beg.

She didn't see anything amongst the dark, but she felt a thin veil of Ciaran's shadows cover her eyes. A mask of darkness and night.

There was the sound of a door she didn't see opening, and then his strong hands were on her hips. He lifted her into the air, her hands gripping his shoulders tightly.

The breeze hit her face first, then her neck and arms. She was sitting on the edge of a horizontal door, and then Ciaran was pulling her upwards. He held her body close to his, his hand crossing over her waist and holding her abdomen towards him, her back against his chest as he guided her a few steps forward.

His closeness, his firm touch on her body, his presence on her back, his shadows on her eyes—she could barely breathe, her entire being consumed by him.

Then his grip pressed firmer against her, making her stop. She wished she could speak, but her words were lost. Everything was lost except him.

Ciaran didn't let go of her, his hand embracing her from behind. She couldn't see, but she didn't need to.

When he spoke, his voice brushed her ear in the most pleasant, outlawed way. "Did you want to keep it quiet?"

The question caught her by surprise. "You mean . . . about my ordeal?"

"That, too."

"The Core Cardinal asked me five questions." That was as much as she could—*wanted*—to tell him.

"Five answers for the crystal feather of a goddess—an apparently sweet deal."

Except, Hope knew, it wasn't sweet at all. It was cardinally bitter. Cardinally cruel. "Nothing is ever as it seems."

Hope felt his nod against the nape of her neck, her shoulders tensing as her head tilted involuntarily towards his face. The shadow veil covering her eyes was so comfortable, so light, she barely noticed it anymore.

"I wasn't talking about your ordeal. Yesterday you lived for a quarter of a century. Twenty-five whole cycles."

Hope sighed. "How do you know?"

"Blame Llunal and his whispers."

"Why does he care?"

Ciaran chuckled. "I will not ask him that."

They didn't talk for a while, the breeze and the distant sound of the sea were the only ones around them. When he spoke, Hope could have sworn he was nervous. "The Core Cardinal didn't pick yesterday for your ordeal for no reason. Twenty-five is a sacred number in Thyria, Hope. Five years for each of the four petals, and five years for the core. Five times five, when a panom is closer to the origins. For each additional quarter of a century we live, the Cardinals bless us with an additional petal."

"The petals you donated." To Sasha, Indianna, Brendon, and Carson. To Lenna, in her second Fifth Ceremony, when he helped her regain her revoked panom powers. "How old are you, Ciaran?"

His chuckle was low. "I don't want to freak you out."

Hope laughed. "You hold me at the peak of a floating mass of metal, with a blindfold made of shadows, and a cliff I can't even see in front of me. Do you think your *age* will scare me?"

He held his breath in, exhaling against her hair. "Does *this* scare you?"

"More than anything ever has."

His grip on her body tightened in the slightest way. "I brought you here to show you something."

Hope's eyebrows lifted at the same time Ciaran's shadows lifted, her blindfold vanishing.

The sunset in front of them overwhelmed her senses. The sky displayed a dance of crimson, orange, and pink. Underneath the hiding sun, a mass of waves caught the lights and colors. The horizon expanded, impossible to not appreciate the full expanse of the universe.

"Bless the Fifth." Her voice was weak, faltering. Her hand reached to hold his metal hand across her abdomen.

She felt minuscule. The sunset was all that existed in front of her; Ciaran was all that existed behind her.

That was all, and all was plenty.

"This is my gift to you, Hope. My gift and my promise: the world."

33

Snow Child

The familiar sensation of fear choked the snow child like the divinity who often claimed his mind choked his dreams—his *nightmares*.

He was used to her, for she was the embodiment of fear. At least now, his consolation was knowing he would wake up when the sun appeared. At least now, his mind was not her prisoner, even if his sleep was.

Her black eyes shone as bright as the crown abandoned in the room. "Come closer," she ordered.

His legs moved as they always did—against his will. He had learned not to fight her magic, so he didn't anymore. Even if the red crystal shackles restrained her naked body to the stone, he wasn't strong enough to fight her.

He was powerless. He was no one.

"I know you are with her," she said, stroking his chin with a nail that opened his skin. "Not here, but there."

Her pale face was impenetrable, his gaze unfocused as he tried not to flinch.

"Tell me, offspring of snow. Tell me what she's like."

He felt the impulse to talk. *She* would make him talk—she always did—but the choice of his words was his.

"Who?" the snow child asked.

"The only one that matters. The one with magic the color of my kin. The one they tried to protect, and the one they will fail to save."

"She's patient and brave," he said. "How much longer will you make her wait?"

The loud laugh of the Cardinal Queen shook the black liquid pooled around them. The liquid was her blood.

"Each of the five spiteful, red-winged ones cursed me with half a century of captivity. *I've* been patient—for over two centuries." Her nostrils flared, her blood-red lips curling as her grip on his chin tightened. "The days are ticking, my curse almost lifting. Patient she is, and patient she will be, for when I come, her end will come with me."

When the snow child woke up, the memory of his nightmare was erased. His nose bled once again, and another black streak painted his hair.

34

Ciaran

Hope breathed in deeply as the sun started peaking on the horizon. They had spent hours side-by-side under the red moonlight, their legs hanging from the edge of the platform at the peak of the navia. Between softly spoken words and peaceful silence, between greeted occasional friction between their hands or legs. And now, the always-returning night was leaving them.

Ciaran felt the whisper approaching, the masculine voice no courtrade knew if it belonged to the darkness or to Llunal himself, speaking softly into his ear.

Protect her.

His eyes jumped to Hope.

Here she was, smiling peacefully at the rising sun.

At some point, Hope had let her braids loose and now strands of black hair moved gently around her beautiful face with the breeze. Her accompanying blades, always present like external appendages of her body, rested on the floor behind them, the biggest proof this woman fully trusted him. Her black eyes were focused, glistening as she didn't take her gaze away from the growing light. Her lips . . . her lips were pink, full, painfully perfect.

He would sell his soul to the Cardinals for a kiss from those lips, for a kiss from *her*, but the goddesses didn't care about what a soul truly craved.

Her chest rose as she breathed deeply, welcoming the sunrise, and Ciaran . . . Ciaran did something precious, something he was allowed—he closed his eyes, inhaling deeply until Hope's sea breeze and sunshine scent filled him like nothing else did. Like nothing else ever would.

He was allowed that small pleasure alone, nowhere as satisfying as the list of fantasies he had, and the merciless Cardinals were the only ones to blame for that.

Protect her at all costs.

He heard the whisper again, and he didn't miss the tinge of urgency in the words. Adrenaline constricted his veins, his arm reaching to grab Hope's—but it was too late.

A violent wind ripped through the air with a deafening roar. A red-tinged wind that didn't touch him. A wind aimed at *her*.

Hope let out a scream as the force pushed her body towards the edge, and then Hope was falling, falling, falling to the deck.

Ciaran's eyes widened, panic squeezing his heart as he held in his breath. Fuck, *fuck!*

No being could survive that fall, not even *her*.

He saw her black eyes begging for help as she fell, her hands reaching towards him even though the distance between them grew bigger and bigger. The desperation when she screamed his name ruptured something inside him beyond repair.

Her body fell backwards, farther from him as each millisecond passed, closer to the deck that would end her life.

It was then that another sudden blast of air hit the upper platform where he stared at his life falling tragically. Again, the wind didn't touch him. This time, it hit the two daggers still resting on the floor.

They were resting no more. They were falling down the precipice, piloted by the air, guided by Cardinal magic. The blades were aimed at Hope.

Ciaran's furious roar filled the sky.

The West Cardinal was wicked.

And the Healing ordeal—*his* ordeal—had started.

35

Hope

The sky above her was cloudless, tinged with blues and oranges and yellows.

The memory of the Core Cardinal's voice thundered in Hope's mind, the sound of the wind deafening as her body plummeted down, down, down.

You may die five times, Hope Nevada. You may rise from each death stronger than before, or you may not rise at all.

"Ciaran," she screamed. A beg, a prayer, and a plea.

Every time she blinked, he was farther; *she* was farther.

Every time she blinked, she was closer to death.

Something shone above her, the rising sun reflecting twice. Something long and sharp she knew all too well. Her daggers were diving down towards her, the tips aimed *at* her.

Ciaran's roar had the strength to stop time, to stop worlds, but in this world, it stopped nothing.

She tried closing her hands to Take the daggers away, she tried Giving herself a shield. Her magic was not answering, which could only mean one thing: a Cardinal wanted this to happen.

Perhaps there was no going back. Perhaps this was it.

Then, Ciaran jumped. He *jumped* from the peak of the navia, his wild, enraged shadows covering him as his upright body fell. The shadows surged from his arms, from his legs, undulating trails pivoting towards the deck.

He was darkness incarnate, dressed in power and shadows.

She felt his shadows wrap around her body, protecting her from the fall. A reckless attempt at saving her life. Desperation made shadows.

Ciaran fell fast, in a controlled way—but not fast enough.

Hope's body hit the deck, the impact cushioned from the life-saving protection Ciaran had granted her. Her body ached, paralyzed, but not dead. Perhaps this was not it, after all.

But when her daggers shone above her chest and her throat, the tips of the sharp, polished blades ready to hit home, she knew it was too late.

The last thing she heard was his scream.

The last thing she saw was *him*.

36

Ciaran

His blood lacked the warmth of most beings, but right now, it was pure ice.

"West Cardinal," he shouted when he landed next to Hope's limp, stabbed, bleeding body. "This was meant to be a Healing ordeal, not a star-cursed *resurrection*."

There was no time to dwell on the whys or why nots. He didn't care why the Cardinal of his House wanted him to prove his worth this way. He didn't care about ordeals, feathers, or the Fifth.

There was a dying woman—*the* woman who was worth everything—for him to save. And he *would* fucking save her.

There was a dagger stuck deeply in her throat, her head shaking in spasms as the blood choked her. The other dagger was in her chest, proudly damaging her lung.

In normal circumstances, if he removed either of them, Hope would bleed to death. But the dual powers Ciaran owned weren't ordinary, and he didn't give a Cardinal-feathered shit if the West Cardinal didn't approve of his methods to Heal Hope. He didn't approve of the goddesses' methods either.

His hands were ready, and her eyes . . . Hope's eyes were glazed, half-open, half-*gone*.

"Hope, don't leave," he begged, his voice broken. "Don't leave me."

One hand atop each dagger, he inhaled sharply, and then, he moved. He closed his hands, Taking both daggers, making them disappear, and thank the darkest night, this time his panom magic worked.

Blood started pouring from both holes like unstoppable rivers, but with a flicker of his hands, blocks of shadows covered each injury, keeping the blood inside. He bent the shadows to his orders, two perfect patches to stop her hemorrhaging.

She wasn't bleeding externally anymore, but she was hurt, damaged, wounded. Hope's eyelids trembled weakly one last time before her eyes closed.

With glazed blood frosting his heart, Ciaran opened his hands again and started Healing. He moved his hands in circles, the palms facing the areas the blades had attacked. Dark green sparks floated from his skin to hers, the shadows in the holes absorbing his panom sparks like the sea welcomed salt, allowing his Healing sparks to reach deep inside her flesh where it was most needed.

Her chest hadn't moved, she hadn't breathed, since he had landed next to her. His hands Healed frantically, fueled by agony and worry. How long could a person survive without breathing? The perforated lung was his main priority.

"Just a bit longer," he promised. "A bit longer, and then you'll be good enough to breathe."

Her head shook slightly, a barely distinguishable movement. Her eyelids fluttered, as if she tried to open her eyes but couldn't.

"I already thought you dead in my arms once before," Ciaran said, knowing at least a part of her was listening. He had to keep her on this side of the dark veil at all costs. "Don't do this to me. Don't let go, Hope."

He just needed time—time and more dark green sparks than he had ever needed—her fragile body covered in them as he kept Healing, and the shadows kept redirecting his panom magic. His inner balance was tilted from so much Healing, but he didn't mind the freezing sensation in his veins, on his skin. He still had a few minutes Healing at this pace, with this intensity, until the inner glacier reached his organs, and only then, would he die.

The bad thing was that Hope wouldn't survive without breathing for so long. The good thing was that if she died because of him, because of his inability to *save her*, then a freezing death would be deserved, and he would welcome it. A death next to the woman of his dreams.

He Healed, and spoke the most secret truths he owned, praying she was fighting to stay here, to listen, praying she didn't let her body and mind lacking oxygen go.

"I waited centuries for you. Since Llunal first whispered of your existence to me, since the Cardinal made me swear on the Fifth I would not give up. They promised one day you would stop being only in my dreams and in the whispers of night. They swore you were real, you would be born, and we would meet." Ciaran's voice trembled as much as his hands. "I said it to you the first time I saw you, and I'll say it another thousand times. You were worth the wait. Hundreds of years were worth it to meet you. And

I did not only get that, but I talked to you, and spent time with you, and saw you. *All* of you. Your pain, your misery, your grief. Your strength, your courage, and perseverance. Your joy, your shyness, and your happiness. I see *you*, Hope. I see all of you and you can't die on me before I say the biggest truth to you. You can't."

The world was as still as she was. His sparks and hands were the only moving things, the only things that mattered.

His vision blurred with icy tears; his eyes closed as he accepted his fate.

He would die Healing her, he would die *with* her, his uneven scale freezing him from the inside out.

Hope's sudden, loud gasp filled her lungs and his heart in equal measure. She was here, her black eyes glittering as she took deep breaths in, struggling to recover the much-needed air she had missed.

He Gave her oxygen, her lungs filling and emptying, recovering, her eyes widened, her exhales loud with relief. Her hand reached for his metallic one, and he stroked her shaky thumb.

He no doubt looked like a fucking mess. His usually smooth, shoulder-long, dark hair was wild, his blue eyes crying above her, shadows disorganized around him, twisting around her ankles and wrists as if they were desperate to bring her back from unconsciousness, dark green sparks still floating from his hand to her lung.

A red crystal feather appeared next to him, and he didn't stop to look at it. He couldn't take his eyes from hers.

A tear rolled down her face. Her voice was thin, labored, but clear.

"I see you too, Ciaran."

He swallowed.

He swallowed his fear, his desperation, his pain. It physically pained him in his heart, in his chest, in the hands that couldn't let go of her body. He swallowed his love.

He swallowed it all, for there was Hope.

37

Lenna

Her golden eyes widened when Ciaran's ink tickled her skin.

We have the West feather.
We're going South to meet you.

Four ordeals finished, four successful strivers, four crystal feathers achieved. One left to go. *Her* fucking one left to go.

"You're quiet," said Jake.

"Good news." Lenna sighed. "Ciaran got it."

Jake lifted his eyebrow, the corner of his lips curling upwards. "Don't be too excited about it."

Lenna covered her eyes with cool, almost numb hands. "Cardinals, I am happy—Am I happy? I'm happy for him, for us, for getting closer to getting the Fifth Power. But I'm not excited one fucking bit about my ordeal."

"I wouldn't say I was exactly *happy* about mine."

"I doubt Hope, Ayla, and Ciaran were either. But—fuck, I just have such a horrible gut feeling about it."

Jake's silver eyes stared into her golden ones. "You don't have to do it if you don't want to."

Lenna snorted. "Sure, and make this whole Fifth crusade a failure. Not only that but also lose the chance to kill the Organ Mandor." They would never stand a fucking chance against the main Ruler of Thyria without the Fifth Power. "Ciaran got the West, Healing feather of his House. Ayla the North, Giving feather from our House. You got the East, Harming feather, and fuck, the East Cardinal point-blank told you that you would make a better Ruler of her Petal. Hope got the Core feather." She pursed her lips, a hand on her waist. "Of course I will fucking do my ordeal. I'm not a rotten quitter."

"Which is precisely why I love you."

Lenna bit her bottom lip, trying to keep a serious face with all her might in the most unsuccessful way. "That, and because I'm the Sovereign Ruler of your hea—"

Jake's hand was covering her mouth before she could finish her sentence. "Shut that pretty mouth, sweet fire."

Lenna grinned against his palm, and then she bit. Not hard, not deep, just enough to make a man remove his hand. But, of course, Jake *didn't* fucking remove his hand, of course his smile widened, his eyes darkening a few shades of grey.

"Wild like that golden cat of yours, are you?" He chuckled, freeing her mouth, his hand lingering on her fire-colored hair, playing with it.

Lenna opened her hand, and her golden sparks appeared, the shape of the lynx cub forming next to her. The wide eyes of the beautiful animal observed Jake and her with a half-interested look before she went to a corner to lick her paw. Such an accurate can't-be-arsed-with-these-pair representation.

"Don't be an asshole. She's a *lynx*."

Jake blinked. "Cat, lynx. Same thing. Does she have a name?"

Of course she hadn't picked a damned name yet for the animal who now growled. "Lover, boyfriend, partner—same thing."

"What did you just say?" His grey eyes narrowed, his hand putting a few strands of her hair behind her ear.

Her eyebrows lifted. "Deaf like a Cardinal post, are you?"

"Lenna Brachyan, you just called me your *partner*."

She put a finger on her lips, pretending to think. "I don't think I did, did I? Maybe I meant lover, you know, all the fucking and that. But I guess it doesn't truly matter. It's all the *same thing*." She tilted her head, frowning, demanding explanations.

"You're wickedly and deliciously exasperating." The way his voice was low as he pinned his stare on her lips made Lenna want to devour him, to get lost in him—*with* him. "When you say partner, what exactly do you mean?"

She stroked his bottom lip with her thumb. "That you better not let anyone else in your ruthless heart and you better not put your precious cock anywhere else, Jake, because I'm so deeply in love with you, I would burn the world down if that happened. I want you all for myself."

He inhaled deeply, his hands trailing down until he held the small of her back. "A burning, raging fire." His hands went lower and lower until they cupped her ass. "*My* burning, raging fire." The way his strong fingers pressed against her cheeks made her core ache in need of more. "My heart is yours, and my cock—worry not, for I will ruin that lush pussy of yours until the very last of our days together. There is no one else I'd rather spend my days—my life—with. I can be your partner *and* your lover. For you, I can be it all."

38

Hope

Nina's footsteps grew louder as she followed the dark green gathering sparks Ciaran had sent. When she entered the room that had become their common area, her white, wavy hair was all over the place, her ocean-blue eyes widened.

"Are you both okay?" she said, holding onto the wall.

Ayla arrived shortly after, her green eyes assessing Ciaran and Hope from tip to toe. Indianna followed.

Ciaran looked at Hope, swallowing. "We are now. We have—"

Raoul entered last, and Ciaran didn't finish his sentence. Hope frowned deeply. The constant, never-ending change was scary.

Anyone could have recognized Nina and Raoul as siblings months ago, but now other than their smooth, pale skin, they looked barely alike anymore. There were dark bags under Raoul's eyes, no longer light blue but a dusky sky tone, and the immaculate white hair Hope had first seen in the cave of Verdania—there were barely any remaining white strands left on his head. The majority of his hair was black. *Black.*

"What do you have?" Ayla asked Ciaran, walking next to Nina.

"The West feather," he muttered. "Raoul, what the Fifth hell is happening?"

Nina's brother shrugged, a failed attempt at being nonchalant, even when it was obvious his state was way past that. "I wish I could tell you. I go to sleep, and when I wake up, I look like crap."

"Real, shit-looking crap, not standard, just-woke-up crap," Ayla added.

"What happens when you sleep?" Hope asked. She had a feeling she knew the answer, and she didn't want her answer to be true.

"I dream."

"About?" Hope insisted.

He looked exhausted when he sighed. "You already know."

The Core Cardinal had warned her after her Fifth Ceremony and then again during her ordeal, and still, this made it so much more real.

"Does she talk to you?" Her voice was a whisper. Ciaran's shoulders tensed when he crossed his arms.

Ayla frowned deeply. "What are you two talking about? *Who* speaks *where*?"

"Black magic," Raoul said.

Ayla snorted, lifting her eyebrows. "Oh, thanks. That explains everything."

When Raoul stopped staring at the floor and met Hope's gaze, she saw it. In his blue eyes there were black speckles that hadn't been there before, either. Speckles that looked like ink. One moment, they were there, the next, they were gone.

"I wish I could tell you," Raoul finally answered. "She talks to me, but I can barely remember when I wake up."

The blood in her veins froze. *Barely*—not *never*, but *barely*.

Nina put a reassuring hand on her brother's arm, pressing gently against his pale skin. "How was your ordeal, Ciaran?"

Ciaran shook his head slowly, the intensity of his stare pinning Hope down. A thin trail of shadows left his fingers, going towards her. In another world, another life, or with another man, she would have been alert, ready to attack. But it was Ciaran.

There wasn't a single person in the world she trusted more than him.

When he spoke, the shadows vanished. "Fucked up."

Hope felt the need to get closer to him, caress his skin, get lost in his embrace, tell him she was fine, that it was all over—because she *was* fine, and it *was* over. Thanks to *him*. She didn't do any of that. Instead, her words left her mouth before she could stop them.

"Can I talk to you in private?" she asked. She clenched her fists to keep her hands from shaking.

"Always."

Without a second glance back, Ciaran opened the door for her, waiting. He didn't have to wait long, because her feet were light and her nerves thick. When she walked by him, her arm brushed his and she had to hold her breath to keep from showing what that slight touch had moved within her, how the glint in his eyes when their eyes met moved her in many ways—many of them forbidden.

It was pouring outside, so instead of going to the deck, Hope's steps were taking them downstairs, to—

"Would you prefer to go to my room or your room?" Ciaran asked from where he was closely following her.

Fifth above and beyond, how grateful she was Ciaran couldn't see the flushed cheeks, her widened eyes or the way she bit her bottom lip.

She surely couldn't take him to her room. What if he sat on her bed, where she had touched herself thinking about him? What if he could *smell* what she had done?

"Yours is closer."

He didn't reply, but when she stopped in front of his metallic door and turned to him, his head was bowed, a curtain of smooth hair falling over his gorgeous face, only his blue eyes and his metal ring distinguishable.

He held the door open for her, and when she entered, she couldn't stop from inhaling deeply. His scent filled her mind, fogging it with woods and night, pines and darkness. It was like entering into *him*. Her knees wanted to buckle, but she tried her best to continue walking. It was almost impossible he'd missed the pause, the shock of what she'd just experienced, of what was surrounding her right now.

Cardinals, maybe going to his room hadn't been the best option.

He sat on the edge of his immaculate bed. "Take a seat wherever you want."

Hope swallowed. She could be wary and clever and sit on the couch, or she could be reckless and dangerous, and sit next to him. Her mind hadn't yet decided when her heart moved her towards him.

His hand stopped on her thigh before she reached for the bed. "Hope," he whispered.

She halted, still standing, his firm fingers still on her. She could have walked, she could have sat, but she must have wished for inner destruction because, instead, her body faced his, standing between his legs. He sat looking at his hand as if he hadn't meant to move it there, but he couldn't have stopped it. The same way she couldn't stop—she didn't *want* to stop—her hands moving to his face, her hands caressing his cheeks, gently tilting his head up until his stare met hers.

She wanted to say so many things she didn't know where to start. She didn't know what she should or shouldn't do, if there was any point in trying to save herself from this. From him.

Perhaps she was beyond saving, perhaps there had never been a saving at all.

His breathing was irregular, his metal ring bobbed. "What am I going to do, Hope?" His other hand held onto the outer side of her other thigh.

The exact same question she had been asking herself for the past few days, for the past few weeks. It was easier when she was able to think rationally, to convince herself she was capable of many things—of avoiding many things. But being here, this close to him, surrounded by his scent, it wasn't difficult. It was almost *impossible*.

His hands moved her legs slightly to the side. It would be easier, *much* easier, to get away from him, back to a safe distance, if he pushed her away, because she was incapable of doing it herself.

But he didn't push her away. He pushed her down, inviting her to sit on his leg. And Cardinals take her blades away, she didn't refuse.

She fit perfectly on his strong, muscled leg, his hand embracing the small of her back while the other rested on her knee. Her arm rested on his metallic shoulder, her hand playing with his hair. It was softer than she thought, thicker than she had imagined.

She had thought he was brutally, fiercely handsome since the very first time. But this close, Ciaran was breathtaking.

"How can the same person save me and destroy me?" His voice was low, as if he was asking himself the question.

The question punctured her heart, but no more than the forbidding of the Cardinals had already punctured it.

"You've saved my life twice now, Ciaran. No words of gratitude will ever match how much this means."

His hand moved from her knee to her throat, where the blade had hit her, where she would've bled to death if he hadn't Healed her.

"No words are needed. I would do it a hundred times again."

The touch of his fingers on her skin made her core and heart tighten. What wouldn't she trade with the Cardinals to allow her to know what his lips tasted like?

"In my ordeal . . . The Core Cardinal asked me if I would keep my feelings and needs aside to protect the land, to avoid a panomquake, and I said yes. She said if my answer turned out to be dishonest or untrue, the crystal feather would break."

Ciaran inhaled deeply. She was expecting an answer along the lines of *I understand and respect it*, *The land must be protected*, or *The feather is more important than anything else*.

His hand trailed up her throat until his thumb stroked her bottom lip. When he spoke, his voice was gravel.

"What needs do you have, Hope?"

She exhaled against his finger, her eyes unable to move from the trap where his eyes and his lips were.

"All the forbidden needs you could imagine. Every single one of them."

The glint in his eyes matched his side smile. "My imagination is very creative."

"Every. Single. One," she repeated, begging she was able to keep her hands off the unmistakable growing bulk between his legs. The growing bulk she had dreamed about.

"Something was allowed that didn't break the land." He flicked the knot of her braid, his fingers skillfully letting her black hair loose. "Do you remember how I . . . confirmed you had Core panom blood?"

She would never forget what she'd felt when he opened the skin on her palm and licked her blood.

"How is that possible?" Her voice came out as a gasp or a beg, she didn't know the difference anymore.

"Llunal is involved in that magic, in blood research and processes, not the Cardinals."

Thank the five damned Cardinals she was sitting.

Research.

Re-search.

Not forbidden research.

If Llunal ever needed a new acolyte, he only needed to ask.

A quiet moan left her mouth. "Do it." The desperation in her voice and her blood had reached a new level of insanity.

Ciaran pressed his nose against Hope's head, his deep, uncontrolled, almost desperate inhale making Hope press her thighs together.

"I could taste your hand again, or a different place."

"Lick me wherever you want, Ciaran."

The metallic hand on her back tensed, holding her flesh with strength she didn't mind one bit.

"Not where I truly want. The Cardinals wouldn't approve if I lick the blood between your legs, and I wouldn't be able to control myself." He nestled his head in the spot above her clavicle, his nose pressing on her throat sending all sorts of explosions to the nerves throughout her body. "Classic old Cardinals, drawing the line at kisses and private parts. A shame, because I would love to thoroughly research every single sensitive part of you down there."

A quiet moan left her mouth. "Lick me, Ciaran. Do with me whatever you can."

"Such a shy moan, that was," Ciaran hummed against her skin. His finger traced a line down her throat, Harming her until she felt her skin open and the thick, red liquid pooling next to where his mouth rested. "It's not enough. I need to know if the way you moan is the way I imagine when I come thinking about all the things I wish I could do to you."

Hope half-opened her mouth, her head tilting backwards so Ciaran had access to the full extent of her neck. Her thoughts blurred with desire, desperation, *need*.

"Lick. Me."

When the touch of his tongue met her open skin, her blood, the world faded—the world *changed*. The world was Ciaran, his tongue, the way he desperately licked as if her blood was what was keeping him alive instead of the air he breathed.

Bless the father of blood research, his shadows, and every single one of his stars.

"Ciaran," she begged, grabbing his hair in her fist to avoid losing the grip between this parallel dimension of lust and reality. If she weren't sitting on his leg, she would have fallen.

His reply was a low growl, his tongue not stopping the tracing of the small, bless-giving wound he had inflicted on her. His hands gripped against her clothes as if they were the most inconvenient poison and curse. Irreverent shadows filled the floor, approaching her ankles desperately, she knew, because he craved *more*.

The sudden, cold touch on her forearm made her stand up with a jump, a hand on her dagger as Ciaran stood, also looking at his biological forearm. Her mind was foggy with lust, her skin wet in various places.

Usually ink from panoms tickled her skin, except when her father was the sender, and the bleeding ink hurt. This time, it felt like the touch of a feather, and the color of the ink was the color of her magic. It was Cardinal-red.

THE FEATHERS ARE CLAIMED.
THE FIFTH JUDGMENT AWAITS.

39

Lenna

"What the fuck does this mean?" Lenna asked.

The ink on Jake's arm from the Cardinals didn't make any sense.

"*The feathers are claimed,* my ass," she spat, looking up. "Excuse me, Cardinal bitches, but you forgot a striver over here. And—*the Fifth Judgement awaits*? Useless revelation of the century. They could have said where, when, how, and what exactly that is."

Jake was grinning at her, his silver eyes glittering with amusement. "The confusion is worth it if it makes you so angry."

She rolled her eyes. "Don't you get me started now, for Cardinals' sake."

With her hands on her hips, she faced the window. The storm outside was significant. The courtrades wouldn't have an easy night.

"We've been going South for days now. Surely my ordeal can't be much farther."

"Have you practiced enough?"

Lenna forced a smile. "I'll never get back the hours I've spent with your ex-girlfriend."

"Fucking someone doesn't make them my *anything*," he said, walking towards her. "Answer me. Have you practiced enough, Brachyan?"

The authority in his voice as he towered over her was hot as fuck.

"Do you miss overseeing my panom training, Jake? Miss being my Panom Guidor? Those were fun days." It felt like it had happened years ago, and it had barely been a few months. How much could a life change in such a small period of time?

He narrowed his eyes, his lips pursing. "Why are you not answering my damn question?"

"Maybe you're not the only one who enjoys riling other people up." She went to leave the room, but Jake held her hand, stepping in front of her.

"It's not that."

Lenna sighed. "Look, I've practiced, okay? Arabella isn't a terrible teacher; I will give her that. Would that be *enough*? Cardinals bloody know, but I am going to do the South ordeal even if it's the last thing I do."

Jake's tense nod was the last thing she saw before the navia disappeared and Lenna's body fell like a dead weight onto a crystal-red floor.

By the time Lenna woke up, the storm was gone, and so was the night.

If the South Cardinal wanted to jinx Lenna by breaking her legs before her ordeal even started, she would have to try again. After the fall, her legs were not broken but—fuck, they were sore. There was no point in Healing them and starting the ordeal with her inner balance uneven, especially when she didn't fancy Harming herself to compensate, and there was nothing else to Harm.

Half-limping, Lenna managed to stand up on the four-petal shaped platform in the middle of the Radel Sea. Looking back, there was no doubt: it *was* the Radel Sea, and that small floating moon-shaped vehicle far from her *was* the navia.

What looked totally out of place was the bright red water in front of her. As if a magical field had fallen atop the sea—a field the color of the Cardinals, vast with red ground, untouched by the waves of the sea surrounding it.

And in its very middle, right where the core of the panom would be, was a floating, crystal orb.

"Red-obsessed," Lenna muttered.

She waited a few moments, but nothing happened. It was clear where she had to go, and it was not clear what the heck she was meant to Take. Remembering everything she knew about the synced use of opposite powers and praying her practice with Arabella would suffice, Lenna inhaled deeply and took the first step out of the platform and into the field, towards the core of the shape.

A curtain of red petals fell thick like the worst downpour. It fell *on* her, everywhere else except where she stood remained completely petal-free.

Lenna snorted loudly, grinning. It was bloody cool to be chased by Cardinal-guided petal rain.

She could see how fast the petals accumulated at her feet, heavier than she had expected them to be, the strength needed to move not appreciated by her sore legs.

The middle of the Thyrian-shaped field was far, the petals fell fast, and her feet were about to be stuck. What was she waiting for?

Run, girl, run.

Lifting her feet above the height of her knees, up to where the petals had buried her in the span of less than a minute, she ran. The falling petals followed, and it took Lenna all of five seconds to realize how hard it was to run with the speed they fell. She waved her arms in front of her to keep from slamming her face against them, but the petals were faster than her.

She knew she had to start Taking them away or it wouldn't be long until she couldn't move. She needed to find something to Give at the same time, something that required the same amount of magic so that she could Take and Give simultaneously, her opposite powers synchronized to keep her scale balanced, or else she wouldn't make it to the center, to where the feather surely had to be.

Something she could Give that didn't give her any more trouble, something that she didn't have to worry about. The Radel Sea surrounded the red field, and Jake's side-smile flashed in her mind before she lifted her hands.

An open hand ready to close and Take petals, a closed hand ready to open and Give fire sparks to the sea. Fire sparks that would extinguish when they touched the water. A release to allow her to Take, Take, Take, because the longer it took her to clear her way, her feet, her knees from the petals raining on her, the longer it would take her to finish this.

It took all her concentration to continue running as fast as she could while allowing the two powers of her panom magic to flow. She could barely keep on top of the Taking needed to avoid ending up buried in petals, and she relied on her Giving to ensure she didn't get dizzy or faint.

The center of the four-petal shaped field was closer and closer, the distance to the sea greater with every step she managed to take, and yet, the middle still seemed suffocatingly far. Her hands alternated opening and closing, her magic Giving and Taking non-stop, the parts of her brain aligning each power to each objective without pause, because if she paused—

A high-pitched scream left her mouth when her ankle twisted, her face slamming against the petals piled on the floor immediately after.

Fuck.

She'd fucked up big time.

It wasn't that these precious seconds had broken her rhythm and would give her a massive disadvantage when trying to reach the core, but that the fire spark she had Given aimed at the sea hadn't reached the water by a few inches with her fall and instead had landed *on* the field. The field that hadn't extinguished the spark like the sea was meant to.

The field that had let that spark become a *flame.*

Big, fucking, royal fuck.

Groaning, she managed to push herself upwards despite the petals piled on her back and shoulders, her legs and arms. The flame was starting to roam freely on the field, and if the path of petals Lenna had left behind caught fire, she wouldn't have enough space or time to run.

Clenching her jaw to the point of pain, she pushed against the force of the petals blocking her way as she Took them, while she Gave shoots of water to the fire starting to surround her. The water was useless against the fire growing exponentially by the second, the fire now burning the petals behind her as if it was its sole reason to exist.

Thanks to Arabella, her inner scale was not tilting.

Thanks to Lenna's own stupidity, a burning world of Cardinal-red petals was going to consume her.

The pressure of the petals around her thighs was worse than the weight of the petals on her feet. She was so close now, the crystal orb standing mere steps away from her. She roared, lifting her arms above her head so the petals couldn't bury the hands she needed to use her powers.

There was no point in continuing to use the powers evenly. The chances of being successful—to survive—were slim unless she Took enough petals away so she could reach the inside of the column. She had no doubt the South feather was there.

In the middle of the field full of petals and fire, Lenna opened her hands wide, her nostrils flaring as her hair waved wildly with the heat emanating from the flames behind her. With a roar that could break glass, she closed both hands with all the strength she had ever gathered, Taking petals away from her legs so that she could take the few steps left to the orb.

She felt her inner balance tilting already, her mind blurry as she blinked desperately to focus. Her feet moved, her hands finally reaching the orb.

The *broken* orb. The side of the crystal sphere was open, exposing the center of the orb.

The very *empty* orb.

She gasped, her limbs stuck with blood-freezing realization as petals, petals, petals and more petals covered her chest, her neck, her head.

There was no feather.

There-was-no-feather.

Therewasnofeather.

The shock cost her deeply.

The petals buried her face, blinded her eyes, covered her nose, filled her still-open mouth.

The fire must have followed, but, by then, Lenna was long gone.

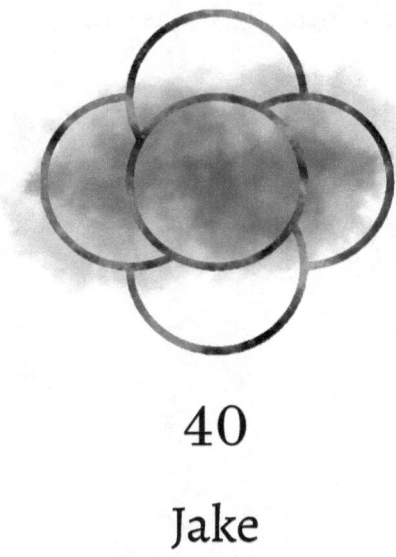

40

Jake

The metal rail of the navia screeched under Jake's clenched fists.

His knuckles were white like the corpses he left many times behind. His clothes were still soaked from the torrential waters he had dived in when he rushed to the deck after Lenna disappeared from his grip.

Disappeared.

He had given up on shouting her name, praying to the Cardinals they would keep her safe.

Bullshit praying, that was. No one was fucking safe in an ordeal.

It hadn't been until sunrise that he saw the red mass interrupting the expanse of the sea, until he chased the courtrades and begged them to move the navia as fast as they could. He probably hadn't asked in the nicest way. He had offered whatever they wanted in exchange. Those were problems for later.

The problem right now was that red mass—whatever the Fifth hell that was—was still too damn far. And there was no doubt Lenna was on it.

Obviously, he was going to try to not interrupt her ordeal. Obviously, he believed Lenna was capable of this challenge and many others. Few beings on Terrha had the will and determination she had. The fire in her veins, in her eyes, in the way she didn't think twice when speaking her mind. The fire that burned worlds down.

Did that mean he was going to sit and watch if his woman was in danger? Cardinals be damned—obviously not.

It had taken all his restraint to watch as red rain started falling on a specific part of the red mass. A person wearing black moved towards the center of the—was it a four-petal platform? A field?

The courtrades moved behind him, the shadows not as helpful as they were at night, the navia still too far as he watched red rain fall, and fall, and fall on Lenna. Whatever that rain was made of it was not letting her run fast enough. Then her magic started, Taking away what kept her feet stuck and—Giving something to the sea.

"That's my woman," he muttered, pride filling his chest and squeezing his corrupt heart. It was awfully difficult to use opposite powers in sync. Very few panoms had mastered it, and here she was. His stubborn, un-yielding woman *doing* it.

His silver eyes narrowed, his nostrils flaring with the need for her to make it, for her ordeal to finish already.

And then, she tripped, and she was on the floor.

"Faster!" he shouted to the courtrades behind him. "Llunal, I'll suck your dick if you have one, but I swear on the Fifth if this navia does not move faster, *I'll burn it down.*"

Burn it down, burn it down, burn it down.

The words echoed in his mind, in his ears, in his life. Because in front of him was a flame, a living, raging flame on the platform where Lenna stood. A flame that trailed towards her, towards her body too full of whatever the fuck the redness falling on her was.

No.

Seeing Lenna fighting harmed him more than all his ordeal put together. The fire was too fast, her pace too slow, the distance to whatever was in the middle of the panom shape too far.

No.

Over his dead fucking body, he was going to let her be tortured again. He didn't care if it was at the hands of his father or the five wicked Cardinals. This was not happening again. *He* wouldn't let it happen again.

Jake jumped out of the navia, cursing Llunal, his slow-as-shit shadows and all his useless stars. The cold water engulfed him, his arms and legs pushing away from the navia with all the strength he could master.

He only needed to swim far enough, far enough to—

He had never been happier to moure in his damned, long life.

The water or the worry swamping him didn't allow him to moure straight to where Lenna was, leaving him at the edge of the four-petal shape field. It was a *field*, and the red rain were petals.

Petals on fire, chasing his sweet fire.

No—it hadn't been the water *or* the worry. There was an invisible wall separating the grounds of the burning ordeal from the rest of the world.

He lifted his hands above the water, and with the wicked delight that not caring about the pain his inner scale inflicted, he Took the whole wall away. The pain would have been enough to stop other beings' hearts. His heart was too sore to care.

He pushed himself up onto the edge of the field, and time seemed to stop.

He couldn't have been that late. It couldn't have happened so fast.

At the very center of the field, he saw a growing mountain of red petals covering Lenna's whole body, piling up and up and up. The wildfire was closing in, advancing faster now the path of petals fueled its flames.

She was going to burn.

Jake didn't have time to run, so he moured. He moured between the fire and the pile of petals, Taking them away as fast as he had ever Taken anything. There were so many petals, and underneath, nothing moved. *No one* moved.

He Took as if his life depended on it, because it fucking did. He would have Given a river behind him, placating the fire that approached his back, but he had never been good at simultaneous magic, and he couldn't stop Taking—he had to get to her.

Torturous long seconds passed until Lenna's hair started appearing as petals were vanishing. Her unresponsive face came later, her mouth choked with redness, the expression of terror marking her face in the same way it marked Jake's soul. *He* had allowed this to happen.

He Took, Took, Took, and when the petals were not holding her body upwards anymore was when she fell limp, cold in his arms.

Lenna. Lenna! He screamed into her mind. But where usually a golden response was waiting, whether angry, heated, or laughing, there was nothing. There was nothing, *no one* to shout at.

"South Cardinal," he roared, his lips curling as tears flooded his eyes. "Take me. Take my feather, take my life. Take everything from me, but don't take her."

The Taking goddess did not answer, did not come, did not care.

The Taking goddess was going to take the true reason for his existence.

His hands shook under her back and her knees, his back barely feeling the fire burning him.

The only fire he cared about had been extinguished.

41

Hope

No being needed to see the sender of the navy ink to feel the desperation in his words.

Lenna's ordeal was not successful.
She's. . . not fully alive. She needs help now.
How far are you?

Jake's message caused very different reactions for Ciaran, Ayla, and Hope.

Ayla squealed, her emerald-green eyes tearing as she gasped. Ciaran ran to the deck of the navia, his dark green sparks heading downstairs no doubt on their way to make the other courtrades aware. Hope's hands were over her daggers, more out of self-reassurance than usefulness. Except there was nothing to reassure herself about, and she needed answers, she needed action. So she ran after Ciaran, Lenna's twin running after her.

The sea around them was not as quiet as other days. Ciaran's shadows were on the move, darkening the space around the navia, pushing the metal mass farther down South. Stevian and Nyraxa joined him shortly after, the three types of shadows working as one against the sun above.

Hope could ask Jake for more details, but she didn't. All that mattered was getting to them as soon as the Cardinals allowed. They were on track, at the precise point that cut the Organ House from the South. The Fifth only knew what distance separated this navia from theirs—from them.

She walked from one side of the deck to the other, testing the wind with her wet finger, red sparks flying from her hands as she tried to work out if her plan was doable.

"The shadows in plain daylight are not as efficient," Ciaran said from behind her.

"I noticed. I'm going to push it."

His eyebrows raised, followed by a slight frown.

"Wind, is it?" A tense smile appeared on her lips at his immediate understanding. The corner of his lips tugged upwards with pride as he nodded. "I'm with you." It was impressive what such a short sentence could do to someone's heart.

"You can't Give wind just like that. It's nature. You'll burn out," Ayla said.

If only Hope had an inner scale to take into consideration. Lifting her hands, her fists closed ready to Give, she looked at the sea around them, at the sky, the clouds, the breeze against the waves. Ciaran walked behind her, his back against hers, and she felt him lift his hands as well.

Hope inhaled deeply, the powers she was gathering from the red panom mark at the back of her neck tickling, fueling what she was about to unleash.

"It's not me you have to worry about," she said.

And then, air currents gained a new meaning.

As if the world had been waiting for her to concentrate her magic on the force of the air, the wind answered her call, allowing the navia to move as fast as the courtrades did with their shadows at night, if not more. Behind her, Ciaran's dark green sparks illuminated his fingers, occasional shadows interlacing with his panom magic. Stevian and Nyraxa did not relax either.

And just like that, the navia moved and moved and moved. When the time Giving had to be close to an hour, her arms ached from keeping them straightened in front of her for such a prolonged period of time. Not that that was any acceptable excuse to stop. What was a bit of sore arms when Lenna was not fully alive? What the Cardinals' Fifth hell did *not fully alive* even mean?

Her arms did not concern her, but Ciaran's body against her back felt cold as ice. Even with his body temperature usually low, he now felt *dangerously* cold. Was this the way his inner balance was uneven?

"Ciaran," she said. "Don't push it."

"Pushing it is precisely what I want to do."

"You know what I meant." Against his lack of response, she exhaled exasperatedly and added, "Not the navia—*yourself*."

"I said I'm with you, and I'll be until we reach them. I'm not going to leave all the fun to you."

Hope chuckled. "Right, because freezing to death is fun. Such a courtrade thing to say."

"Breaking the laws of magic and nature with you is fun. Even if it includes freezing to death."

"Right. Much more reasonable. Will you be able to Heal Lenna when we get there? Because out of all of us, the panom with the most expertise in that field is you. It was proven quite recently, you shall not forget."

Of course, Indianna and Nina also knew non-magical healing, and Hope had zero doubts they had been packing their supplies and remedies since Jake's ink had arrived, preparing for whatever emergency the situation required, very likely with the help of Ayla as well, who left the deck when they started commanding the wind. With Stevian and Nyraxa and their shadows somewhere at the opposite end of the navia, here there were just Ciaran and Hope and their magic.

His deep inhale followed. "Forget shall I never."

It was impossible to guess how much longer they needed to reach their navia, how far they were, how long Lenna had to wait, what Jake was doing to keep her from going to the only state that could follow being *not fully alive*. The only state that had to be avoided.

"My permanent inks," Ciaran said from behind her, his voice getting lost as he spoke towards the sea.

Hope's eyebrows raised, her back straightening and making even more contact with his own. "Yes?"

"You asked about them."

"And you didn't answer."

"I can answer now."

Hope opened her mouth, her jaw dropping. "*Now*? Of all moments? When I cannot even see you and can barely hear you? Not to mention this half-hurricane we have in our hands." The one that swallowed and pushed the navia through the world.

Ciaran turned swiftly and Hope gasped. His chest was breathtakingly in front of hers, his extended, Giving hands above Hope's shoulders. Her arms found a new home on the sides of his very terse, very muscular chest.

A wind-Giving embrace.

"Now, of all moments, Hope, I have to tell you." His low voice finally reached her fully, the short distance between his mouth and hers dangerous and painful, the way his blue eyes and her black ones met as powerful as their magic.

It was only because she had been Giving for over an hour without stopping that her mind switched to a sort of autopilot magic, enabling her to focus on him, his words, his mouth, his voice. She aimed for, "I'm all ears," but her traitorous subconscious opted for, "I'm all yours."

Ciaran's throat bobbed, his arms bending slightly as if he wanted to relax them and caress her.

"Each time I stopped believing you would come, Llunal sent me an ink. Every permanent ink on my arm, on my chest . . . Every ink is made of shadows. They're made of you."

Words had vanished from existence. But luckily, Ciaran continued. "Now . . . Now their purpose has been fulfilled."

"What purpose?" Her voice was hoarse.

"To remind me to believe in the fates the gods laid out for us. To remind me to be patient, that you were real, and one day I was going to meet you."

She swallowed, praying the ongoing wind would continue pushing for a while even if she needed to use her hands for something else, because she was physically unable to stop her fingers from caressing his skin, from tracing the shadow inks that marked his biological arm. Ciaran's eyes closed at her touch, his head tilting slightly back as he inhaled deeply.

He had been patient. He had been patient *for her*. For *centuries*.

Feelings that could wipe Terrha in one go were surging from a very specific part of Hope's chest.

"If they're made of shadows, could you make them vanish now?"

His eyes opened to look at her, his brows furrowed. "I would never. They've shaped who I am. They were there when nothing else was. They've been my compass and my moon. I owe them my life."

He caressed her cheek as a tear rolled down. She hadn't noticed her eyes watering, she was too busy feeling everything else, understanding the brutal impact of what he was revealing.

"The inks are getting all the credit, but don't be fooled." He cupped her face, the tip of his nose touching hers. "*You* have been my compass and my moon, Hope. You kept me going when the world seemed hopeless. I begged the Cardinals for answers, for any little hint about you. They gave me *nothing*. And then you appeared, blades in hand, panomquake under your feet, shaking this world like no one else had. You shook my world. The moment I saw you, I knew—I knew the wait had been worth it."

Hope's breath shook and he didn't let go of her face. Her arms reached to hold his—to hold them as if she was holding on for dear life. Every time he spoke, it felt as if a new dagger stabbed her heart, a dagger full of the most meaningful and the most destructive venom to ever exist.

"You are more than I could have ever dreamed. You are fearless, humble, loyal, lethal. There was never a chance I wouldn't love you."

The air between their lips was tense, in static suspension. She wanted to kiss him. She *needed* to kiss him so badly.

"I hate them," Hope whispered, her voice shaking between the tears. "Why make you wait all your life, waste all your precious years, for something *they* never allowed? Why make us suffer, why break us by forbidding—"

Ciaran's bit his bottom lip in a way that had to hurt, his eyes glittering as if he was shattering in a million pieces. She didn't want to say the words out loud, but it was too late to stop them.

"—our love."

For a second, Hope thought her words had been the cause of a panomquake. But when she managed to look at something other than the man in front of her, the man who had overtaken the reason for living and breathing, she understood.

It hadn't been a panomquake, but the crash of one navia against another.

On the deck of the other navia, a man covered in burns with black hair and silver eyes—Jake—held the limp, pale body of a red-haired woman—Lenna.

As one, Ciaran and Hope were on the move before the next heartbeat, sprinting to the rail and jumping into the sea, ready to climb on the navia as if their lives depended on it.

42

Lenna

Death was warm and wet and windy.

Death was painful and quiet and not relaxing at all.

If this was death, she was not up for it.

As she was not up for having the last memory of her life being quite literally choked by petals right, left, and center, thanks very much. Were those petals still in her mouth, her nostrils, her ears? Cardinals bloody knew. Other than being uncomfortable and in pain, she felt nothing, saw less than nothing, heard a whole load of nothing, and had below-nothing idea of what was happening, if anything was happening at all.

If death was this annoying limbo, Lenna was going to be the angriest, least-conforming dead woman ever.

May the Cardinals guide you to peace, Thyrians usually prayed when beings lost their lives.

No, the Cardinals would not be able to guide her anywhere—let alone *peace*, if that even existed—because the moment she saw a red wing, the moment she saw the *hint* of a red feather, she would riot. From her immobile, totally constrained, absolutely useless limbo—she would riot. One could bet the Cardinals were shaking in fear.

Then, she heard him. No, not heard, *heard* him. Mind-heard, mind-listened, mind-felt—whatever the fuck it was meant to be called—it was *him*.

Jake. And his mental voice was full of bossy, authoritative threatening.

If you go, I'll go with you, Lenna. Don't you fucking dare.

Her snort in her mind was loud. As if she could *go* anywhere.

Snorting at me? Don't take the piss, Brachyan, his voice penetrated her mind with a tinge of anger.

Wait—

a fucking—

minute.

No. It couldn't be. He couldn't hav—

Death was confusing as fuck.

His voice was full of amusement the next time—and something else that sounded like . . . hope, perhaps?—and she knew exactly how his silver eyes gleamed and the corner of his lips tugged upwards when he spoke like that. Pity she couldn't see him.

I've been waiting more *than a fucking minute. The only confusing thing here is why it's taking you so long to open your eyes, so instead of giving me mental backtalk, collaborate.*

She cracked a laugh. *Collaborate.* That was actually very funny.

Centuries, eons, or seconds passed, the limbo limbing in silence, the confusion confusingly lonely. Maybe she had lost the little plot she ever had.

As if someone had woken her with a sudden backslap, she felt her body again and—*fuck*, it was awful.

Every part of her body hurt. Her unmoving limbs, her shallow-breathing chest, her impenetrably shut eyelids, her excruciatingly dry mouth, and every damned cell.

Every. Single. One.

But hey, at least she owned a body again. A distant, rottenly sore body, but a body after all. A body that felt better by the second in different places, a body held by strong hands that were familiar, a body that was being Healed.

She had been Healed before, by the man who held her as if she would break if he'd let go, but this . . . This was different, more intense, more varied.

Her eyelids fluttered weakly. It felt as if she had to push against the whole Radel Sea to move them even the tiniest bit, but after what seemed like a decade or five, her eyes half-opened, her wide pupils readjusting.

Ciaran, Hope, and Ayla were in front of her, their palms extended, dark green, Cardinal-red, and silver sparks floating from their Healing hands towards her body. They were absolutely soaked, their expressions a nice combo of fear and worry and determination and whatever else.

"Lorolbol," Lenna muttered.

"Oh, dear. We've lost her." Ayla frowned. "Her brain is fried."

"Say that again, Brachyan," Jake ordered, his breath against her ear sending a delightful sensation towards her.

"Lookorrible," Lenna repeated.

"You can't honestly care about how you look like right now," Ayla spat, pursing her lips.

Lenna cleared her throat. Her not-as-achy, thank-fuck-already-much-better throat. What a pleasure to get one's body to act the way one wanted.

"*You three* look horrible," she repeated for the third time. "And you're getting me wet."

Ciaran laughed, tilting his head back. "Fuck you."

"Welcome back, Lenna." Hope grinned, and her black eyes moved to examine the way Ciaran was grinning. His blue eyes met Hope's and then danced towards her grin, lingering way-too-long on her lips. Cardinals above, this pair.

"Have you two fucked yet?" she managed to say.

Ciaran's expression switched to grave and anguished, but his eyes still did not move from Hope.

"What?" Hope coughed, her eyebrows shooting to the sky.

The sky was spinning. "I'm dizzy as fuck," Lenna whispered, and Jake put some red strands behind her ear. "What happened?"

"You were in your ordeal. Don't you remember?" She didn't know how long she had been gone but she had missed Jake's voice in the quiet limbo.

She exhaled with effort, sitting up, and readjusting her sore back on Jake's chest. His arms around her waist were a welcome blessing.

"I remember too well. It was a trap. There was no feather."

"What do you mean, *no feather*?"

"I honestly couldn't put two and two together by then, but I remember an orb where a feather was meant to be, and there was no bloody feather."

"Maybe it didn't appear because the ordeal wasn't completed the way they wanted?" Ayla asked.

Lenna had been wondering the same. "If I wasn't worthy, you mean? After petals half-drowned me, I pushed my inner balance to a new limit, and I almost incinerated myself? The South Cardinal can shove her crystal feather up her ass, then." She sighed. "I don't know if I fucked up, if I wasn't good enough, or what the Fifth hell happened, but I only know there was no feather. I'm sorry."

"Never be sorry for trying your best," Jake said.

"Even if my best wasn't enough?" Lenna asked, looking up at him.

"Even more so."

The kiss he planted on the spot behind her ear made her close her eyes. She inhaled deeply, enjoying how his embrace filled her with his leather and ginger scent. When Lenna opened her golden eyes, Ayla's green ones were observing her, an amused smile on her lips.

"You enjoy looking, Ayla?" Lenna asked.

Her twin chuckled, biting her bottom lip. "I'm simply happy to have a non-dead sister." She tilted her head and added, "And to see you two together. You look like cute, traumatized lovebirds."

Lenna slammed her hand against the deck floor, a painful idea that she immediately regretted. "Can everyone do me a damned big favor and not mention flying creatures for a while?" Lenna asked, covering her forehead with the other hand.

"You mean not even the Cardin—"

"*Especially* not them." Lenna's fuck-you-smile was greeted by a cough that sounded very much like *traumatized-indeed*.

Hope finally removed her Healing hands. "You're safe, everyone is alive. Fine, we have no South feather, but we have the other four. It could be worse."

"Could it?" Lenna lifted an eyebrow.

"We could have *zero* feathers. We could all be dead." Hope's tone was as matter of fact as her stare.

Lenna opened her mouth to argue but then settled for, "Point taken."

"So, who got the ink about the Fifth Judgment?"

Jake, Ciaran, Ayla, and Hope raised their hands. Lenna bit her tongue. How very kind of the flying creatures to exclude Lenna and then try to kill her.

"Any clue about where the Fifth Judgment could be?" Hope asked.

Ayla clicked her tongue. "Will they even accept us at the *Fifth* Judgment with *four* feathers? The math of this crusade isn't in our favor."

Hope narrowed her eyes, crossing her arms. "Surely we can't just go back to Thyria as if nothing ever happened, as if all of *this*—all these weeks, traveling, suffering, ordeals, near-deaths—was worthless."

"It wasn't worthless," Ciaran said in a low voice, looking at Hope. "And no, we aren't going back to the same island ruled by the Organ Mandor with empty hands."

"Even if the Card—" Ayla started, but rolled her eyes when Lenna faked a coughing fit and continued, "Even if *they* will not give us the Fifth Power because we lack the *fifth* feather?"

"Maybe we can exchange something equally important that convinces them we need the power. If they care about their island, surely, they can't just look and clap at how my father destroys every living being in it."

"Bargaining with goddesses," Ayla sighed. "Fabulous plan."

Ciaran shook his head slowly. "Not bargaining—*trading*."

43

Hope

"Not bargaining—*trading*," Ciaran said, and his voice echoed in her mind.

Trading.

The idea of trading with the Cardinals came with a wave of grief towards Hope's mother and her previous life in Verdania, of the many times they had attended Trading Day for twenty-four years.

What Hope needed was the absolute certainty that the next time she saw her father, she would be able to kill him. If she had to trade with her life to get the Fifth Power, she would.

The corner of Jake's lips tugged upwards. "I don't care what they ask for. We are getting the Fifth Power, and we are killing our father. There is no alternative."

Hope nodded with a side-smile. She was all in for this type of family bonding.

Perhaps the Cardinals read minds, perhaps they read intentions, perhaps they were present everywhere. Perhaps they would never know what triggered what happened next.

The four crystal feathers moved at the same time. Ayla's flew from her cleavage, Jake's from his pocket, Ciaran's from the sleeve covering his metallic arm, Hope's from the blade sheath she had been keeping hers. They floated in front of them, suspended mid-air, the redness of the crystal reflecting the world surrounding them, and then, Hope heard the Core Cardinal, speaking from her feather.

The five strivers will be welcomed at the Fifth Judgment for your futures to be gambled with. My sisters and I will greet you where the darkness meets the sparks at the light of red.

When the message was over, Hope grabbed her feather, putting it back in its safe place. There was no doubt no one else heard the Core Cardinal, but each of the other successful strivers had also heard messages, their feathers speaking to them. The question was if they all had said the sam—

"Where the darkness meets the sparks at the light of red," Ciaran repeated.

"At the light of red?" Lenna asked, who was clearly pissed at how the Cardinals were treating her, or—more accurately—*not* treating her.

"At night, when the red moon shines," Hope said, thinking out-loud.

Jake nodded. "Where does the darkness meet the sparks, though?"

"*Why* darkness, is the question," Ciaran wondered. "Panom magic is about light, sparks, colors."

"Courtrades, Llunal, shadows, night. Darkness is all about you," Hope said, and the way Ciaran smiled back at her filled parts in her heart she didn't know she was missing.

"There must be a connection between the two, somewhere. Somewhere both magics meet," Ayla guessed.

Ciaran lifted his hands and thin trails of shadows going in different directions left his fingertips, some of them going to each navia, and some towards the sky. Was he sending whispers to Llunal?

It didn't take long for the courtrades to arrive. Two men, Franklin and Nevan, with a woman, Annie. The ones who had guided, pushed, and moved the navia through the Radel Sea from the East to the South, allowing Jake and Lenna to find their ordeals.

Stevian and Nyraxa appeared shortly after. The latter repositioned her eye-patch after the descent and climbing from navia to navia. Stevian's blue eyes, surrounded by wrinkles, were wary and clever as always, assessing. He bowed his head with a kind smile when Hope looked at him, and she didn't hesitate to smile back. It was easy to sometimes forget how nice it was for beings to be kind to each other, how the smallest, simplest things were the ones that mattered most.

The courtrades listened, the shadows around Ciaran's feet moving in dark swirls as he asked for their help. He explained what they knew, what the inks had read, what the voices had spoken.

Stevian didn't take his eyes off Ciaran while he talked, nor when he stopped talking. The silence that followed was brief, thick, and full. He seemed to be focused on him, but Hope didn't miss the way his white hair moved with an infinitesimal nod, the way the shadows around the old, wise man shifted, as if pushed by another, darker force. When Stevian spoke, he had the answer they had been waiting for.

"There is a sacred place in Orizane. A mountain where Llunal was known to live when he built his land. No courtrade sets foot in that place, because the few who ventured never returned, and from afar, one can see the light. The trees, the rocks . . . they are marked with red sparks, as if red magic had rained above the woods, inking it forever despite the shadows of Llunal."

Not any red magic, but Cardinal magic.

Red, the color of Hope's sparks.

44

Lenna

Sasha was sobbing nonstop, her dark curls a hot, wild mess and her brown eyes somewhere between irritated-flood and I'm-going-to-slap-you-with-compassion.

"I cannot believe you were in your *ordeal* and almost didn't make it, and I didn't even look for you because I thought you and Jake were fucking your brains out, as usual."

Lenna considered her answer, biting her bottom lip in a failed attempt to keep a serious face. It was definitely better to not go into detail about how close to *almost didn't make it* she had been. The way the memory of her death limbo caused her absolute fucking terror and an irresistible need to laugh hysterically in equal parts was probably concerning. But what would life be if she didn't ignore the concerns and moved on?

"That's what we'd have been doing otherwise, to be honest."

"But you *weren't*, Lenna. You were fighting for your lif—Don't look at me like that, okay? I'm not going to ask you again about the damned ordeal. You keep it all for yourself, because why would anyone need to talk to a friend, anyway? Am I even a friend if instead of worrying about you I was busy with a blond distraction?" Sasha wiped her soaked eyes angrily, making her pretty face even redder.

"Oh. What blond distraction, miss?" Lenna tilted her head, lifting her eyebrows repeatedly. "I didn't know Arabella was your type."

Sasha rolled her eyes, pointing at Lenna as she said, "You talk, I talk. You don't talk, then I will *not* fucking talk."

"Brendon's cock has to be huge. The day he was wearing those sweatpants, I swear on the Fifth I could s—"

"Lenna," Sasha shouted, interrupting her. "For the love of all feathers and my own sanity: *talk to me*."

Lenna pursed her lips, avoiding Sasha's stare. "I don't give a shit and have no sympathy for any feathers, but I do value your sanity, and yes, you are my friend—a bloody good friend—so stop blaming yourself for something you had no idea about."

Silence followed, and when Lenna made eye contact with her, Sasha's arms were crossed, her pinning stare demanding more. Lenna exhaled theatrically and obliged.

"The ordeal was crap. Imagine being inundated by petals, not being able to make them disappear fast enough to keep from being trapped, being stupid enough to think giving fire to the sea was a good way to compensate for it, then burning the whole thing down because, you know, why not? And then when my man came to save me, because he is way better than what an idiot, pyromaniac like me deserves, I didn't even realize because I was so far gone."

"Jake saved you." Sasha's words weren't a question, her smile was genuinely happy, proud, her tears not angry ones anymore. "Of course, he did. He's fallen deep, *your* man."

Lenna bit her tongue, this time to keep her own tears from falling. "He's good, Sasha."

"You don't need to convince me."

"Sometimes I need to convince myself. He cares like no one else has ever cared about me before, he treats me as if I'm something precious, valuable, something unique that deserves to be loved. And he . . . he doesn't hold back. He gives me everything he has. His ruthlessness, his trust, his passion, his devotion, his love."

"His sex." Sasha grinned.

Lenna winked. "Times fifty."

"I'm so happy for you, Lenna. You deserve to be loved well."

Loved, fucked, *saved*.

Lenna gave her a tight hug and a kiss on her still wet cheek. "If you ever say you're not my friend again, I'll rip these sexy-ass curls of yours."

Sasha gasped dramatically. "Savage bitch."

"Warning has been served."

Sasha's laugh accompanied Lenna to the door.

After the unanimous decision to abandon the other navia in the middle of the Radel Sea, they traveled like a happy family towards Orizane. The crescent-shaped island, creation of Llunal and apparently where most courtrades lived, was somewhere towards the East of Thyria.

Thanks to the united efforts of the six courtrades and—shock-not-shock—Hope, their travel speed was incomparable.

Hope, for all non-feathered-creatures' sake.

Whereas the shadows worked more efficiently at night and culminated their strength at ante meridiem, Hope's magic was formidably scary at any time of the day. For the past thirty hours, the black-haired woman had stopped a handful of times, barely long enough to sleep or eat. She didn't seem to care. And her constantly open palms, Giving as if the sole purpose of her life was to move them through? Lenna's—*anyone* else's—would have cramped or fallen into pieces by now.

But that wasn't the most impressive.

She had been using panom magic Giving wind.

Wind.

Wind.

What the actual Fifth blessing was that? Did a woman with such power truly need the Fifth power?

A flash of the Organ Mandor and his lovely Red and Black Lawful Stabs, of death and torture and endless pain, broke through Lenna's thoughts. Okay, maybe Hope needed the Fifth power if she was to beat *him*.

The other panoms had tried to join her with their best efforts at moving the vehicle through the waves. Ayla's eyes were sore and she couldn't open them after a few minutes. Lenna had to use her magic like an old woman while sitting in a bloody chair as otherwise she was dizzy, and even doing that, she didn't last long. Jake took a while until he joined his half-sister, but when he did, they were a marvelous sight of unhinged power, his silver eyes glittering as the sky changed above them.

Ciaran had been there from the beginning, and he was still there. Not using his magic constantly, as sometimes his shivering took over and his hands couldn't aim properly. But he was still there, looking at Hope, drinking her in.

The men joined and stopped, rejoined and eventually stopped again. And Hope fucking Gave, Gave, Gave. What could someone's inner scale be, so that unceasing, relentless magic didn't seem to touch her? It was as if she didn't have one.

The way Ciaran admired her, though. In all the years Lenna had known him, she had never seen the blue-eyed man be lost in another being. He looked at Hope as if she was everything that mattered, as if she was his guidance and his saving.

He didn't leave her, not for a second. Every moment Hope Gave, he was there; anytime she accepted minimal rest, Ciaran took over, his shadows loose and more present than ever. Perhaps being surrounded by other courtrades, in a vehicle created by his dark god, had allowed him to embrace his shadows with freedom.

Lenna walked downstairs, looking for Jake, but he found her first.

"Here you are." His eyes sparkled with something that could be excitement.

"I have questions."

His side smile was challenging and amusing. "I love an interview."

Lenna held his hand and dragged him towards one of the under-deck rooms. He closed the metallic, black door behind him and Lenna put her hands on her hips. "Can I mind-talk to you now?"

"You mean mind-annoy me? I don't know, you tell me."

That was not promising. "I've tried to tell you things multiple times in the past few hours, and either you're an asshole who ignores me to annoy me, or it doesn't work."

His black hair covered his forehead when he tilted his head. "I haven't ignored you. I would have loved to hear your inner monologue."

Lenna's brow furrowed. "It wasn't *meant* to be a monologue."

His side smile didn't move when his voice echoed in her mind. *I know. I meant I would have loved to know what you so desperately wanted to tell me.*

She snorted. "Well, there was a bit of everything, to be honest. A few *for fuck's sake just answer*, some *I know you're listening*, a couple *you'll never get rid of me now*, and a very, very detailed description of how I would love your cock to fuck my mouth."

His eyes darkened to a shade of grey immediately. "Very detailed, huh?" His hoarse voice and slow pace towards her made her core tighten. "Did it include how would I grab your hair in my fists while you do it? How I would fill you deeply into your throat until I made you gag? How would my cum taste in your mouth?"

"Yum." Lenna grinned, the tip of her tongue sliding over her teeth as her golden eyes followed Jake's until he towered over her. He put his hands under her thighs, lifting her until her back was pinned against the wall.

"I never want to get rid of you, sweet fire."

His leathery scent and his strong body pressing against her were absolutely distracting and greatly welcomed. "I'm not sure I like to be called sweet fire anymore."

"Why?"

"Nothing sweet about being too fucking stupid to burn myself and my ordeal with me. If anything, I'm fire-cursed."

He shook his head slowly, his black waves brushing against her cheeks and neck.

His hand was on her jaw before she could blink, his lips meeting hers with longing and need. Her breath was ragged as their tongues collapsed in a dance that could last forever. It wasn't only heated need, there was more.

There was the raw desperation and consuming rage they'd suffered. This kiss was suffocating the vivid possibility that one could have died without the other, the pure fear when the end felt so close. But here they were—very-fucking alive, together, closer than they'd ever been. Stronger than they'd ever been.

Her hands wandered under his shirt, his defined abdomen greeting her touch as his teeth bit her bottom lip, his low groan in answer to her peaked nipples asking for more. Her fingers moved towards his back, his very muscled ba—

She gasped, widening her eyes, panic cooling her blood as she jumped to the floor, walking behind Jake.

"It's nothing."

She Took his shirt, words not finding her mouth as shivers traveled up her thighs. It hadn't been her imagination. What she had felt with the tips of her fingers, what she was looking at right now, was Jake's utterly scarred back.

She knew what had caused that burning, painful destruction to his skin, to his body. *She* had fucking caused that, and how badly must have that hurt?

Tears flooded her eyes, her heart sore as if she'd been stabbed. "You should have told me."

Jake turned around to face her, his fingers wiping away her tears as he sighed. "Told you I have scars that prove I would do anything to save you?"

"Maybe I can Heal them," she managed to say between jagged breaths. "Maybe I can make your skin smooth again."

"Lenna, look at me." His still dark grey eyes narrowed until hers met his stare. "I don't want them Healed. These scars will forever remind me to never take for granted how lucky I am to see you smile, to hear you laugh, to touch you, to kiss you, to *be* with you. I wear them with pride."

Her heart squeezed with overwhelming guilt, pain, and love. Her arms surrounded him, losing herself in a tight embrace he returned with the same passion.

"I love you, Jake. Thank you, and I'm sorry, and . . . I told you . . . I'm fire-cursed."

"No, Lenna. You're my fire-blessed."

45

Hope

It was the second time the world became pitch-black while Hope Gave wind to push the navia. It was impossible to know if she'd been here for forty, fifty, or fifty-five hours, and it didn't truly matter.

Her mind was an exhausted mumble of panom power and blurry focus, of thoughts that didn't last long enough to fully understand their meaning to assess if they were important or not. Everything had moved to a second plane, her hyper-fixation being an island she had never set foot on.

The feeling this time was different. She felt it in the way the red moon shone like a red bulb in the middle of a black sea. She felt it in her blood, in her magic, in her heart.

She couldn't see the island, but she *felt* it—Orizane was close.

Since the sunset was over, the six courtrades had reined their distinct shadows swirling in a joined effort to reach their goal. Perhaps they also felt the island approaching now. Perhaps their night-vision even allowed them to *see* the place their god created. Perhaps it was ante meridiem already—the peak of the night—when Llunal's magic had more influence than any other time.

The corner of her eye caught the glimpse of dark green sparks leaving Ciaran's fingers.

"Nearly there," he said next to her, and a gentle shadow caressing her skin made her smile.

He hadn't left her side while she'd been here, Healing her when her arms cramped due to being extended for too long, her hands from being open, her fingers from being tense. He had taken over the few minutes she had stopped; he hadn't slept while she hadn't slept; he had barely eaten as she had barely eaten. She was not glad that he'd put his body under the same strain—he hadn't needed to. But still, it had been his choice, a choice that screamed *You're not alone, I'm not abandoning you*, and *We'll do this together*.

The exact same choice Hope would have made for him.

Now, his shadows were as strong and unstoppable as they'd ever been, the metallic shine of his arm pushing them through the night to join the other five beings blessed with Llunal's shadows. His panom sparks had vanished down the stairs heading off the deck, and she had a good guess why. His dual powers in use for the same cause.

The door to the deck opened, and loud footsteps sounded.

"Mother of all Cardinals, how dark is it?" Ayla asked. If ante meridiem wasn't already dark, the constant shadow-wielding of the six courtrades made it impossible to see.

"Bloody Fifth hell! Whoever stepped on my foot—*be more careful*," the pretty, blond panom woman said angrily. She had traveled with the others, and Lenna described her as a *non-important-but-a-bit-useful-guest*.

"So sorry, Arabella," Lenna's voice sounded as innocent as a killing blow. "I didn't mean to. It's just *so* dark."

"Orizane is right in front of us," Ciaran said. "If our shadows and magic work together, we'll get there soon."

A ball of navy sparks illuminated Jake's hands, the light reflecting his face from underneath as his silver eyes assessed everyone's positions. He stepped behind Hope and Ciaran. Lenna, Ayla, and Arabella followed, the color of their sparks illuminating their paths. Then the sparks vanished, leaving space to Giving from all of them as the shadows took advantage of the night.

"Final stretch," Hope whispered, more to herself than the others.

"Final sprint," Lenna answered. "Fifth Judgment, here we fucking come."

Cardinals only knew if she'd been sleeping for a day or two, but when Hope finally managed to scrape through the thick wall of dreams in her subconscious, she didn't remember falling asleep on such a comfortable, warm bed.

She was quite sure there had been red wings in her dreams, but she couldn't remember if it was her imagination or if the Core Cardinal had truly visited her. There was something like a warning and a sense of urgency that her utterly destroyed physical state didn't let her grasp.

She had never pushed her body and her magic that much, for that long, with such intensity. It had been worth it, but totally draining in every single sense. She was glad it was over, even if the uncertainty and the bargaining—the *trading*—that would come next wouldn't be any easier.

The Core Cardinal had protected her since she was little, visiting her in her bird form while in Verdania, then guiding her through the Vessels when the roixers almost caught them. The times she had spoken with her, she had seemed caring, invested in Hope's wellbeing and future.

Yes, the questions of her ordeal hadn't been easy, and the threat that her crystal feather would break if any of her answers were untrue was present every single time Hope looked at Ciaran, wished to touch him, *needed* to kiss him. But if the Fifth Judgment was a meeting with the Five Cardinals, the Core Cardinal being one of them, Hope couldn't help but feel hopeful that they'd be granted the Fifth Power. Once they got it, once *she* got the power, she would kill her father without a second thought, avenging the death of her mother and every other innocent life he had ever taken.

"Hope? Are you awake or still in dreamland?" Lenna's voice was close, and Hope opened her black eyes to meet her golden ones. She sat in a black armchair, her red, wavy hair was wet as if she'd just showered. "Hi there. Your escort just left to shower, sorry me as your waking view is not as good."

"My escort?" Hope chuckled, propping her elbow up, taking in the bedroom and the weak sun penetrating through the see-through black curtains. Her bed was gigantic, the thick blankets covering her made of intertwined wool and shadows. The black walls were covered with abstract painting with different shades of grey and white.

Lenna nodded, interlacing her fingers and putting them under her chin. "The one you can't fuck. I was just thinking about it. You know that glint in his eye when Ciaran looks at you?"

Hope's eyebrows shot through the roof. She knew *exactly* what glint she was referring to. That glint in his blue eyes had made her core squeeze countless times, and it had inspired her self-gratification up to seven times in the space of a week.

"Of course I know that glint."

"That glint can *only* mean one thing, Hope." Lenna lifted her eyebrows repeatedly, grinning. "He has to be fucking filthy in bed."

Hope inhaled sharply, a weak moan leaving her throat without her permission at the thought as the door opened and Ciaran walked in. His nostrils flared, and his eyes—his very-much-*glinting* eyes—trailed from her ones to her bottom lip. The bottom lip her teeth raked.

"Oh, perfect timing." Lenna snorted. "Well, I'll leave you two to it." With a casual wave and a side glance that wished for filthiness, she slammed the door and left them alone.

Ciaran's eyes didn't move from her mouth, and his feet didn't move from the other side of the room, as if he was trying to control himself. "You're awake," his voice was low.

Hope coughed. Yes, she was *very* awake. Definitely too awake for her own—for their own—good. "Awake indeed."

"Were you and Lenna—? Did I interrupt—"

Her jaw dropped open as she held the blanket up to her chest. "No, you didn't. Nothing that couldn't be interrupted."

He swallowed, his eyes glazing. "I can smell how awake you are, Hope."

Her eyes widened, her core tightening. She should shut her mouth and talk about the weather, the bedroom, the island they were on. Talk about anything that wouldn't feed this ever-growing hunger and soul-consuming need that could end both them and their world.

"We were just debating." She cleared her throat.

"Debating?"

"Whether you'd be filthy in bed or not."

His eyebrow cocked, the metal ring on his lip bobbing as he tried not to smile. "And what conclusion did you reach?"

Now it was Hope's turn to swallow as she sat against the headboard. "You said you come thinking about what you'd do to me. Perhaps . . . Perhaps you're not the only one who is thinking about the other."

The low groan emanating from his throat made her core wet and ready. "I'd fuck you senseless in every possible way. I've had centuries to gather ideas."

She couldn't take her eyes away from the long, hardening shape protruding against his pants. "I'm glad we at least have a good time imagining." If they wanted a country or a world to live in, their desires and fantasies *had* to stay in their imagination.

"We could imagine . . . at the same time." His metallic hand ventured inside his pants, and when he freed his length, Hope gasped. His cock was *huge* and thick, veins marking across its magnificent side. She never thought she'd wish to be a metallic hand so desperately.

She wet her lips as one hand repositioned the covering blanket and her other hand found the rim of her underwear. Her underwear was as wet as her core.

"I wish I could rip that off with my teeth," Ciaran growled, his metallic hand pumping his length with a tight grip, his other hand clenched in a self-restraining fist.

Her two fingers circled around her clit with the same fast pace as he pumped himself. She would never be brave enough to say it out loud, but Hope wished she could pump him herself. She wished she could suck his beautiful cock until she left him dry.

She looked at him, still dressed in black as he continued the work she was so jealous of. When she lifted her hand, she Took his clothes one by one, the muscles on his arms and legs, on his abdomen and chest, tense and marked as he tilted his head backwards in anticipation.

He groaned, his eyes darkening to a shade of dark blue. "I want to see you, Hope."

A part of her wanted to stay covered even as she touched herself while admiring him. Another part wanted to stop resisting the urge to remove her cover, to allow him to see her as well.

The bravery won against the shyness, and Hope Took her blanket and her trousers. Ciaran moaned when he saw how wet she was, the shape of her hand pushing against her underwear as she touched herself without pause. The shirt came after, her bare breasts exposed, her peaked nipples hard and begging for touch and taste they wouldn't get.

"Fuck, Hope," his voice was hoarse, his pumping harder, faster.

Her head tilted backwards, her eyes half-closing as she gave her clit a hard, painfully enjoyable time. Only then, she Took her underwear away.

Hope opened her legs on the bed, bending her knees, allowing him to see her. *All* of her.

She couldn't be more exposed. She was a forbidden offering to him.

The desire in his heated eyes, on his extremely hard length, on his non-stopping arm, was desperate and raw. His moan met her own. "What I would do to you isn't of this world." Dark green sparks and shadows jumped from his clenched fist. "Let me—Just let me try something."

She needed whatever he wanted to try, and she trusted him fully. He wouldn't put them and their world at risk. "Be. Careful," she begged between ragged breaths.

He bit his bottom lip as he wielded shadows from his fingers towards her. Towards her exposed, soaked core. She gasped, begging for them to come faster. The blood-tasting blessed by Llunal was permitted, so why wouldn't shadow—

Her gasp interrupted all her lines of thought. His shadows wrapped around her hands and pinned them above her head against the headboard. More shadows covered her breasts, pressing them together and pulling her nipples. His hand moved in the air, ordering the movements of the shadows, guiding them to his will, and when the last swirls of darkness arrived, there wasn't a trace of gentleness in Ciaran's dark, pleased eyes.

Shadows circled her clit, and the cold touch against her flesh was delightful and unexpected. The way they circled her masterfully was otherworldly. He wielded his satisfying shadows as he pumped, pumped, pumped himself.

Her legs shook with pleasure, her loud moans not stopping, and when she tipped over the edge, he did with her.

They came together, and the world was still whole.

46

Lenna

B y the time the navia reached the shore of Orizane, the sun peaked through the horizon, illuminating the black, loose sand of the beach, expanding as far as Lenna could see. Stevian, the oldest courtrade, guided them to his family home. Thank the Fifth, his place was close and big enough to hold them all.

It was only now that she realized also how heartbreakingly *empty* it was.

There hadn't been a living soul until they arrived, the silence prominent and present. Her footsteps echoed as she stepped into a room full of black wooden furniture. *Children's* furniture. There were two small tables and four small chairs with marks of black pens—or were they shadow stains? Red, green, and yellow wooden blocks were half-piled, half-splayed on the table and the floor.

A knot sat on Lenna's throat. How many years had those blocks been there, purposely untouched? Untouched, yet cared for. There wasn't dust anywhere, not even on the frames sitting on a shelf next to a wide piano.

She approached, unable to step away from this invasion of privacy of the man who had been generous with them. The privacy of his *family*, for in the frames were images of a younger Stevian with dark hair, a beautiful, grinning dark-haired woman ruffling the hair of two small kids. One was older than the other, but neither could be older than five, and they were both laughing. Carved on the black frame, white words read: *May the stars not hinder their darkness. May Llunal shade them.*

Goosebumps took over her skin as Lenna covered her mouth, keeping her sob as quiet as possible as tears struck down her cheeks.

"No need to cry, Miss Lenna," his voice sounded from behind her, and she was so overwhelmed by the sudden sadness that she forgot to apologize for being there.

"Are they . . . aren't they—I'm so sorry."

Stevian joined her side, his wrinkled finger tracing the face of the woman in the image with a melancholic smile. "My wife lived a long, full life, and is patiently waiting for me in the stars until Llunal claims my end."

The hand covering Lenna's mouth became a fist, her knuckles pressing against her lips. "Are they your daughters?"

"They were and will always be. They were the light even the deepest darkness couldn't tame." His white eyebrows met as he swallowed, his throat bobbing as he looked at the girls.

"They look like you." The same oval shape, the same blue eyes. "How lucky wer—are they to have a father like you."

"A father who swore to protect them from any harm. A father who failed." He sighed. "Sometimes it's not possible to control life, to control what others do. Llunal was graceful to bless me with a second chance, to offer my guilt a path to redemption."

She barely knew him, yet Lenna couldn't see any scenario in which this man would've allowed harm or failed to protect his daughters from harm intentionally. They admired the beauty and innocence of the past together, in silence, until the rest of the house started to wake up.

It was obvious there was no point in Lenna attending the Fifth Judgment when she hadn't got any crystal bloody feather to offer the winged, godly creatures she was still angry at. But was she going to miss her opportunity to tell them off for tricking her into an ordeal that had no feather? Not in fifty-five years.

"The words the crystal feathers spoke to you said *the five strivers will be welcomed at the Fifth Judgment for your futures to be gambled with,* correct? Well, I am a striver. An unsuccessful, pissed off one, but a striver nonetheless. All five of us are going," Lenna insisted, ignoring Jake's stern-and-very-much-unhappy stare and Ayla's rolling eyes. "How long will it take us to get to that sacred place?"

"The Birthing Pit of Blackness is in the middle of the Veiled Mountains, at the other side of Orizane," Stevian said.

One second, Jake was behind her, his hand on her hip. The next, he was at the other end of the room. Lenna cocked an eyebrow. "Having fun?"

"Just testing if his god allows us to moure."

Fair point, since mouring was part of the red-feathered females' magic.

"We have the name of the place and its location. That's enough to moure there," Hope said.

Stevian blinked, looking at her. "I can go with you. Make sure you get there safely."

"Thank you, but I'm sure we'll be fine." Hope's reassuring smile and very broad explanations of mouring were not *that* accurate and definitely not inclusive of all the risks and things that could go wrong, but Lenna wasn't going to tell her off. "What exactly are we looking for when we get there?"

"You will see the woods, the place where the trees are marked with red sparks, as if red magical rain had fallen on them."

"*Where the darkness meets the sparks at the light of red,*" Hope remembered, staring at Ciaran, who nodded slowly. "Where the Birthing Pit of Blackness is covered in red sparks. When the red moon will illuminate it—at ante meridiem."

In an hour, they'd be where courtrades who ventured never returned, to gamble with their futures with the five goddesses that had attempted to kill them during their five ordeals.

If that wasn't a wonderful plan.

47

Hope

It made no sense that the Fifth Judgment, the moment when they would present the crystal feathers to the five Cardinals to determine whether they were worthy of the Fifth Power or not, was here. Not in Thyria, the four-petal island the goddesses had created. Not in the Vessels, the undersea net that helped keep the land balanced.

No. The Fifth Judgment was *here*, in Orizane, the island created by a god of darkness and shadows not related to panom magic. Yet the Fifth Power was the extreme form of *panom* power.

There had to be an explanation Hope was missing, something she failed to understand.

It was impossible to know what the night would bring, what the Cardinals would have waiting for them. The only comfort was the weight of her multiple blades on their sheaths, and knowing she was not going alone.

A year ago, Hope would have thought relying on others was a sign of vulnerability and a liability to one's survival. Her life had changed, though. *She* had changed.

Confronting adversity with people who would do anything for each other was not a weakness, but a strength. The greatest, most powerful strength.

Over the past hour, the usually loud and bubbly group of friends had become increasingly quieter. Now, a few minutes away from mouring to the place Stevian indicated, the silence in the living room could be cut in half.

Indianna, Sasha, and Brendon sat together on a couch, the former tapping a nervous finger on her leg, the middle one curling and uncurling her already curled curls, Brendon combing his blond hair more times than were necessary. Nina held Raoul's hand, and she didn't take her worried eyes off Ayla, who paced up and down and up again. Lenna sat on Jake's lap, her red waves covering her face as she leaned on his shoulder as he stroked her back distractedly, his silver eyes narrowed and focused on a spot in the wall. Arabella was nowhere to be seen, but no one seemed to miss her. Who Hope was impatiently missing still wasn't here, and it was after the fifth time rearranging her daggers on her belt and the second time re-braiding her two plaits that she decided to go look for him.

Hope didn't question why her feet knew which way to turn, or why her body seemed to know where his was. She followed her instinct, and two corridors and a few closed rooms later, she found him.

"Ciaran," she said.

His curtain of dark hair moved as he looked at the door, at her. His usually straight posture looked affected and . . . Was his jaw trembling? He held a wooden frame with both hands, tightly, as if he'd fall if he let go of it.

"What's the matter?" she asked, frowning, walking towards him and putting a hand on his metallic one.

"I think I know who this is," he whispered, his voice shaking as much as his hand as he lifted the photography of a family of four members so Hope could see.

Her eyes widened. She thought she knew, too. She knew the blue eyes of one of the little girls in the picture like her own heartbeat. Which made Stevian—

"I think he is my grandfather, Hope."

There were so many feelings to unpack, so many questions to ask, so many things to discuss, so many answers to get—and yet, that truth was irrevocable. Her own eyes glittering, her arms surrounded his chest, and she gave him a tight hug that he welcomed as if it was the first breath of his life.

When Hope and Ciaran returned to the living room, Lenna sighed. "Why so many weapons, Hope? You're making me feel empty-handed."

"Call it a comfort thing."

"Sure. You're not planning on killing any birds tonight, are you?" Lenna's side smile with a cocked eyebrow was dangerous.

Hope chuckled. "I'm planning on getting the Fifth Power tonight, trouble-seeker. Are we going?"

Lenna stood up in a jump, a hand on her hip as the other flicked the mass of red hair back. "For once and once only, I'm not going to make any theatrics with goodbyes, okay?" Lenna's tone was matter of fact and take-no-shit at the same time. "There is no reason to be overly dramatic. We go, you get the Fifth Power, I tell the Cardinals off a bit, we come back. End of."

Hope smiled. "And then I will destroy the Organ Mandor, and we'll live in peace forever after."

"He killed my mother, too, and amputated my arm trying to get rid of my courtrade blood, I remind you," Ciaran added, clenching and un-clenching his metallic hand. "Share his death. Don't be greedy."

"*Our* father tortured me during childhood and for centuries of my life, and I saw him torture Lenna in front of my eyes. Surely you can spare half his head for me to have fun with, sister?" Jake winked.

Hope grinned. It was the first time Jake called her 'sister'. "I'll have a think."

"We moure, then?" Ayla asked.

"We moure." Hope nodded. "To the Birthing Pit of Blackness in the Veiled Mountains of Orizane."

48

Lenna

T he Birthing Pit of Blackness was anything but black.

Whoever had given this place its name was a liar, and a bad one at that. *Someone Likes Red Sparks*, *Massacre After a Head Smashes*, or *Pretty-Explosive Bloody Shower* would have been more suitable names.

The red moon shone as bright as ever in the dark sky, its red shade falling over the tall trees, its light peeking through the narrow spots between branches until it touched the rocky ground. The tall trees were covered—*covered*, from leaves to trunk to branches—in red sparks. The same color of—

"Cardinal red," Ciaran muttered. "Fuck."

"I've never been here before," Hope said, her voice trembling. She walked towards the closest trunk, her hand suspended in front of the shining redness before she inhaled deeply and touched it. The sparks didn't move, didn't react.

They didn't react because they weren't sparks. "It's like . . . permanent ink."

"The color of your magic, your sparks, your mark," Ayla said, looking at the equally red, four-petal mark at the back of Hope's neck her two braids left exposed.

"Yes, and no. The color of my magic, but also . . . The color of the Cardinals." Her black eyes narrowed, as if she couldn't make sense of it.

"They told you all to come here, didn't they? Casually leaving me out of their messages. Well then, where the fuck are they?" Lenna asked.

It could have been Hope touching the ink or the presence of five panoms in the Birthing Pit of Non-Blackness, or it could have been Lenna's words. It could have been ante meridiem striking the night's clock or everything at once, but a path appeared between the red-painted rocks and moss. A path of red feathers, guiding them *into* the pit.

Hope didn't hesitate, her steps not faltering. Ciaran followed her lead, Ayla in the middle before Jake and Lenna holding hands closed the rear.

Feathers and sparks led them into a narrow opening into the rocky surface of the Veiled Mountains, and when they stepped inside, shadows engulfed them.

"It's safe," Ciaran said as Hope halted. "The shadows are welcoming us."

Lenna lifted her eyebrows, a sarcastic smile already on her lips. Well, it was nice to know these spiraling dark forces surrounding them were *welcoming* and not planning to *strangle* them.

Despite the moving darkness that had been waiting for them behind the veil, they walked for a few minutes with their sparks as the only source of light, until their path became wider, and they reached a—

"Shut the fucking fuck up," Lenna gasped.

They were in the land of the courtrades, the land created by Llunal, in the mountains *he* had lived in, according to Stevian. So why was there a four-petal chamber as big as the Cardinals Temple of Thyria, with the same massive dome carved inside the mountain—inside *his* mountain?

Unlike the one in the Organ House, this dome wasn't made of crystal, but of the smoothest rock, polished until perfection by hands or magic, or both.

Each petal of the wide chamber hosted an empty red throne facing the center of the panom. Four thrones of red feathers and red crystals. In the center of the four petals, in the very middle of the inner circle, there was an intricate circular pedestal.

"Interesting," whispered Hope as she stepped cautiously into the flower, clearly wanting to reach the center.

Ciaran stopped her with a hand on her shoulder, and Hope turned to him, her fingers meeting his. Her black eyes glittered with what she must have read on his face, hidden from Lenna.

"Be careful if you trade, Hope. There's more to life than giving everything until there is nothing left to give. No bravery should get you killed."

Her black eyes blinked as she swallowed, her fingers tightening on his touch. "Ciaran."

His metallic hand caressed her cheek slowly, his touch lingering as if it was the last time he would ever touch her.

"Lenna," Ayla's pissed off voice made Lenna stop contemplating the pair. The green eyes of her twin had an edge of fear and worry on top of the anger that her words let go. "You have no feather to offer, you failed your ordeal. Remind me why are you here again?"

"I'm here to have a civilized conversation with the South bird and demand some answers."

"No civilized conversation is going to end well if you call her *bird*." Ayla's green eyes were sharp, unforgiving. "And you don't *demand* answers to goddesses, for Fifth's sake." Ayla's voice broke at the end.

Lenna smirked. "Watch me."

"Your pretty mouth better not get you killed this ante meridiem, sweet fire." Jake's grip on her wrist was tight, his other hand holding her chin until her stare met his, the silver in his eyes burning.

"Oh, my pretty mouth can do many useful and skillful things," she winked, "and maybe it's not your favorite, but one of them is talking." Against his cold, dubious stare, she sighed. "Honestly, I don't plan on getting myself killed. You will not get rid of me so easily, Jake."

"I don't want to get rid of you at all, Lenna. Ever." His grip tightened on her chin as he lowered to reach her lips, his other hand fisting her mass of fire hair. His kiss was warm, definitive, unforgiving. A warning and a threat. Proof of his love in its purest essence that she could get lost in forever.

Ayla made a scoffing sound that no doubt included rolling her eyes.

When Jake pulled back and left Lenna with her mouth half-open, begging for more, he tilted her head sideways and whispered against her throat. "Behave. I can't lose you." Then he stole towards the red throne marked with the word *East*.

Lenna sighed, hands on her hips. If he only knew she was here to not so much have a word with the cheating goddess who had tricked her into an already-lost ordeal, but to make sure the Harming bitch who almost destroyed him inside and out during his own ordeal didn't harm him again.

By the time Lenna managed to drag her determined stare from him, everyone was in position. Ayla was directly opposite her, standing in front of the throne in the North petal, her arms crossed with her smooth curtain of red hair falling over her shoulders, her chin tilted backwards, and her lips pursed. Her silver dress fell to the floor, a tad more modest than Lenna's golden gown with a side slit that went farther up than her hips and met a drastic line of exposed skin from her shoulder. Lenna felt a sudden rush of pride. Her twin looked fearful and magnificent, a true deserving heir of the North House.

Ciaran and Jake were opposite each other, the former a few steps away from the West throne, her man eyeing the throne in the East petal he stood in. Ciaran, dressed in black leathers very similar to Hope's, stood with his legs slightly apart, his whole focus on the dark green sparks he was conjuring atop his biological hand. It was always difficult to know what he thought, but it was even harder now, for so many feelings were no doubt layered behind the blueness of his eyes.

In the middle of them was Hope, slowly circling the crystal pedestal in the Core, her black eyes slightly unfocused, no doubt taking in every single movement, every single breath in the chamber. Her steps were surprisingly silent despite the amount of metal she had clinging to her tight leathers.

When Jake turned to face Lenna, his side-smile and the wink of his silver eye made her want to cross to his petal and kiss him even more, and maybe she would have, if five goddesses hadn't appeared from thin air.

The North, West, South, and East Cardinals stood in front of their respective thrones.

The Core Cardinal stood in the middle of the four-petal flower, beneath the center of the dome. Her red eyes gleamed with something difficult to identify as she examined the five panoms in the room, her stare meeting Hope's for seconds that seemed to stop time.

Then, the Core goddess opened her arms wide, her body spinning atop the rotating pedestal. When she spoke, her voice echoed throughout the chamber, in their heads, and by the way Lenna's blood trembled, it might even have been inside their very veins.

"Strivers, welcome to your Fifth Judgment."

49

Hope

The sight of the five Cardinals splaying their magnificent, red-feathered wings was breathtaking.

Each of them was unique, and yet there were so many similarities between the sisters who had brought Thyria and panom magic to life. Their irises and hair were the color of their wings, the color Hope was more than familiar with. Their dresses were cut in different shapes, all of them made of red feathers that trailed down to the ground.

The North Cardinal wore a thin diadem crowning her hair and her feathers faded to a lighter tone of rose on the tips. She was glaring at Ayla intently in a way that lifted the hair on Hope's arms.

The South Cardinal's face could have been sculpted in stone, and it would have shown the same amount of emotion. Her impeccable face was utterly impenetrable, and she didn't even look at Lenna, who observed her with her arms crossed and her golden eyes narrowed.

The skin of the West Cardinal was covered in small, symmetrical red marks that trailed up the tips of her middle fingers, up her shoulders, and disappeared behind her back. When Ciaran met her apparently candid stare, she blinked.

The East Cardinal was the tallest. Her face—Hope held in a gasp. Her face was a wicked canvas of innumerable white scars, and when her blood-stained teeth flashed at the sight of Jake in front of her, her grin was vicious and cruel.

The biggest force came from the Core Cardinal, right in front of Hope, standing on the pedestal in the middle of the four-petal flower-shaped chamber. Her eyes were pinning, and there was no trace of the kind smile Hope had seen on the two occasions they'd met. The only sign of acknowledgment towards Hope was the smallest nod, and a whisper that didn't move her Cardinal-red lips, meant only for her. "Daughter of Red."

Hope smiled, feeling her blood rushing with excitement and adrenaline, her hands on the sheaths of her blades like anytime she welcomed a challenge.

"Sisters, you may sit," the Core Cardinal indicated, and the four goddesses who created the petals sat on their thrones, theirs wings fitting perfectly, allowing for their full splendor to shine. "Strivers, present now the crystal feathers, tokens of your worth, that grant you entry into this fateful gamble."

At once, Jake, Ayla, Ciaran, and Hope moved, freeing the feathers they had gained in their ordeals. The feathers they had suffered for, the ones they had almost died for. The red crystal shone in Hope's hand, and she swallowed the tinge of doubt that came with understanding the Cardinal's words.

The feathers didn't grant them the Fifth Power. They granted them a place here and now, in the Fifth Judgment.

If the Core Cardinal minded that Lenna didn't have a feather in her hands, she didn't say or hint that she had realized.

"The Cardinal of your ordeal will demand her due. Should you desire the Fifth Power, the price must be met, or an offering of equal worth presented in its stead."

These winged goddesses had pushed them to their limits, had toyed with their lives as if they meant nothing, and clearly, that wasn't *price* enough.

Hope clenched her jaw, hoping she didn't have to wait much longer to find out what her price was meant to be. She needed the Fifth Power to kill her father, and there was little she wouldn't offer to obtain it. Luckily, she didn't have to wait at all, for the Core Cardinal towered from her pedestal over her.

"Hope Nevada, successful striver of the Core ordeal. Do you present your feather to unveil the fate of your gamble?"

Hope lifted her open palm, the crystal feather shimmering under the dim lights around the dome. "Here it is. What price do you want me to pay?"

The Core Cardinal smiled, her eyes gleaming with pride and hope as she made the feather float between them.

"The only price that will annihilate the risk of destruction of our beloved land: the life of the man you love."

The blood in her veins froze, the image of Ciaran's blue eyes in her mind freezing any rational thought she could have ever had. She could hear her heart thundering in her chest, her forced breaths struggling to keep their usual pace.

There was no point trying to pretend this price was anything she had expected.

There was no price that could hurt more.

It didn't matter how much she wanted the death of her mother avenged and her father wiped out of the living plane of Terrha. It didn't matter how much she wanted—she *needed*—the Fifth Power.

She didn't need to look at Ciaran to know her answer, but she couldn't resist looking back. When their eyes met, she inhaled as if it was the first gulp of fresh air she had taken in years. The deepness of his blue eyes was enough to fill the Radel Sea and her own heart.

Ciaran had prioritized her, cared for her, saved her. Ciaran had made her feel desired, wanted, protected—*loved*.

"I'd rather die myself." The absolute certainty of her thought left her mouth before she could rephrase it, her voice echoing in the chamber.

"No." The sharpness in Ciaran's voice was no match to her best blades.

The Core Cardinal shook her head slowly. The finger of the goddess touched her red-stained bottom lip in a way that was too similar to an order of silence to be a coincidence. "Is that the price you offer in place of mine?"

"I offer my own death, to be claimed when Terrhan peace is ensured."

Never mind that it had been precisely the Core Cardinal who had told her she'd die up to five times. Never mind that it seemed it was precisely this goddess who had been more interested in Hope surviving and coming out alive.

The red eyes staring at her narrowed. "A life for a life. I accept your price."

Hope's eyes widened; a part of her disbelieving how easy it had been. It was almost as if the Core Cardinal had already known what her answer would be when she asked for Ciaran's life. As if the goddess knew she'd rather have a forbidden love than lose the man she had fallen in love with.

The Core Cardinal circled the floating feather with her fingers. The crystal melted, its shape shifting as it became a liquefied, living mass of Cardinal-red magic.

It was like nothing she had ever seen. The waves emanating from this power were deadly, devastating, and dominant. They were incomparable and unmatched.

The Core Cardinal guided it to Hope's mouth. "You may drink your Fifth Power."

She wouldn't have been surprised if the touch of such substance killed her instantly, but an irrational part of her trusted the goddess who had always seemed to protect her.

The Fifth Power burned her throat with electricity, ice, and fire. She couldn't scream in pain as she swallowed the mass of magic, the air not finding the way out of her lungs while this new power took over her whole body, changing her—reforging her.

She'd never know how long it took for the transformation to happen, but when she lifted her head and removed the hands from her throat, she felt it.

In her blood, there were no longer four powers to access. From her panom mark at the back of her neck, she could not only pull the four petals to Give, Take, Harm, and Heal.

She could also now pull the Core, the unification of all powers, to use the Fifth.

50

Lenna

H ope looked the same, and yet the power emanating from her every pore was not that different from the omnipotence of the Cardinals themselves.

This type of magic could end worlds and create new ones, and now, the bastard daughter of the Organ Mandor, who he had discarded and abandoned as a newborn, who was the only living female with Core panom blood—owned it now.

There were few words to describe the awe in Lenna's heart at the determination, stubbornness, and perseverance of the woman in front of her, the woman blessed with the Fifth Power.

There were even fewer words to describe how fucking annoying she found the loud, slow claps of the East Cardinal resonating in the chamber.

"Such generosity, Core, yet alas, *disappointingly* uncomplicated for your girl." The disgust of the Harming goddess was palpable in her spiteful words and the hateful stare towards the Core Cardinal. "I don't think I can cope with the pretense that this was not long-planned by your secret lover and yourself, my dear."

The Core Cardinal narrowed her red eyes, and the sight was terrifying. "We must not interfere with the writings of fate, sister, nor forget the unwavering, unified front we represent."

The East Cardinal scoffed, the scars on her face crunching together as she grinned. "But of course, why would I wish to interfere with the intricate affairs between you and His Darkness?"

"You ought not to speak of that which lies beyond your understanding, East."

The East goddess curled her upper lip, her white teeth splashed with what looked like dry drops of blood exposed. "I long to leave this putrid pit where you two copulate, and the sooner, the better." Her red stare turned from her sister to Jake, who—Fifth damn him five times—wore a side smile full of amusement and not enough wariness to deal with the hatred of such a being. "Jake Coralt, successful striver of the Harming ordeal. Do you present your feather to unveil the fate of your gamble?"

"Yours to take. Say your price."

The silence that followed as the East Cardinal examined him as if she could read his mind sent goosebumps all over Lenna's thighs. She didn't like this goddess one fucking bit.

"I will not demand one price, but two." She lifted a hand up as the Core Cardinal opened her mouth. "My opportunity to grant the Fifth, my gamble, therefore *my* rules."

The silver in his eyes glittered as he narrowed them. "Say your prices."

The East Cardinal stood from her throne and paced until her eyes met his. "I like you, Jake Coralt." Her fingers caressed his cheek, leaving an open, bleeding wound behind. He didn't even flinch.

Do not move, Jake whispered in Lenna's mind. *It's all a game.*

How was he worried about *her* and not about the abusive creature touching *him*? Lenna's nostrils flared, her jaw aching from clenching it so hard, the inner side of her cheek bleeding to keep from jumping and attempting to rip her throat and wings at once.

"Once I name my prices, refusal will not be an option. In return, you will be granted the Fifth Power."

Any remote sign of amusement or nonchalance left Jake's body, his shoulders and arms tense with the risk she posed in front of him. Lenna didn't have any doubt—it was a fucking trap.

"I will not go into such gamble blind. There are conditions," Jake demanded.

The East Cardinal tilted her head. "Two conditions you may name."

Jake inhaled deeply. "Lenna Brachyan will be alive and unharmed, untouched by you or your sisters, by this gamble or any others."

Lenna's heart squeezed so tightly it could fit inside her fist. She wanted to shout "Don't trust her" so badly, but it would be useless, because Jake already didn't trust the wicked mind of this goddess.

"Repulsive, but agreeable. One more condition you may name before I reveal the prices you will pay."

"The woman I share blood with, Hope Nevada, will remain alive, unharmed, and untouched."

"Wise, but not wise enough, Jake. The obsessive protection of my dear sister over your half-sister is unmatched. You wasted your second condition, but I respect your first. I will now name your due, and you will receive your well-deserved Fifth Power." Her finger touched his lip, breaking it in half, blood droplets pooling at his feet.

"Get your fucking hands off him, spiteful winged creature of Hell," Lenna shouted. The moment her voice left her mouth, Jake's widened silver eyes were on her, a warning and a plea that she was not going to comply with anymore.

To Lenna's utmost shock, the East Cardinal took her finger off him, but it was the utterly delighted and satisfied smile on her red lips that froze her in place.

"By the time the sun rises, I will have killed every member of the East House. You will become the new Ruler of my House, Jake. You will bear your title with the honor it deserves, and I expect you to make me and my House proud. The second price, though, is the highlight of my night." The East Cardinal looked at the Core Cardinal as if this was her personal vengeance, as if whatever hatred she was putting in Jake's gamble was fueled by much more than the man she was making bleed. "It's a favor you will one day thank me for. To become the ruthless panom ruling the Harming petal, you must let go of what makes you weak and vulnerable."

Jake shook his head slowly, blood dripping down his chin and cheek as his strong fists clenched at his sides, as if he had realized something that was too late to undo. He turned to meet her golden stare, and his eyes showed the biggest terror Lenna had ever seen.

Terror bigger than losing one's life, terror greater than witnessing the end of the world.

"From now on, Jake Coralt of the East House, you will not be able to love."

51

Hope

Lenna crumbled to her feet, gasping for air as if every particle of oxygen had burned with the final words of the East Cardinal. Her shaking hands covered her devastated face. Her golden, tearful eyes clearly debating the need to stop watching at how Jake drank his Fifth Power. Hope tried to walk towards her, but invisible magic held her inside the circular center of the chamber.

Lenna was alone, crying at the foot of the throne belonging to a goddess who still ignored her. Jake had ensured she was alive, unharmed, and untouched, and yet, Lenna was the vivid image of someone dying inside, her heart being ripped raw from her chest without asking for permission or forgiveness.

The North Cardinal cleared her throat, claiming the attention of the panom who had also tried to leave her petal to be with her twin with no success. "Continue we shall. Ayla Brachyan, successful striver of the Giving ordeal. Do you present your feather to unveil the fate of your gamble?"

Ayla stared at the Cardinal of her House as if she wished to *stab* her feather into her red eyes, and Hope couldn't even blame her. It hurt her deeply to see how Lenna was ruined, and she wasn't her blood, birth-twin. Whatever Ayla was feeling wasn't patience and understanding.

"Am I dealing with a deaf striver?" The North Cardinal chuckled.

"I present my feather," Ayla muttered between clenched teeth. If she held the crystal feather any tighter, there was a real risk it would explode.

"You are the current heir of my House, and in your ordeal, you proved how incapacitating the imbalance of your inner magical scale is." Her smooth hands repositioned the white diadem atop her cardinal-red hair, and then Hope saw it. By the small, backwards step Ayla took, it was evident she'd seen it too.

The small white pieces forming the diadem of the North Cardinal were *teeth*. Teeth of beings. Human beings.

The goddess fluttered her eyelashes as she saw the focus of Ayla's green eyes. "Beautiful, I know." She sighed; her grin seemingly genuine. "Your blindness limits the use of your magic. If you didn't have that painful impairment anytime your inner balance tilts, *and* you had the Fifth Power, you would be unstoppable. How badly do you want the Fifth Power, Ayla Brachyan?"

When she spoke, Ayla's voice was a whisper. "You want my eyes."

The North Cardinal laughed, pure joy and happiness on her face. "Clever girl. Your emerald-green eyes would make a pretty necklace. It would look *lovely* amongst all the red. So, what do you say?"

Ayla didn't say anything. She lifted the palms of her hands to cover her eyes in the exact same way Hope had seen her protect herself when her balance was uneven, when the use of one power broke the even balance of the panom powers.

After a while, Ayla sighed. "I accept, on one condition."

"Which is?"

The red-haired twin hesitated, and finally said, "If I am to lose my sight for the rest of my life, please allow me to see Nina Avert one last time."

"As the Giving Cardinal, I find pride in being benevolent." The Cardinal splayed her wings, her hands moving with sparks the color of her feathers, and then, Nina was there.

Hope inhaled sharply; her brow furrowed as the tips of her hands touched the hilt of her daggers. The white-haired young woman looked so out of place, her hesitant ocean-colored eyes taking in everything and everyone around her, her eyebrows shooting to the sky when she saw the five Cardinals in the room, her mouth half opened with endless questions that wouldn't be answered. She wore a plain, pale pink dress over her pale skin, and she had never looked more fragile and vulnerably *human* than in this chamber of powerful panoms and cruel goddesses.

"Ayla, what's happening? Are you okay?" Nina asked, her hand reaching Ayla's, her eyes trying to decipher the emotions behind the green eyes of the woman in front of her.

Ayla smiled, a tear rolling down her cheek as she caressed Nina's, putting a wavy, white strand of her hair behind her ear. "I will be okay. Sorry for disturbing you so late. I just needed to see you. I wanted to see you."

Nina swallowed. "I'm glad to see you, too, but I don't like seeing you cry."

Ayla's lips widened with a tense smile, her green eyes drinking Nina in for the final time, before she said to the North Cardinal. "Thank you. She may go back now, please. Nina, I'll s—meet you very soon."

A disconcerted frown didn't suit the face of the North Cardinal. "But I granted you one condition, not two. Your friend here is welcome to stay the rest of the Fifth Judgment. Consider it a kindness. Now, if I may . . ." The joyful grin was back, and then, moving Nina to the side with a swipe of her hands, the Cardinal stood in front of Ayla, her hands in front of the green eyes she had gambled for.

There was no warning. One second, Ayla was staring with shock and determination at the goddess. The next, her eyeballs were floating out of her sockets and into the palms of the grinning Cardinal. Her ear-piercing screams filled the chamber as Lenna's raging sobs resurfaced loudly behind Hope as she cursed, and Nina choked on any words, holding the wall with both hands as if that was all her body could do.

As if these noises were pure musical background, the North Cardinal hung Ayla's eyeballs from a silver chain and placed it around her neck. She sat down on her throne with an unwavering smug smile, and when she looked back at Ayla, the North Cardinal lifted her hands, making everyone quiet, and somehow stopping Ayla's pain. "Forgive my manners, I got overexcited. These are for you."

Two metallic eyeballs floated from the Cardinal's Giving hands, and replaced Ayla's old ones, and when the heir of the North blinked, silver was all that was visible in her eyes.

Silver, the color of Ayla's magic, her sparks, her ink, her mark, her dress. Silver, the color of her soul.

The powerful, liquefied mass of magic the feather of her ordeal had transformed into floated towards Ayla, and she seemed to sense it approaching, for she repositioned herself to align with it.

"Here is your Fifth Power, silver heir. Now, drink."

52

Hope

Fear was not a feeling she was used to, and it was deeply uncomfortable. Her heart raced, her muscles were tense, the slight sweat on her palms felt clammy where they touched the hilts of her daggers. Hope couldn't tell if the heightened senses—the way each sound was perceived and processed, every minuscule part her peripheral vision captured, the hyper-awareness of the contact of her feet on the ground—were caused by the Fifth Power or were part of the physical reaction of being scared.

How could she not be, when the Fifth Judgment was massacring their futures, their love stories, and their bodies. How could she not be when Ciaran was next?

The West Cardinal placed one hand over the other on her lap, sighing deeply as she removed her red stare from the new necklace her sister from the North was wearing.

Was there any point in praying the Healing goddess of the West would not be as cruel as her North and East sisters? That she'd have some mercy with Ciaran? That she wouldn't ruin him as much?

Hope knew how desperate her thoughts were, fueled by the frustration and impotence at play in this wicked gambling game, fueled by the biggest fear that he would suffer. The Giving goddess hadn't Given shit, so why would the Healing goddess be any better.

In fact, hadn't it been the *Healing* Cardinal who had thrown Hope from the peak of the navia and stabbed her with her own daggers to what could have been her end? The only reason Hope hadn't met her end then was Ciaran. And it was to him that the Cardinal spoke.

"Ciaran Castel, successful striver of the West ordeal. Do you present your feather to unveil the fate of your gamble?"

He swallowed, and Hope knew it wasn't in doubt, but preparation. "I have the feather of your ordeal, and I would like to offer an exchange."

The red eyebrows of the Cardinal rose. "You might exchange the feather and my price for the Fifth Power."

"I seek a different exchange. I wish not for the Fifth Power, but for something else." Ciaran's low voice held no trace of hesitation.

"You wish not for the Fifth Power, and yet you risked joining the Fifth Crusade and surviving your ordeal?" The West Cardinal leaned forwards on her throne, some feathers on her wings readjusting.

His chin dipped once. "I have no need for the Fifth Power. Being a striver on the Fifth Crusade was the only way to show my commitment to this cause and present my offer to you, West Cardinal."

The eyes of the West Cardinal met those of the Core Cardinal for the briefest moment, and then they were focused again on Ciaran's blue ones.

"What is it you offer, son?"

"I offer all my panom blood." Ciaran bowed his head, a sign of respect and an apology at once.

The West Cardinal frowned, the shine in her eyes very similar to human disappointment. "Why, I wonder, do you want to offer the most valuable treasure you own?"

When Ciaran spoke, his voice was a whisper. A whisper too loud in the silence that was going to shatter Hope's mind.

"The whispers have spoken, and her life is full of death. I offer my panom blood, until the very last drop, so when she dies, Hope Nevada can be reborn. The world can't risk losing her again. *I* will not risk losing her again."

"You were so patient, and you've protected her well."

The muscles on his shoulders tensed when the West Cardinal didn't continue speaking, but he didn't speak either. After painfully silent seconds that seemed endless, she spoke.

"If you gift me your panom blood, you will not be complete ever again."

It was then that Ciaran turned to look at Hope. Her tearful eyes did not forbid her from appreciating the unfaltering conviction in him. She wished there was no one else here. Here, in Terrha.

She wished their lives were different, uncomplicated, not so complexly influenced by fate and powers of gods and goddesses.

She wished their love was free and not forbidden.

His eyes glimmered as he said, "I have never been complete before. I am now."

Hope felt the Core Cardinal nodding from her pedestal.

"You must swear to seek a suitable, deserving candidate to inherit the West House from your father when he passes," the West Cardinal said.

"I've been raised in the West House and will endeavor to ensure the continuity of its line in a way that respects our beliefs." He smiled, more to himself than anyone else. "I have a few candidates in mind. I would like to discuss such a responsibility with them, but I swear a candidate will be chosen and presented to you."

"In that case, I accept your offer, Ciaran Castel. Your panom life finishes now."

Hope gasped as the West Cardinal inhaled sharply, lifting her hands as she stood. Ciaran's back arched in an inhuman way, his long hair floating backwards, his feet not touching the floor as ten tendrils of blood left different parts of his body and floated to each finger of the West Cardinal.

His thick blood was red, dark green sparks intertwined with it, and there was *so* much. The Cardinal's fingers sucked, sucked, and sucked his blood as she redirected to a crystal vase, filling it without cease.

Fear rushed up Hope's veins at a new speed. Panom or not, he needed *some* blood to live.

Just when she stepped forward, ready to stop whatever this nonsense was becoming, the blood stopped floating from his body to the Cardinal, and his body fell like a dead weight on the ground.

The West Cardinal put a crystal lid on the vase and made it float towards the Core Cardinal. "Sister, keep it safe."

The voice of the Core goddess sounded next to Hope, but she could have been miles away for all the attention she gave it. "I will."

Hope's focus was on the stillness of his body. Ciaran's hair covered his face but thank the Fifth and all these five cursed and blessed Cardinals one by one, his fingers grasped the floor.

Shadows from each corner of the chamber went towards him, like magnets unable to resist a huge metal force. They trailed up his legs, up his biological and metallic arms, swirling around him—*with* him.

The first thing Ciaran's eyes searched for when they opened was Hope.

He stood up, owner and master of shadows as ever, every single dark trail readjusting and finding a way to hover around his feet and hands.

It almost was as if Llunal was welcoming Ciaran to his new version of life. A life where he was not the heir of any Thyrian House. A life where he was not dual powered, but courtrade.

A life where they could be together.

Hope felt the skin on her forearm tickle, and tears of happiness filled her eyes when she saw not dark green ink but shadow ink with Ciaran's handwriting.

I love you beyond petals and magic.

53

Lenna

S he'd been staring at the scarred fingers of the East Cardinal, unable to believe they weren't talons. The pain she felt in her heart after the goddess had stolen the ability to love from Jake was physical. Talons had clawed her heart, now a miserable organ left in shreds.

The next cursed, winged female had taken her twin's eyes to make a fucking necklace.

Her sister would never see the red moon, the Radel Sea, her silver sparks, or the face of her lovers again. She wouldn't see the face of her children, if she ever had them. She wouldn't see anything or anyone else again, because the North bird wanted a *pretty* necklace.

A. Fucking. Pretty. Necklace.

The voice of the Organ Mandor in what seemed like another life echoed into Lenna's thoughts. *Female minds, twisted indeed*, he'd said. Maybe he hadn't been so wrong after all.

These feathered deities were creatures of malice.

They were brutal, barbaric beasts. And for the first time since the five Cardinals had appeared, the South Cardinal was now looking at her.

"Lenna Brachyan, unsuccessful striver of the South ordeal. You don't belong here."

"Thanks for the reminder that almost dying was not good enough. I came seeking answers," her voice broke between ragged breaths. She couldn't remember if she'd ever cried this hard, this much. The answers she had wanted seemed minuscule, irrelevant problems now.

"So I heard." The South Cardinal's face was severe, impassive. "While I wait, and because your attempt at my ordeal demonstrated courage, I will answer one question for you. Pick wisely."

Lenna narrowed her sore, golden eyes. What was the Cardinal *waiting* for? She was the last goddess, and Lenna was the last one in this chamber they could fuck over. Whatever she meant, Lenna was not going to lose her chance.

The list of questions she wanted to ask was longer than her life was likely to be. What was the future of Thyria going to be like? How would Hope kill the Organ Mandor now that she had the Fifth Power? What would happen to the West Petal now that Ciaran was not the heir to his House? Would Raoul ever stop having nightmares and his hair turning darker with each one? Would Ayla ever be happy living without seeing? How many panomquakes had happened in Thyria this ante meridiem, with so many changes in the Houses and their powers?

There were other questions, too . . . Questions that hurt too much to say aloud.

What would happen to Jake? Was the Cardinal's price he had agreed to pay irreversible? Would Lenna survive loving him for the rest of her days, when he would not—he could not—reciprocate? Why the Fifth fuck had these Cardinals ruined the two beings she loved most? Why were they so perverse? Why, like the Organ Mandor himself, did they deserve to live and destroy lives without consequences?

Nothing in her life was certain anymore. *Certain* things changed in a matter of seconds.

Love ended as if it had never existed, sight was stripped as if someone had never deserved it. Certainty was an empty concept, a fantastic creation to give reassurance to beings who craved it.

Lenna didn't crave certainty, though. She craved something bigger, more dangerous and wilder. She craved the truth, and she had one chance to get it.

"How can a Cardinal be killed?"

The impassive features of the South Cardinal finally changed. She tilted her chin up, her red lips pressed tight in a line. "The life of a Cardinal can only end when her wings are torn by the weapon bearing her own blood, and her heart is struck by the weapon bearing the blood of her Queen."

All Lenna had time to do was save the valuable information for later, because firm steps approached the entrance to the chamber through the path they had walked under the mountain. And when she turned to see who it was, her blood froze.

"Precisely the five beings I wanted to see. And as always, it's an honor to see you, too, my Cardinals."

The grin on the face of Rhei Coralt, Organ Mandor of Thyria, was as repulsive as it had ever been. His silver eyes, identical to Jake's, shone with excitement, his obsidian black hair shorter than the last time Lenna had seen him. The suit he wore was impeccable, accentuating the tall figure of his body and every marked angle of his face.

"You're late," said the South Cardinal.

The Organ Mandor walked in front of her throne, bowing his head as his hand did a stupid flourish. "My sincere apologies. I couldn't understand the cryptic clues of where the Fifth Judgment was happening. This . . . *location* was quite unexpected."

The Core Cardinal's nostrils flared, and her voice was angry. "If you didn't understand it, how is it that you are here?"

"A little bird told me." His smug smile was even worse than his vomit-inducing grin. "Since I'm here, we might as well proceed."

He put his hand inside his jacket, and a few gasps echoed in the room when they saw what he held tightly inside his fist.

The Organ Mandor had the crystal feather of the South ordeal.

"Why the South ordeal, Ruler of the Organ House?" the Core Cardinal asked, her eyes narrowed to slits that surely could spit red fire.

"If male honesty is ever allowed, I have no doubt you'd have ensured I wasn't successful in your ordeal, Core Cardinal, which I think is deeply unethical and unfairly biased. Your interests and mine have never aligned. But the truth is, by the time I realized what these five beings were doing, my precious bird told me the South ordeal was the only remaining one to be completed."

"South?" Core Cardinal asked, her voice raising an octave and making the rocky dome tremble, some small stones falling to the ground.

"I didn't say anything."

"I missed your bleeding inks, Father. I wondered why." Was Hope—

Lenna narrowed her eyes, trying to confirm that—Yes, Hope was fuck-ing *smiling*. Of course, that woman was bloody smiling when her biggest enemy was in front of her.

His silver eyes were cold and sharp as he stared at the black irises of his bastard daughter, heir to his throne. "I stopped sending you inks because I had bigger commitments in mind."

Then, it hit Lenna.

The outlandish force of water that would have hit their navia when they traveled to the South ordeal, the one Jake stopped before it could drown them all. He hadn't been able to identify what it was, but he had known it wasn't nature.

The ink from the Cardinals *before* Lenna had arrived at her ordeal. *The feathers are claimed*, it had read on their skins. The message had been Cardinal-cursed clear, and it hadn't been sent to Lenna.

And when Lenna had entered the ordeal, after stubbornly promising "I am going to do the South ordeal even if it's the last thing I do."

The South Cardinal had *allowed* her to enter it, but there was nothing to gain. Because the feather of the Taking ordeal, shining in the fist of Rhei Coralt, had already been claimed.

How had she been so painfully narrow-minded and dumb? All the signs had been there. Signs, inks, and even a gigantic water force against their navia, for Fifth's damned sake.

Everything had been there, except her opportunity to pause, analyze, understand, and prepare, and now it was too fucking late.

"Rhei Coralt, successful striver of the South ordeal. Do you present your feather to unveil the fate of your gamble?"

The hairs on Lenna's spine rose with the words of the South Cardinal. The Organ Mandor lifted his fist and opened it, the crystal edges marked on the skin he had held tightly.

"Yours to take."

"For the Fifth Power, I will take your feather, and I will take the life of someone who gave you something."

His grin was immediate, and his silver eyes met Jake's. From the look on his face, Jake's ability to hate had multiplied exponentially for every bit of love he would never feel again.

"Please take the life of my wife, who gave me my son."

The growl that left Jake's throat was not of this world, his fists clenching as navy sparks raced around his hands, charging.

The South Cardinal nodded, and a woman with the same full lips and straight nose as Jake's appeared in front of her throne. Before the woman could blink, the South Cardinal Took her heart.

Lenna lifted her hands to her throat, running to the dead body that crashed to the ground a few steps away from her. Organs couldn't be Taken, but clearly the Taking Cardinal could do whatever the fuck she wanted.

Lenna's skin tickled, and she tried to cover it as she read Hope's words on her skin.

The invisible barriers are down.
The Mandor must not drink
the Fifth Power.

When Lenna looked up, she saw Ciaran lifting his head from his biological forearm, too.

"Where is it?" Rhei Coralt asked impatiently, not even glancing at the dead woman at his feet.

"Your Fifth Power is here. You may drink."

The South Cardinal left the levitating liquefied mass of Fifth Power in the air, and then, as if their duties were completed and the Judgment had finished, the five Cardinals vanished.

54

Hope

The instant the five Cardinals vanished, Rhei Coralt opened his mouth, walking towards the mass of Fifth Power floating in front of him as if nothing else existed, ready to drink it.

It was also that instant when Hope unleashed her hands.

Her blades flew across the chamber, their hilts burning with Cardinal-red sparks as they followed their course with flawless precision. One blade stabbed his hand, the second struck the Organ Mandor's open mouth, blocking the entrance of the power he didn't deserve.

Before her next two blades were ready to attack him, an immensely powerful surge of navy sparks flew from where Jake stood towards their father's body. The navy sparks hit him straight in the chest, making him lose balance as he stumbled sideways, choking on the blood the dagger made pool in his mouth. He fell on the crystal pedestal the Core Cardinal had occupied.

When Hope reached his body, Ciaran was next to her. The horror in the silver eyes of the man on the floor was blatant, but Ciaran was unforgiving. His dominant shadows squeezed his throat and chest, not allowing the Organ Mandor to take full breaths.

Ayla arrived last. "At least he's quiet." She opened her hands, Giving thick chains across his body to hold him down.

Despite their efforts, he still moved, and Hope saw their mistake half a second too late. Her blade ensured the Organ Mandor couldn't use his panom magic with one hand, but the other—

Jake traced a precise line with the side of his palm, Harming him, separating his wrist from his hand. Even the Organ Mandor would have screamed if he could speak.

Ayla suddenly frowned, looking up at—Nothing. She wasn't looking at anything at all, but when she spoke, her voice was tinged with sadness.

"Raoul says he has his Stabs on his back."

On one side of the chamber, Nina gasped, her eyes full of tears as she covered her mouth.

Hope didn't understand exactly what Ayla wanted to say, how Raoul could be involved in any way without being here, and why she knew, but she slid her hand behind her father's back and—

Two cold, crystal hilts met her touch, and she pulled them out.

The Red Lawful Stab, used for torture and pain, created with blood of the five Cardinals. The same blade he had tortured Lenna, Ciaran, and Jake with.

The Black Lawful Stab, used for death, born from the blood of the Cardinal Queen. The same black crystal blade Rhei Coralt had used to kill Hope's mother.

The eyes of the Organ Mandor were closing, his breaths barely noticeable under the thick silver chains and the strain of shadows.

Hope extended her hands towards his chest, Healing his heart and lungs with circular motions.

"What on Terrha are you doing?" Lenna spat.

The cold calculation in Hope's eyes was terrifying. "He doesn't deserve a merciful, unknowing death. He will see us being his end. His soul will forever remember who killed him, and why."

Ciaran's hand was on her shoulder, squeezing tightly, and she felt the shadows release their grip slightly to aid her goal.

After long seconds, the heavy eyelashes of the Mandor fluttered, his silver eyes full of exhaustion and hate staring back at her.

"Much better," she smiled.

She held the Black Lawful Stab over his heart and halted. Her father once said this dagger only obeyed the Organ Mandor of Thyria, yet she didn't feel the magic opposing her. Perhaps the Fifth Power overruled this, or perhaps it was the fact that *he* was not going to be the Organ Mandor for much longer.

Hope looked at Ciaran, Jake, Lenna, and Ayla. They all had reasons to be here, to want this man dead. Ciaran's dead mother. Jake's tormented childhood and the woman who gave birth to him lying on the floor. Lenna's torture, removal of panom powers and her revoked heirloom. Ayla's vengeance for the pain inflicted on her twin.

"Whenever you are ready," Hope said.

Ciaran understood her first, placing his hand over hers on the hilt of the Black Lawful Stab. Jake was next, and Lenna followed, her eyes lingering on the point where her hand touched Jake's, as if she was wondering when, if ever, she was going to be this close to him again. Ayla topped the hilt.

The Organ Mandor of Thyria, murderer, torturer, and discarder of countless innocent beings, looked at them as the Black Lawful Stab perforated his heart on its last beat.

55

Hope

S he had done it. *They* had done it.

Rhei Coralt was dead.

Revenge had been served twenty-five years late, but it had been served well, with the deadliest dagger at the hands of the five people who hated him most. Vengeance came with sour satisfaction and nerve-wracking responsibilities.

The moment his life ended, the Birthing Pit of Blackness engulfed all of them in shadows and red sparks. Ciaran, Hope, Jake, Lenna, Ayla, and Nina were moured by the god-sent magic to the entrance of Stevian's house.

When they left, the beach had been empty, and their navia had been anchored. Now, mere hours later, the beach was crowded with busy people dressed in black, and fifteen navias stood in line in an impressive exhibition of metallic crescent shapes.

"What the—" Lenna started.

Her voice made Stevian look back at them, and the old man grinned, tears filling his blue eyes as he lifted his palm to his heart. He sent a twirl of shadows above every courtrade at the beach, getting their attention. He looked from Hope to Ciaran and back at Hope, and when he kneeled, so did the two hundred courtrades behind him.

Hope clenched her jaw. She didn't know why these courtrades were kneeling, but there was respect, admiration, and loyalty in such gesture. How many emotions could be thrown at someone in one night before breaking?

Ciaran, next to her, held her hand. She would not be able to look at him *without* breaking, and she couldn't break in front of the people kneeling in front of them. *For* them. Hope squeezed his hand, not wanting to let go ever again.

Stevian lifted his head. "The whispers of night commanded me to gather your army and to prepare to leave Orizane. For the safety of Terrha, we must head to Thyria when the sun leaves the sky."

An army of *courtrades*.

Hope smiled. Perhaps the grand plan of the Core Cardinal and Llunal hadn't gone wrong at all. Perhaps fate was truly playing a key part here. Perhaps this was the destiny that had been written for them centuries ago.

She whispered to Ciaran, "Your army is waiting for you to speak."

He inhaled sharply. "This is not *my* army."

"Don't be rude," she whispered back, elbowing him.

A loud breeze hit them, and Hope knew Llunal or his whispers had spoken to him.

"Shit, okay, okay," he muttered. He sighed, cleared his throat looking at the dozens of courtrades gathered, and then he spoke. "It'll be my honor to navigate the darkness with every one of you. The night is nothing but shadows and stars."

"The night is nothing but shadows and stars," the courtrades repeated, bowing their heads deep.

The Radel Sea was calm. Hope's blood, like her future, was not.

The future held many worries, but her father wouldn't be one of them.

It had been hours since the red moon shone in the sky and the courtrades had started pushing the navias from Orizane to Thyria, the sun starting to rise again. It was impressive how fast navias moved with the shadows of two hundred courtrades acting as one.

When they arrived in Thyria, Hope had moured to the protected clearing in the woods where they had buried her mother's body. She missed her mother and the woods so painfully much.

The black and red crystal daggers sheathed on Hope's belt were heavier than any metal blades she had ever carried. She knew, though, their weight was not on their material but on their history, the punishments they had inflicted, their magic. They thrummed, calling her to release them like a wave waiting to crash against the shore. Luckily, Hope was well versed in the arts of resistance and perseverance. She'd be cautious, though. These blades, like any weapon, were as dangerous as their wielder.

The Fifth Power was as dangerous as the Lawful Stabs, and its three wielders were here. Jake, who hadn't crossed a word with Lenna yet, Ayla, who would never see again, and Hope.

She was the Ruler of the land approaching on the horizon. The highest authority of the Roix, owner of the Organ House, and Supreme Ruler of all Thyrian Houses.

She was the new Organ Mandor of Thyria.

Hope had been observing the night and shadows pass from a room under the deck. She felt someone approach from behind, her heart beating faster at the recognition.

"You haven't slept yet," Ciaran said, his long hair a mess from wielding shadows for hours.

She hadn't, and she doubted the constant influx of thoughts and worries would ever stop now. "You haven't either."

Ciaran sighed. He looked exhausted, and she knew she couldn't look any better. The past couple of days had been more intense than whole years. He caressed her cheek and took her hand. "Come with me."

She was too tired and too eager to spend time with him to object, so she let him guide her. He closed the door of his bedroom behind him, and she lifted her eyebrows.

"I like this kind of sleeping," she chuckled, a blush rushing to her cheeks.

He shook his head with a smile. "The first time we make love won't be while knackered and sleep-deprived after using all types of powers for two days and nights in a row."

She tilted her head to the side. "Why not?"

The glint in his eyes shone bright as ever. "Because I need you in full form and strength for what I will do to you."

"Oh, in that case, the wait better pay off."

"It *will* pay off. Not tonight's wait, Hope, but my *centuries-long* wait. So, sleep, now. Organ Mandors need to sleep too."

"And commanders of armies of shadow wielders too."

He chuckled. "Apparently, they do."

She Gave herself clean clothes made of soft cotton, undid her braids until her long black hair was loose, and laid down on his bed. He removed his shirt and laid down next to her until their eyes were mere inches away.

She inhaled deeply, her black eyes closing at the pleasing envelopment of his night and pine scent. When she opened her eyes, she pushed a strand of dark hair behind his ear and gently touched the metal ring on his bottom lip. It bobbed when he smiled.

"You can't imagine the number of times I've dreamed about this," he whispered, his blue eyes glittering as his metallic hand rested on her cheek, his thumb stroking her flushed cheek, moving to the corner of her lips.

"Dream no more, shadow warrior. It's time to live."

When their lips met, their souls met as well, colliding with each other in the most intimidate dance ever danced. Hearts had never felt full before, taste had never had a worthy meaning until then, touch had never been experienced like this.

It was a kiss between cultures, magics, and history. It was a curse of forbidden love finished, broken by his love for her.

It was a promise.

Epilogue

Her black shoes echoed in the empty throne room of the Organ House.

"Idiot, power-blinded male," she muttered from her black-painted lips.

It was common knowledge that the Organ Mandor must never leave Thyria, for it was too great a risk to leave its throne unprotected.

The snow child, consumed by her black thoughts and vile, had finally succumbed the last of his white strands to the color of her blood. A dead snow child not made of snow anymore, since blackness had killed him, his lifeless body abandoned in a corner, discarded.

She climbed the steps to the throne, savoring the deep inhales of long-missed fresh air in her lungs. Her black, wavy hair fell on her pale breasts. The black feathers of her majestic wings shone with the power they had been blessed with—the wings she hadn't been permitted to fly for over ninety thousand days.

Her black eyes assessed the room. After over two centuries restricted to a limited space, she was here. She would have smiled if she remembered how.

No one alive was here. Not even her lover, the one who had mistakenly fallen in her net of wicked feelings, the one who visited her in his sleep, the one now dead at the hands of his daughter.

She had waited two-hundred and fifty years for her curse to break. After such a long time, she had no rush to meet the new Organ Mandor, the Daughter of Red the prophecies had spoken of since Fate existed.

The one protected by the Core Cardinal and her lover, Llunal himself.

She, more than anyone, knew it wasn't an easy feat to be the first-born, the chosen one.

The most feared, the most powerful, the one others rebelled against.

She lifted her black crystal crown over her head.

Centuries ago, she had been the first to sit on this throne.

The Cardinal Queen would also be the last.

The Panom Saga

Petals for Vicious Secrets

Petals for Deadly Power

Petals for Broken Wings – coming in 2026

Author's note

Thank you so much for reading Petals for Deadly Power! I hope you enjoyed following Hope, Ciaran, Jake and Lenna on their quest for the Fifth Power. The third and final book in the Panom Saga, Petals for Broken Wings, is coming soon!

If you enjoyed this book, I would be extremely grateful if you would consider leaving a review on Amazon or Goodreads. Reviews are extremely important for authors, and they do make a difference!

I would love to keep in touch! If you'd like to be the first to know about new releases, exclusive content, and magical bits, you can find me on Instagram, Tiktok and Facebook. You can also join my newsletter at marthamonteval.com.

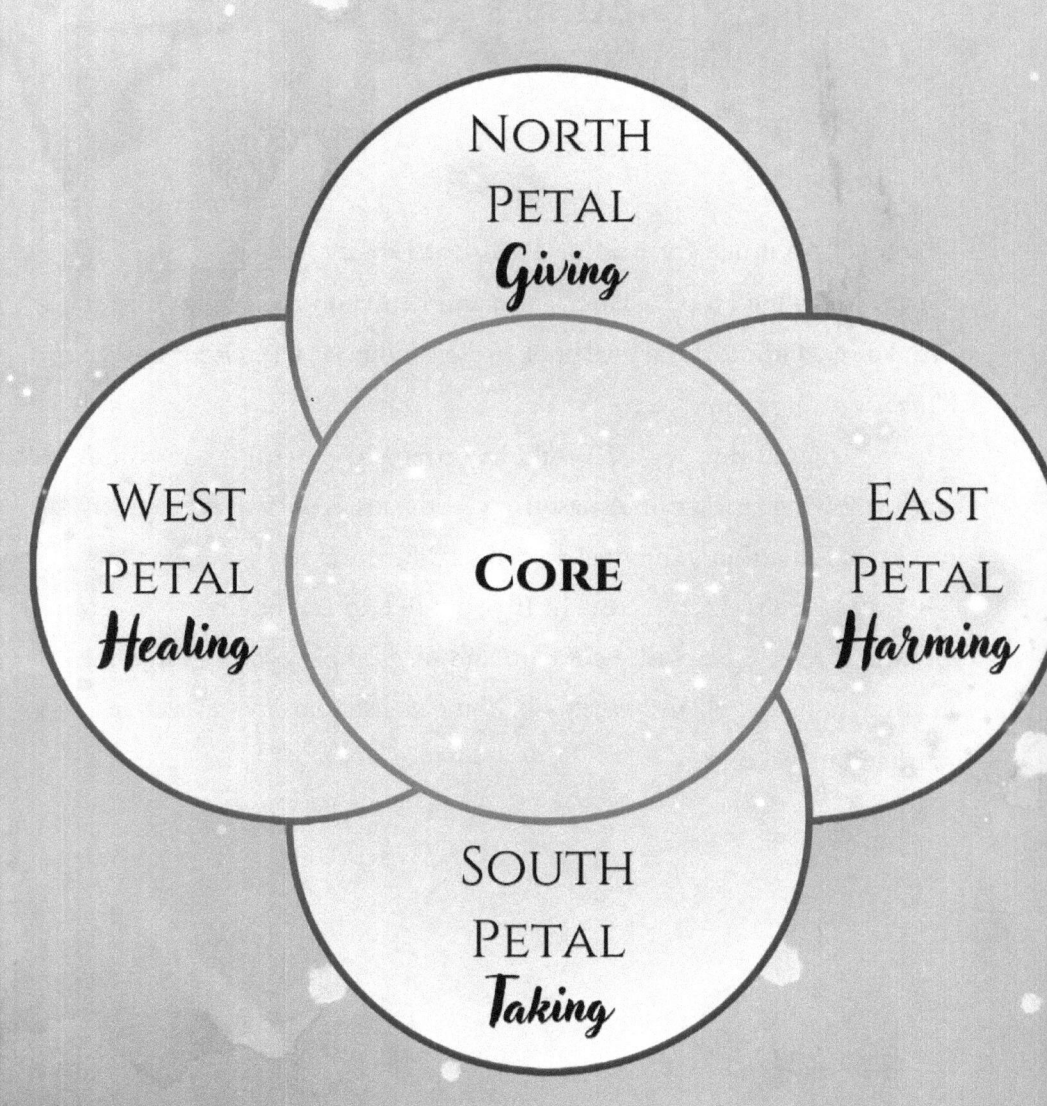

Hope Nevada

Lenna Brachyan

Ayla Brachyan

Ciaran Castel

Indianna Halia

Rhei Coralt

Jake Coralt

THE CARDINALS

Glossary

Ante meridiem – Time since the death of night until the sun is at its highest point in the sky.

Beftac Center for Injured Beings – Biggest healing center in Corentre.

Being - Any individual in Terrha, such as a human, a panom, a cour-trade, or other.

Black Lawful Stab – A legendary blade made of black crystal, with lethal powers to kill irreversibly. The Black Lawful Stab only obeys the Organ Mandor of Thyria. Blood of the Cardinal Queen was used to create it.

Borealia – Capital of the North Petal in the North of Thyria.

Cardinal Houses – A term to refer to the North House, South House, East House and West House of Thyria.

Cardinal Queen – Queen of Cardinals.

Cardinals – Five goddesses of panom magic, creators of the Petals and builders of Thyria. The North Cardinal, East Cardinal, South Cardinal, West Cardinal and Core Cardinal are sisters.

Cardinals' Temple – Sacred temple in the Organ House in the very center of Thyria, where Fifth Ceremonies take place.

Compassom – A rare device that allows invisible panom marks to be seen on the skin of a panom-to-be or potential panom.

Core Cardinal – Goddess of the Organ Core, inner circle of the panom mark, and the Organ House, responsible for keeping harmony between the opposite magics so the land doesn't collapse.

CoreCode – A game played with dies and cards.

Corentre – Capital of Thyria, in the Organ Core, home to the Organ House.

Corolla - Petal-shaped snack, sold in the cities of Thyria.

Courtrade – Being blessed by Llunal and gifted with the god's powers: shadow-wielding and whispers of night.

Crois – A courtrade metallic weapon with the shape of a semicircle.

Crystal Clear Safehouse - Safehouse in Corentre owned by Ciaran Castel, protected from unwanted visitors, invisible to the eye of any being he hasn't allowed access.

Deliseen – An interactive panel found in exclusive Elite manors and some Houses.

Discarded being – An individual exiled to the cruel island of Verdania, usually as punishment. Discarding is a responsibility of the panoms belonging to the Organ House.

Dual-powered - Being who is both a panom and a courtrade.

East Cardinal – Goddess of the East Petal and the East House, creator of the Harming power.

East House – One of the five political houses of Thyria, in the East Petal and governed by the East House Ruler.

East Petal – Physical location on the East of Thyria, home to the East House. The East Petal of the panom mark is the one responsible for the Harming power, and must be balanced with its opposite power on the West Petal, responsible for Healing.

Elite – A selected group of humans who hold a significant amount of power, wealth, or influence. Humans can gain entry to the Elite by donating generous amounts to the five Houses of Thyria, or by earning their value because of unique abilities, knowledge or skills.

Epitellia – Invisible barriers that protect a place and restrict the entrance from unwanted beings.

Fifth Ceremony – A sacred ceremony that allows a panom access to their unleashed magical powers and gets the four-petal mark magically inked on their skin.

Fifth Crusade - A five-trial journey to prove to the five Cardinals the worth of five panoms who aim to earn the Fifth Power. The Fifth crusade consists of five ordeals, undertaken by five strivers. Each ordeal belongs to a Cardinal, and requires dominance of their pertinent power in order to succeed. The North Cardinal's ordeal needs a striver who has full control of the Giving power. The South Cardinal's ordeal demands the striver masters Taking. The striver for the West Cardinal's ordeal has to dominate Healing, and the one for the East Cardinal's ordeal must be an adept at Harming.

Fifth Power – An ancient power which is extremely dangerous and difficult to get.

Giving – One of the four panom powers, originally from the North Cardinal, which requires the panom to use the North Petal of their panom mark. Its opposite power is Taking.

Groll – The lowest-value coin in Thyria. There are twenty-five grolls in one valer.

Harming – One of the four panom powers, originally from the East Cardinal, which requires the panom to use the East Petal of their panom mark. Its opposite power is Healing. This power is more complex to dominate than Giving and Taking.

Healing – One of the four panom powers, originally from the West Cardinal, which requires the panom to use the West Petal of their panom mark. Its opposite power is Harming. This power is more complex to dominate than Giving and Taking.

Ink – A message sent from a panom to another being, which appears on the skin of the recipient with the color of the sender's magic and with the sender's handwriting. The message disappears once the recipient has read it.

Inner balance / Inner harmony / Inner scale – Essential scale individual to each panom that must be balanced when using opposite magics (Giving and Taking are opposite magics, and Healing and Harming as well). When the inner harmony is uneven because one power has been used more than its opposite, the panom suffers certain signs and symptoms that can incapacitate and be fatal.

Interpetal Bullef – Communication center that ensures respectful harmony between the Houses and its Rulers.

Invisible Grand – The most secretive organization of Thyria.

Jofryo River – River that surrounds the inner circle of Thyria.

Llunal – God of shadows and darkness.

Mouring – The ability to transport from one place to another using panom magic. A panom can moure independently or moure two other beings at the same time by touching the back of their necks.

Myster – A drink with alcoholic properties.

Navia - Crescent-moon shaped vehicle that stays afloat in the seas, owned by courtrades, fueled by the power and magic of Llunal.

Necroseer - Being who can see, listen and speak with the dead.

North Cardinal – Goddess of the North Petal and the North House, creator of the Giving power.

North House – One of the five political houses of Thyria, in the North Petal and governed by the North House Ruler.

North Petal – Physical location on the North of Thyria, home to the North House. The North Petal of the panom mark is the one responsible for the Giving power, and must be balanced with its opposite power on the South Petal, responsible for Taking.

Ordeal - A challenge or trial where a panom proves their worth to one of the Cardinal goddesses, in order to obtain a red-crystal feather required to earn the Fifth Power. Also see: Fifth crusade.

Organ Core – Circular shape in the middle of the four petals of Thyria and the panom mark.

Organ Mandor – True Ruler of Thyria and Ruler of the Organ House. Every human and panom being must answer to the Organ Mandor, including the four Rulers of the Cardinal Houses.

Orster – Scientific center of research and investigation with the laboratories better guarded by the Organ House.

Panom – Being with magical abilities, blessed by the Cardinals and gifted with their magic. A panom gets access to their powers after the Fifth Ceremony.

- **Acquired panom / Converted panom** – Being who gets their panom mark by marriage.

- **Blood panom** – Being who gets their panom mark at birth.

- **Potential panom / Panom-to-be** – Being with an invisible panom mark on their skin who will only become panom after a Fifth Ceremony takes place.

- **Recipient panom** – Being who gets their panom mark by donation.

Panom Guidor – Experienced panom assigned to guide and teach a new panom how to control the four powers after their Fifth Ceremony.

Panom mark – Four-petal-shaped mark with a circular inner part, with the same shape as Thyria. This mark is permanently inked on the skin of panom beings and allows them to perform magic. Before the Fifth Ceremony, this mark can only be seen on a panom-to-be by using a compassom. The panom mark of each panom has a unique color, the same color as their ink and sparks.

Panomquake – A sudden violent shaking of the ground, typically causing great destruction, because of instability amongst the balance between the five Houses of Thyria.

Past meridiem – Time since the sun is at its highest point in the sky until the death of night.

Red Lawful Stab – A legendary blade made of red crystal, infused with powers for centuries. Blood of the five Cardinals was used to create it. It affects females worse than males.

Roix – An organized military organization equipped for fighting and establishing order.

Roix Reigner – Highest authority in the Roix, to whom all roixers must obey.

Roixer – A military member of the Roix armed and trained to fight, who obeys orders from the Roix Reigner and the Organ Mandor.

South Cardinal – Goddess of the South Petal and the South House, creator of the Taking power.

South House – One of the five political houses of Thyria, in the South Petal and governed by the South House Ruler.

South Petal – Physical location on the South of Thyria, home to the South House. The South Petal of the panom mark is the one responsible for the Taking power, and must be balanced with its opposite power on the North Petal, responsible for Giving.

Striver - An aspirant taking part in the Fifth crusade. Also see: Fifth crusade.

Sweetgum Beech – The biggest square of Corentre.

Taking – One of the four panom powers, originally from the South Cardinal, which requires the panom to use the South Petal of their panom mark. Its opposite power is Giving.

Terrha – World inhabited by beings.

Thyria – A four-petal-shaped island in the middle of the Radel Sea, with five political Houses.

Trading Day – A day every week when the Rulers provide supplies and resources on the Trading Table for the discarded beings living in Verdania.

The inhabitants of Verdania can suit themselves to the whatever the Trading Table provides.

Valer – The highest-value coin. One valer is worth twenty-five grolls.

Verdania – An island in the Radel Sea where discarded beings are sent to.

Vessels – Underwater net of tunnels connecting different islands in the Radel Sea. Vessels are circular-shaped empty tunnels, with blue-tinged membranes separating them from the water of the Radel Sea. A vessel always connects to another vessel, creating a net to ensure the flow of the magic above them.

Vitam tradere – A blood bound effort between two beings to start killing to keep living.

West Cardinal – Goddess of the West Petal and the West House, creator of the Healing power.

West House – One of the five political houses of Thyria, in the West Petal and governed by the West House Ruler.

West Petal – Physical location on the West of Thyria, home to the West House. The West Petal of the panom mark is the one responsible for the Healing power, and must be balanced with its opposite power on the East Petal, responsible for Harming.

Acknowledgements

To Hannah, for being the best friend every being dreams of having: the perfect one to have simultaneous, parallel conversations and synchronized reads with; the first in line and the biggest supporter of any project that comes to my mind; the one who gets to read the very first raw drafts and fuels my soul with her feedback, passion, and excitement; the one who is always just a message away from sharing her opinion on the things that make this magical world unique. Thank you, thank you, thank you. I couldn't do it without you.

To Neil, for being the very first reader who handwrote me a card as a fan—I'll keep it safe till the end of time—a firm advocate of *Petals* and its characters, and a true lover of Jake. Oh, about Jake—oops, I'm sorry (am I?). For your glinting line and all the little bits you inspired in this saga. Thanks for forcing me to look after myself when I forget, for caring, and for making sure I don't push myself too hard.

To the Bears who read my books and support my career as an independent author: thank you beary much. It makes me smile to realize how lucky I am to be surrounded by people who are always ready to cheer me on and celebrate wins together. Thank you, Rachel, Jenna, Gemma, Jess, Demi, Patricia, Adam, Margarida, Lydia, Becca, and every other Bear who has been part of this journey as a reader.

To the magic or destiny that brought North and South together, that gave purpose and meaning to things that had lost them long ago—thanks for proving that life can be joyful, exciting, and surprising, that there is more to it than darkness and scars. ThanKs for bringing hope back.

I couldn't be more grateful for having worked with you, Jennifer, and I can't wait to work with you again. Thank you for your passion, kindness and speediness. You're a gem!

Thank you Bianca for another amazing cover that truly reflects the soul and story at its core! It's always a pleasure to work with you.

My most sincere thanks to the amazing members of the ARC Team, who have been excited and patiently waiting for book 2 since they finished reading book 1! Every minute dedicated to bringing this story to life, every word typed, was worth it to deliver this novel to you. Thanks for your continued support!

Thank you, Emma, for making me take a step back and breathe when I need it most.

The loyalty of a mother can't be beaten, even when she ends up reading the spice her daughter writes. S.O.S. and thank you, Mom. I promise I'll give you a *Petals* shirt soon—no need to ask again.

Mabel, Laura, you're the answer to so many questions, the fundamental pillars that never falter, the ones who are always, always there. Thank you from the bottom of my heart.

To every reader, thank you for reading *Petals* and for helping bring this world to life. May the Cardinals bless you and gift you with magic in your life.

About the author

Martha Monteval has been in love with books since she was five. She reads anything in the fantasy romance and dark romance realm, especially if morally grey characters with dubious manners are involved. When she is not reading or writing, she is practicing martial arts, eating way too much sushi, or playing with her two little ones.

Her debut novel, *Petals for Vicious Secrets*, was published in 2024.